PRETTY LIES

BOOK ONE IN THE WATCH ME BURN SERIES

R.E BOND

Copyright © 2020 by R.E Bond

All rights reserved.

No part of this book may be reproduced in any form or by any electronic or mechanical means, including information storage and retrieval systems, without written permission from the author, except for the use of brief quotations in a book review.

This is a work of fiction. Names, characters, places, and incidents either are the product of the authors imagination or are used fictitiously, and any resemblance to actual persons, living or dead, business establishments, events, or locales is entirely coincidental.

Cover design by Samantha La Mar

TalkNerdy2me | www.tlknrdy2me.com

Editors: Dark Raven Edits & Diamond Editing and Proof Reading.

*To my Instagram bestie, Megan,
who's talked me into this fuckery since day one.
This one's for you, soul sister.*

CHAPTER ONE

RORY

"You're joking, right?" I exclaimed as I crossed my arms tightly across my chest and glared at my father.

He gave me a stern look from his seat behind the desk, his voice rough with warning.

"Aurora Donovan, don't even *bother* to argue with me on this. This new school will be perfect for you, and you should be grateful for the opportunity."

Was he for fucking real? Grateful?

"I didn't ask for a new school, or a new mother," I snapped, hurt and anger lacing my tone, but he turned his attention back to his paperwork as he spoke again.

"I didn't ask to have a spoiled bratty daughter, but I sure as hell got one."

"How the hell am I spoiled and bratty? We're broke and have been for a long fucking time! No thanks to the debts that you keep racking up. That's the only reason you like this woman, isn't it? You love her money, not her," I spat.

I wondered how long I could argue with him before he

completely lost his temper with me again, and I didn't have to wonder for long.

I didn't flinch as he slammed his fist onto his desk, his dark blue eyes boring into my light blue ones.

"Josie and her son are expecting us, go and get ready so we can leave."

I rolled my eyes, my arms still crossed firmly.

"I *am* ready."

"Like hell, Aurora. You've got to make a good impression. Tattered jeans and a ripped shirt won't work," he gritted out, making me frown and look down at my outfit with annoyance.

The black ripped skinny jeans and white crop top didn't look that bad if I was being honest.

I thought I looked pretty alright for a casual meet.

"I always wear this?" I finally questioned, making him look away from me, disgust in his voice.

"Exactly. Find something nice for fuck's sake."

"This *is* my nice outfit, unless you want me to wear overalls or my pajamas?"

He was such a fucking prick.

I headed from the room, needing to get away from him, grabbing my black combat boots and lacing them up.

I leaned against the wall to wait for Dad, brushing my long black hair with my fingers and tying it up in a high messy ponytail.

Well, Max.

I only called him Dad when I had to.

He finally emerged from his office, shaking his head at me with irritation as he walked past, grabbing his car keys.

"You know, you could at least pretend to like the idea of not having to get a job so badly now. Maybe Josie can take you shopping and you can get some nice new clothes? Maybe even a haircut?"

I gave him a dirty look before walking out the door behind him.

"I still need a job, and no, Josie won't be taking me out to do shit, because I don't give two shits about her money. I've had to look after myself for a long time now, so I'll be fine, thanks."

He was such a freeloading piece of shit.

Once we were in the car, he sighed in defeat, a soft tone in his voice.

It was fake, it always was.

"Look, I know you miss your mother, but Josie…"

"You make it sound like she's dead. She just couldn't stand you and your spending habits. When I find her, I'm gone, you got that?" I gritted out before he could finish his sentence.

He always pushed thoughts of Mom to the side, and I fucking hated it.

"She left without you all those years ago because she didn't want you, Aurora. Stop living in your head with your happy stories of having a home with her again," he said in a low voice, causing my heart to tighten.

He was fucking wrong.

Mom wanted me, I just knew it.

We drove the rest of the way in silence, my face scrunching into a scowl as we drove up to a massive mansion to park the car.

Seriously? That belonged to Max's latest piece?

She actually lived there?

"Bit overkill, isn't it? Who is she, the fucking queen?"

He ignored me as usual, climbing out of the car and strolling towards a huge door as it opened, and a slender blonde woman walked out to greet him.

I climbed out but hung back until he gave me a frustrated look.

"Josie, this is my daughter, Aurora."

Josie's smile was sweet, but I dodged her as she tried to hug me, not that she seemed to be offended by my lack of affection.

"It's nice to meet you, Aurora. Your father's told me so much about you."

All bullshit, I bet.

"I prefer Rory."

"Well, Rory, come inside and make yourself at home. Would you like a sparkling water? Your father said you love them."

I gave my father a sideways glance before replying in a relaxed voice, trying not to sound rude.

"Well, he's lying because I hate them. It tastes like television static in a plastic bottle."

She let out a genuine laugh as she led us inside the big ass mansion, and I tried hard not to be intimidated by everything.

It literally spelled out *money*.

The corners of her lips lifted into a small smile.

"My son will like you. He's in the gym at the moment, I'm sorry."

My eyebrows shot up in surprise.

"You have a gym?"

Of course they had a fucking gym.

"We have a gym, pool, movie room, bar, and so many bedrooms. You can use anything you like, okay?" She beamed, making me realize the woman wasn't some snot-nosed cow like I'd originally thought she'd be.

I gave her a small smile, warming up to her a little.

"Thanks."

Josie showed me through the entire house, beaming even more when she stopped in front of a huge bedroom that our entire house would have fucking fit inside.

"This one's yours!"

"Pardon?" I asked with confusion, taking a small step back as tension rolled through me.

Max cleared his throat, managing to at least look slightly embarrassed.

"Your bedroom, Aurora."

I narrowed my eyes and took another step back silently, but Josie scowled at him, winning herself a few bonus points from me.

"Max Donovan, you didn't tell her?"

"We're telling her now, aren't we?"

Father of the fucking year.

Josie shook her head and glanced at me with an apology in her friendly green eyes.

"I thought you knew, honey. I asked your father to move in, and I asked him to bring you around so we could meet each other properly first."

My back hit the wall and I sneered at my father, my fists clenching by my sides as I tried to contain some of my anger.

I could *kill* him.

"Wanna drop anything else on me today? New mom, new house, new school. I'm glad I haven't sorted a job out yet, or you would've fucked that up too, wouldn't you?"

"Aurora, what did I say at home?" He asked sternly, but I was pissed off and not feeling too agreeable.

He shouldn't make a habit of upsetting me at important times, then maybe I'd stop embarrassing him in front of people.

Fuck him.

"I'm not fucking moving. No way in *hell.*"

"Well, tough. You aren't eighteen yet kiddo, so you don't have a choice," he said smoothly, acting as if he had me under control.

He didn't, and he hadn't for a long goddamn time.

Josie seemed concerned, so I gave her a small polite smile, knowing it wasn't really her fault our little tour went sour.

"Thanks for showing me around, Josie. I might go and wait in the car while you and Max finish talking. You have a beautiful home."

I could be polite when I wanted to be.

She went to hug me but stopped herself last minute as my whole body visibly tensed.

"That's okay. We won't be long," she nodded before I excused myself and stalked back through the house.

As I wandered through the kitchen, I heard a snort, making me glance up to find a guy my age with hazel brown hair scowling at me like I was the devil incarnate.

"So, you're the girl that's moving into my house to spend my mother's money?"

That got my hackles up instantly and I clenched my hands into fists, deciding against punching his lights out.

Fucking rich prick.

"No, I'm the girl that had no idea she was moving in, and don't worry, I don't want your mother's fucking money. I look after myself."

"You're just a charity case that my mother's taken interest in. You know Max has been coming here for years, right? I've heard a lot about you, and I'll tell you right now that you need to stay out of my way," he said bitterly.

Who the fuck did this guy think he was?

Hate burned under my skin as I managed to speak confidently.

"Gladly. Spoiled over-privileged rich kids aren't exactly something I like to hang around anyways, so maybe you should be the one to stay the fuck away from me. Got it, *rich boy*?"

An amused smirk hit his face just as our parents walked in, halting when they saw the stand-off between us.

Josie frowned with confusion.

"What's going on? Do you two already know each other?"

Her son chuckled almost cruelly, grabbing a beer from the fridge and popping the top to take a sip, his eyes landing on me again before he smirked.

"We were just talking, weren't we, *Aurora*?"

I rolled my eyes, figuring it would be better than telling him to go fuck himself.

"Sure, if that's what you want to call it."

"Aurora," Max warned in a low voice, but I raised an eyebrow, biting one of my lip rings for a moment before answering him.

"You don't get to decide how to parent me now. I raised my damn self, and you know it. So, if you want to put on some act in front of your coincidentally rich girlfriend, then be my guest. I'm not playing along, and I sure as *shit* won't be lounging around by the pool, acting grateful to be here. Josie's too fucking good for you, and I hope she learns that you're a using piece of shit before you spend the last fucking cent she has. Does she know about the gambling and the drinking? How about the illegal poker games and hookers? You only care about yourself. It was nice to meet you, Josie."

I ignored the furious look on my father's face and the stunned one on Josie's son's as I turned and headed out the door, shutting myself in the car.

It was worth being backhanded once we got home.

Caden

Aurora was a fucking brat, plain and simple.

I was going to destroy her piece by piece, and Jensen was going to have a fucking *field* day with her.

He liked crushing people more than I did, and that said a lot.

Problem was, she seemed more broken than I first realized.

Watching her with her dad made me wonder what the hell he did to her to make her the way she was.

Max hadn't done anything wrong towards my mom or I, but I still had never grown to like him.

I'd heard my dad talk about him before, and since dad liked him, I knew Max was a piece of fucking shit.

Dad had warned me that Aurora was a little cunt, so I guessed I had to find out for myself.

Who was Aurora Donovan, and why the hell did I have to fight my smile when she shot Max down like she did?

I headed up to my room, watching her from my bedroom window as she sulked in the car, but my eyes narrowed as Max stalked out after a while and waved his hands around, shouting in her face.

I didn't miss the way she flinched.

I needed to know what the fuck was going on, and I had every intention of finding out what kind of man my mother was dating.

I had to be fucking nice to her, didn't I?

If she wouldn't tell me the easy way, the guys and I would get it out of her the hard way.

No matter the cost.

Rory

A sigh escaped me as I glanced around my new school the next day as I walked through the gates.

Fucking rich pricks.

I'd never really made close friends anywhere, so I knew it would be like every other time I went somewhere new.

I'd just stick to myself like I always did.

I wandered to where my locker was assigned, slightly surprised to find Josie's son leaning against it, and the way people stayed out of his way made me realize he was a big deal.

His arms stayed crossed as I approached, but he silently moved out of my way as I jammed my jacket inside.

I turned to face him and scowled when I found him still watching me.

I sneered. "What?"

His eyes scanned my face, pausing as he noticed the bruise on my cheek, before he met my hard gaze.

"The fuck has my mom gotten herself into with Max?"

My body relaxed slightly at his concern as I shut my locker with a sigh.

"Honestly? He's a piece of shit and she should get the fuck away from him. She's too damn nice to deserve what will happen if she lets him stay. He ruins everything around him, and I like your mom, so you need to convince her to leave him."

I turned and walked away, chewing on my lip ring as I went, but I was surprised when I noticed he was walking beside me when he spoke again.

"The gambling and shit's true?"

"Yep. My aunt gave me money for my birthday every year as a kid. She stopped when she found out Dad was stealing it to gamble," I shrugged lazily.

"The hookers?"

"Basically thinks he's Charlie Sheen after a big night of

booze. I watched him snort coke off a hooker's tits one night, so *that* was fun," I muttered, heading across the yard towards my classroom and trying not to shiver at the horrid memory.

He suddenly grabbed my arm, instantly letting go as I spun around and yanked myself away from him, my whole body tense from his simple touch.

He seemed curious by the way I reacted, but he masked it quickly and leaned against the wall, his voice serious.

"Is he violent towards women in general, or just you?"

My face remained unreadable as I shrugged.

"I've never seen him hurt a woman in my life. Look…"

"Caden."

"Huh?" I asked, his lip twitching with amusement as he fought a smile.

"My name's Caden."

Good for you.

"Oh, okay. Well, Caden, I've watched my father get into trouble that he can't get out of so many goddamn times, so listen when I tell you to get your mom to leave him. He's poison, and the only people who get hurt are those around him. He'll throw anyone under the bus to save himself if he needs to. Trust me on that."

He gave me a nod and turned to walk away, talking over his shoulder at the last minute.

"Careful around here, Aurora. He's placed you in the lion's den. Girls like you don't last."

I smirked at that.

These fuckers could bring it on.

"Yeah? Well I'm not like most girls, and I already live in hell at home. I may as well live it at school too, huh?"

He hesitated, looking like he was going to say something, but he continued to walk away, disappearing around the corner just as the bell rang.

I walked into the classroom and sat down, noticing

people staring at me and whispering, but I ignored them throughout the whole lesson and kept my head down in my books until the lunch bell rang.

I quickly made my way down the hallway and put my books in my locker, grabbing my bag before heading to the cafeteria to eat.

I instantly regretted it though, when I sat down and a cold sticky drink was tipped over my fucking head.

People erupted into laughter, but the only reaction I gave them was to glance up at the blonde girl who did it, with a small smile on my face.

"Probably best you didn't drink that anyways. I mean, it can't be good for your waistline." My eyes roamed over her and I smirked. "You could lose a few pounds."

Petty, I know.

The prissy bitch's lip lifted into a sneer.

"Who the fuck do you think you are?"

I rolled my eyes, sounding bored as I spoke.

"How about you fuck off before I show you who I am?"

She went to slap me, but I grabbed her arm, bending it around behind her back and slammed her chest down onto the table to pin her there, speaking in her ear sternly.

"You rich kids like to pick on people who you think are below you, but you forget that we've had to survive more than you. We know how to fight, we play dirty, and we aren't afraid to get blood on our hands. I'm Rory Donovan, nice to fucking meet you."

I let her go, grabbing my bag and stalking from the room, noticing a table of three boys in the back watching me.

Caden was one of them, and he had an amused expression on his face, but he didn't make it obvious that he'd watched how the situation was handled.

The guy beside him watched me with dark eyes, his short light brown hair spiked to look deliberately messy.

The other guy sat opposite them, his messy chocolate brown hair covered his eyes slightly, but the intensity in his curious stare burned through me.

When he realized I was watching him, his eyes narrowed and he said something to the others as I held his stare.

I didn't back down to fucking anyone.

The girl that I'd just had restrained was waving her arms around dramatically, yelling at Caden and his friends to do something about dealing with my trashy ass, but I pulled my eyes away from the stare-down I was having and was out of the room, heading towards the bathroom before anyone answered the fucking drama queen.

The rest of the day was basically the same.

The girls would bully me relentlessly and no one stopped them, but I let them think they had the upper hand.

I'd dealt with worse over the years, and a bunch of prissy high school girls weren't going to get to me.

I was walking to the bus stop when someone called my name, making me glance over to find Caden and his two friends leaning on his car.

I kept my expression blank, but inside I was basically having a fucking orgasm over his car.

The shiny black Dodge Challenger STR Demon was begging me to drive it, but I wouldn't admit my appreciation of it to him.

"The fuck do you want, Caden?" I asked harshly as I approached, earning a cruel smirk from him.

He went to speak, but someone joined us and spoke instead, causing my heart to slam into my chest as they moved into my direct line of sight.

There was no way in fucking *hell* that he went to my school.

"Rory? What the fuck are you doing here?" He asked with

horror as his familiar almond eyes stared at me through the black hair that hung over his face.

"Hey, Lukas. Long time, no see," I replied bravely, despite wanting to throw up as anxiety and hate rolled through me.

Lukas James had been my best friend from the first day of preschool.

He remained my best friend up until he walked away from me when I'd needed him most.

That happened at the end of middle school, and I'd been glad when he'd gone to a different high school than me.

It also helped me move on when my father continued to move me to different schools every few months.

I was running out of schools, honestly.

Caden frowned, seeming confused by us.

"You two know each other?"

Lukas ignored him, moving up to me and jabbed a finger against my chest.

"You're the new girl that everyone's talking about? You took on Claire Davidson at lunch?"

I shoved him back firmly with a glare.

"She's lucky I didn't beat her to a bloody fucking pulp, and you know it. Nice to see you turning a blind eye as usual, not that I needed your help. A spoiled little rich girl is the least of my problems."

Lukas hadn't been there, but that wasn't the fucking point.

Caden growled, inserting himself between us and pointing at his orgasmic car, his angry green eyes on mine.

"Get in, Aurora."

"Doubt it, dickhead," I scowled, giving him an unimpressed snort.

Was he for real?

Lukas frowned with confusion, drawing my attention to his eyebrow piercing as it moved with the motion.

"Hang on, how the hell do you two know each other?"

Caden went to answer him, but I spoke over the top.

"We don't. Now, if you'll excuse me."

I only got a few steps away before Caden muttered not to touch me, but a hand grabbed me anyway.

I spun around, jerking my elbow into the side of Lukas's head as panic overtook me.

He let go, rubbing the tender skin with a scowl, his black choppy hair sticking up with the motion as his angry eyes peeked out from behind his hair.

"What the fuck, Rory?"

I shoved him, and I knew I was visibly panicked.

"Don't fucking touch me, Lukas. *Ever.*"

His expression softened, but when he reached for me again, Caden pulled him back a step, trying to give me the space I desperately needed.

"She said don't, so leave her."

"But…"

"I said, fucking leave her," he warned in a low voice, and Lukas finally backed up to his spot next to the others, biting his lip ring with annoyance as he glared at me silently.

Caden watched me for a moment before turning towards the driver's side of his car, speaking over his shoulder.

"Are you sure you don't want a ride?"

I'd die if I got in that fucking car.

I'd probably come all over the seat when he started the engine and the vibrations hit my ass, so I waved him off with my hand and shrugged.

"I'm fine."

His green eyes met my blue ones, and it felt like he was looking into my goddamn soul as he stared me down silently until he finally snorted.

"You're far from fine, if you want to be honest with yourself," then he climbed into his car and slammed the door without another word, making me bite back a moan as the engine roared to life.

I quickly turned and headed to my bus stop, only just managing to make it on time.

I sat in the back and put my head in my hands with a sigh.

Things just got fucking difficult.

"What the fuck?!" I snapped as I walked into my bedroom when I got home, finding it basically empty.

The only thing left was my fucking bed and an empty set of drawers.

I stormed through the house, frustration sinking in when I noticed Max wasn't home, but I found a note in the kitchen stating that everything had been moved to Josie's and to make sure I'd join them by dinnertime.

I scrunched it up in my hand and tossed it in the trash with more force than necessary, detouring back to my room.

I snatched my cigarettes from the hidden panel in my bedroom wardrobe, before stomping outside to light one.

I sat on the porch with my back pressed firmly against the wall and closed my eyes, not opening them again until a car rumbled into the driveway.

Caden climbed out from behind the wheel, making me snort.

For fuck's sake, really?

My eyes closed again in hope that he went away, but he slid down the wall beside me, lighting his own cigarette.

"Figured you might want a lift?"

I didn't look at him as I took a long drag, exhaling as I answered.

"You figured wrong. I'm not fucking going anywhere."

"You might want to once it gets dark and cold. He shut

the power off, apparently," he said lazily, blowing smoke into the air.

"Of course he did," I muttered, opening my eyes to flick the butt of my cigarette onto the lawn.

"How do you know Lukas?" He asked bluntly, and I instantly tensed.

I wasn't about to tell him my deepest, darkest secrets.

"We used to be friends."

"Friends?"

I was quiet for a moment before a small sigh left me, deciding to give him just enough to get him to back off and stop digging.

"He was my best friend from the first day of preschool until the end of middle school. Shit happened and I'll never forgive him, okay? Drop it, because I won't talk about it anymore with you."

He nodded, not seeming convinced by my answer as he glanced around the sad excuse I'd called home for most of my life.

"Mom wanted to set your room up, but I figured you probably don't like people touching your shit, so I told her to let you do it. After dinner they'll probably fuck off for the night, so you'll basically have the house to yourself. I've got somewhere to be later, so I'll be home late. C'mon, let's go and I'll show you how everything in the movie room works. Got a Sony in there too, if you like gaming."

I kept quiet for a second before glancing up at him, his green eyes staring back at me intensely.

"Why are you being nice? Yesterday you said…"

"We aren't buddies or anything, but you despise your dad even though he's all you really have, and you don't take anyone's shit. So, I figured we can at least not kill each other, okay? Get in the car," he mumbled, but he didn't sound bothered.

I stood, locking the house up before walking over to his car with him, hiding my excitement as I slid into the passenger seat and felt the soft leather under me.

I was right about nearly having a fucking orgasm as the engine rumbled to life.

We didn't speak the whole drive to his place, and once we got there we wandered into the kitchen together, making Max frown with disapproval.

"Where have you two been?"

I snatched a banana from the fruit bowl on the bench and shrugged.

"School."

"School's been out for over two hours."

"After school, I went home."

"This *is* your home now, Aurora," he said patiently, but I knew on the inside he wanted to strangle me.

I popped a shoulder up in a half shrug.

"Nah, this is Josie and Caden's home. You and me? We're like tourists. Once the money runs out, we'll fucking go."

I peeled the banana, ignoring how his eyes narrowed to slits.

"Would you stop that? Believe it or not, I believe you'll be happy here if you just tried."

I glanced at Caden with a smirk.

"I mean, at least I have some *super* good company while we're here playing house. Did you know that Caden's best buddies with Lukas James?"

My father stiffened, and Caden glanced between us as he tried to figure us out, but Max forced a smile.

"Well, isn't that nice for you, honey? Does Lukas come around here often?"

"Oh yeah, all the time. We all share classes and stuff too. Maybe I'll hang out with him after school tomorrow? I'm not sure yet. Oh, Caden? Can you show me the movie room now?"

Caden gave me a curt nod, seeming unsure with what was going on.

"Yeah, sure thing."

His eyes watched me closely as I took a big mouthful of my banana, chewing it slowly and swallowing, before turning to my father who looked pretty pissed at me.

"You don't mind if we hang out for a while, do you?"

"Aurora…"

I faked a giggle and forced myself to press my body against Caden's, resting a hand on his solid chest and smiling sweetly up at him.

"C'mon, Caden. Since we toured my home, I say we tour yours. You know, *every* room."

He raised an eyebrow but smirked, deciding to play along with my little game, moving slowly so he didn't startle me as he reached out and tucked loose strands of black hair behind my ear with fake affection, a soft tone in his voice.

"As if I could say no to you?"

Max watched us for a moment before storming from the room, a smirk of satisfaction stretching across my face.

I removed myself from Caden who was looking pretty amused himself.

"Your dad's going to think we're fucking now."

"Good," I shrugged, heading down the hallway with him trailing behind me.

Once in the movie room, he plonked down on one of the couches, watching as I sat beside him before he spoke up.

"You know you'll just piss him off, right? I mean, I personally love pissing people off but why do you want to?"

I met his gaze, giving him a bored shrug as I drew my knees up to rest my chin on them.

"He doesn't give a shit about how I feel when he fucks

with my life, so I'll at least try to have fun in upsetting him back. Besides, maybe if I push him far enough, your mom will see the man he really is."

"Which is what, Rory?" He asked, his voice tight and irritated.

My eyes darted away from his and my arms tightened around my legs.

Fuck.

"Nothing."

"How often does he hurt you?" He asked gently after a moment, my jaw clenching in response.

I ignored him, staring at the huge TV screen on the wall, my body tensing up when he shuffled closer and reached out to tuck my hair behind my ear like he had earlier.

I hated the fluttery feeling in my stomach from his touch.

"Well, if he knows what's good for him he won't lay a hand on you when I'm around."

I flicked my gaze to his, my voice breathy as I forced out a response.

"Why's that?"

"Because, I'll fucking kill him," he answered in a low voice as he stood, taking the remote and explaining what I needed to press to make the PlayStation work, then he left the room quickly.

I didn't see him again for the rest of the night.

CHAPTER TWO

RORY

"Dead bitch walking," Claire pealed with laughter as I wandered into the cafeteria at school the next day.

I grabbed a can of soda from the vending machine, turning to walk away, but I ran into Claire and her friends who had managed to sneak up behind me.

I gave her a dirty look and snorted.

"Move."

"As if. You didn't seem to understand me yesterday, so I'll tell you in another way. You aren't welcome here. Also, what the hell are you wearing, you trailer trash whore?" She sneered, making me roll my eyes and give her a small smirk.

"We call them clothes. I know you aren't used to them, but most people wear them all the time. It's in chapter one of *How not to be a little tramp guide for beginners*. I'm assuming no one ever gave you a copy?"

She snarled, swinging her hand back to slap me, but the room went quiet as Caden's voice cut through all the noise from his usual table with the other guys.

"Claire, back off."

Claire's eyes widened a fraction before she scowled, obviously not used to being told what to do.

"What the fuck, Caden? You know she's a problem here and has no right to prance around like she paid her way. She couldn't afford to go to school here, so some rich prick's paying for her. She's trailer trash, and…"

"I said, back off. Rory, get over here and stop winding her up," he snorted, jerking his head to motion me in his direction.

Well, the cat was out of the fucking bag now, wasn't it?

People whispered as I made my way over to the guys, and Caden moved over so I could sit between him and his friend with the spiked hair, who ran his gaze over me without being discreet about it in the slightest.

Claire noisily snorted, drawing everyone's attention to her to see what she'd do.

"Um, what the hell are you doing? She's a nobody!"

Caden gave me one of his sandwiches before glancing at her with a bored expression on his face.

"You done fucking squawking now?"

She looked horrified, but he gave her a small smile and faked a thought popping into his head. "Oh, I completely forgot. Everyone, listen up!"

The room went silent as all eyes turned to our table as Caden stood, motioning towards me with a big shit-eating grin. "Everyone, meet Aurora Donovan. She's basically my new stepsister, so if anyone touches her, they will be dealing with me. Got that?"

Whispers and gasps sounded around the room as he sat back down, but Lukas stared at us from across the table with shock on his face, his fingers tugging on his lip ring absently.

"Hang on, the guy your mom's banging is Max Donovan?"

Caden grinned, leaning back in his seat as he spoke.

"Yeah, they just moved in. Groovy, huh?"

His friend with the messy chocolate brown hair and pretty blue eyes checked me out without shame, finally smirking at Caden.

"Live-in pussy? Nice, bro."

My gaze snapped to his as I spoke in a low dangerous voice that made me sound tougher than I really was.

"No one fucking touches me. If you even try, I'll slice your diseased dick off and choke you with it."

A wicked grin stretched across his face, but Caden snorted and gave his friend a serious look.

"Back off, Jense. Rory, this is Jensen Gilbert, and the guy beside you is Tyler Johnson."

Jensen reached a hand across the table and I grabbed my knife from my pocket, instantly slamming it down between his fingers and leaving it to stick up in the table.

Everyone in the room stayed silent as I kept my hard gaze on Jensen's, and he looked slightly worried when I didn't back down.

Fucking pussy.

I lifted my lip into a nasty smile, my voice dripping with sarcasm as I pulled my knife from the table and slid it back into my pocket.

"Like I said, don't fucking *touch* me."

"Jesus, okay. Holloway, she's fucking crazy," he mumbled, but that just made Caden chuckle with amusement.

He was such an asshole.

"Yeah, she is, so watch it. You guys all up for meeting at my place tonight? Pizza and movies? I can't be fucked hosting a party."

I zoned out, letting the guys talk as I ate the sandwich he'd given me, but his voice snapped me out of my thoughts after a while.

"Rory? I asked if you were coming or not?"

I blinked with confusion, glancing around the table at the others.

"Where?"

"Home. Ride with me, yeah? It's only study period, and no one sticks around for that shit," he said lazily, watching me intensely as he waited for my answer.

I hated how everyone in the room seemed to be waiting for my response.

I finally shrugged.

"Yeah sure, why not. Did you need me to fuck off tonight for your guys night thing? Because if you want..."

"You're invited too, stupid," he rolled his eyes, standing and clearing his tray before waiting for the rest of us to follow his lead.

As we walked past Claire's table, Caden moved from one side of me to the other, and I could hear the muttering and protests under people's breaths at it.

I didn't get why it was such a big deal.

Word had already spread through the school that Caden and the guys had put an end to the bullying on me, and everyone seemed to want to catch a glimpse of me as we all walked through the school and up to the parking lot together as a group.

Everyone split up to go to their cars, and Caden gave me an amused smile as I climbed into his Challenger and we drove towards home.

I was worried I'd moaned out loud about the car or something stupid, but before I could worry about it for long, he spoke.

"You know, you're about to become the most popular girl at school, right?"

"You mean *unpopular*. You saw how people glared at me. Why did you stand up for me anyways?" I muttered, peeking over at him to see him offer me a cigarette.

I hesitated before accepting it, lighting it and putting the window down.

"Because, you aren't who I thought you'd be and to be honest, you cop enough bullshit at home. Besides, now I've said you're with me, no one will mess with you. Claire might, but you just let me know and I'll keep her in line, okay?"

"Caden…"

"Okay?" He asked sternly, waiting for me to nod before giving me a sly smile.

"So, do we make it look like we're up to no good together in front of your dad, or what?"

"You'd be up for that?" I asked with surprise, causing his smile to widen.

"Hey, you wanna fuck in the kitchen and get caught, I'd be up for it. I mean, you're hardly difficult to look at, Rory."

Did he call me hot?

I was quiet for a while before giving him a small smile, hoping I didn't look panicked by the thought.

"Maybe we could upset him a little? No fucking though."

He laughed heartfully, "You want me to give you a sappy cute nickname then? I've noticed you actually freak out when you're touched, and since I know you won't talk about it…"

"It's not so horrible when it's you," I mumbled softly, watching him pause before lighting his own cigarette, giving me a curious look.

"You ever going to talk to me about it?"

"We're only on day three, Caden, but if you wanna hold my hand or something in front of Max, that's okay."

My face heated with embarrassment, but he didn't seem to notice as he took a drag of his cigarette and turned into our driveway.

Once he parked the car, we climbed out and waited for the others to park close by before we all headed towards the front door together, Caden giving me a cheeky grin.

"C'mere, troublemaker."

I moved closer, letting him put an arm around my shoulders and pull me closer.

I knew the others were watching us with curiosity as we walked into the house, but I didn't comment about it as we moved through the front room.

Max and Josie were in the dining room talking when we walked in, and Max instantly noticed Caden's arm around my shoulders.

Josie gave us all a big friendly smile though like the good mom she was.

"Hey guys, good day at school?"

Caden smiled back, not moving his arm from around me.

"Yeah, pretty good day. We're having a movie night, so if you're looking for us, we'll be in the movie room."

"Alright. Don't drink too many beers, okay? You know I don't like it," she replied, but Max snorted as he looked at me.

"Don't you have *any* beer, you got that, Aurora?"

I smiled with fake sweetness at him, sarcasm in my tone.

"Of course, Daddy. Only enough room for one alcoholic in this family, right?"

His jaw tightened, but Josie rolled her eyes.

"One or two never hurt anyone, Max. She's seventeen after all."

"Yeah, not twenty-one. I'll check on you when you go to bed, okay?" He frowned at me with annoyance.

How fucking embarrassing.

I went to speak, but Josie laughed, my body relaxing.

I wasn't used to someone being on my side when it came to Max.

"Leave her be, sweetheart. Besides, they'll all camp out in the movie room for the night. The boys normally have movie nights at each other's houses. It's good to see them including Rory too."

He silently fumed as Caden smirked and moved behind me, wrapping his arms around my middle to rest his chin on top of my head.

"Don't be silly, Mom. We love Rory being around. Did Max tell you Lukas was her best friend until he started high school with us?"

Josie beamed, giving Max a swat on the arm.

"You didn't tell me that! Oh, how wonderful! Don't be too loud tonight, okay guys? I don't want to be kept awake by you."

Caden met eyes with Max, making sure to give him a sly grin as he answered and started walking me towards the hallway.

"Trust me, we'll try *really* hard to be quiet. C'mon, Rory."

Once we were in the movie room, Lukas gave us a filthy look.

"What the fuck was that?"

I glared at him, about to tell him it was none of his fucking business, but Caden chuckled and spoke first.

"Nothing man, it's just funny to stir her dad up, that's all."

"Won't be funny when he beats her fucking bloody over it and she ends up in hospital. *Again*," he growled, shoving past us and angrily sitting down on one of the couches.

Caden's eyes moved over to me and he frowned, looking like Lukas just pissed in his cornflakes.

"Rory…"

"Leave it, Caden," I replied softly, sitting down on one of the couches as he set a movie up.

He sat beside me, hesitating before putting an arm out for me to curl up under.

I could feel Lukas's eyes boring into me as I let Caden pull me as close as possible, and by the time we'd started the third movie for the evening and had a few beers, I was comfortably sitting on his lap.

It scared me how relaxed I was with his arms around me, if I wanted to be completely honest.

The moment Caden headed upstairs to get some snacks, Lukas plonked down beside me and narrowed his eyes.

"What the hell is up with you and Holloway?"

Fuck me, really?

"Nothing, why?"

The other two chuckled, but Jensen gave me a smirk as he leaned back in his seat, managing to make lazy look a little bit sexy.

I needed to calm down on the beer or some shit.

"Babe, Holloway doesn't cuddle. Not even after a good fuck. So, tell us what's going on? Be a team player and share the gossip."

Lukas gave me a concerned look as he spoke again.

"How can you sleep with him when you hardly know him? Especially after what happened to you?"

I was officially starting to panic, and I'd lost the relaxed feeling I'd had all night.

I curled into myself and choked out, "Lukas, fuck off."

He didn't take the hint, continuing to speak and make me even more fucking nervous.

"Seriously, Aurora. You don't even know him. How can you just trust someone after what you went through?"

"I trust him more than I'll ever fucking trust you. I'd trust almost *anyone* more than you," I snapped defensively, his almond eyes dropping with shame as he sighed.

"Look, I know I fucked up and wasn't there for you, but you don't understand what actually…"

I wasn't going to have that conversation with him.

"Drop it."

"Rory, I'm sorry," he said gently and reached for me, but I scrambled off the couch, landing on my ass almost painfully, but I kept moving backwards.

I needed distance between us before I couldn't breathe.

"Stop it, Lukas! Leave me alone!"

"Damnit, Rory. I get that they fucked you up, but just listen to me for a second," he asked as he went to stand, but I pressed my back against the wall firmly, becoming worked up as I shouted at him.

"You fucked me up! Don't you get that? It's what *you* did that fucked me up! I would have been okay if I'd had you!"

Tyler finally took pity on me and my obvious fear, giving Lukas an impatient glance.

"C'mon, man. Leave her alone."

"She just needs to listen to me and…"

I slammed my hands over my ears as the guys continued to argue, and it wasn't until a hand touched my shoulder that I uncurled from myself and swung my fist up hard, zoning back to my surroundings as it connected.

I glanced up, my breath coming out hard and fast as I tried to get control of the panic that was consuming me, finding Caden squatting beside me, rubbing his eye where I'd punched him.

A small smile was on his face, but it didn't quite hide his concern.

"That'll teach me for sneaking up on you. Didn't mean to scare you, are you okay?"

I peered over his shoulder to find the others all gone, making me relax slightly.

"Yeah, sorry I…"

"It's fine. Jense said Lukas was being a prick. They've all gone upstairs because Ty suggested you needed a minute or two. Lukas is heading home, too."

I sucked a breath in as he slowly took my hands in his, uncurling my fists and wincing slightly as he saw the blood on the palms of my hands from my fingernails.

"C'mon," he said softly, my eyes peering at him with confusion.

"Where are we going?" I asked as I went to stand, but he carefully put his arms around me and lifted me against his chest like I weighed nothing.

He walked silently up to his bathroom and placed my ass on the sink so he could rummage in the cupboard, grabbing a clean cloth and some ointment.

He washed my hands as I watched him cautiously, putting ointment and band-aids on my palms once they were washed and dried.

He gave me a cheeky wink once he was satisfied that he'd sorted it.

"All better. Do I need to kick Lukas's ass?"

Did I blush a little?

Fuck.

"No, it's okay."

"You sure?"

"Positive. Can we go and watch another movie now?" My voice sounded shaky, but I didn't care.

I just needed to forget about my meltdown and hoped the others did too.

"Of course. I've got you," he smiled, lifting me from the bench, and I instantly wrapped my arms around his neck so he could carry me down to the kitchen.

Jensen raised an eyebrow at us, and I instantly wriggled so Caden would put me down.

I kept forgetting that I didn't trust these guys.

Tyler's concerned steel grey eyes were on me as I put some distance between me and them.

"You all good?"

I nodded, giving him a tiny smile.

"Yeah. Sorry if me being here is ruining guys night or…"

"Don't be dumb. Lukas is the one who couldn't leave well

enough alone," he stated, surprising me that he was taking my side.

We headed back into the movie room, and Caden made sure I was curled up on his lap again by the end of the night.

I actually enjoyed myself, despite being tense.

I couldn't let them get close, not until I knew that I could trust them.

"Rory, wake up."

I jolted awake in a panic, my eyes frantically glancing around in the dim light until I noticed Caden beside me, giving me the space I needed to calm down.

When I realized who it was, I let out a deep breath and absently reached for him, trying to calm my breathing as he tucked me against his chest and ran his fingers through my hair in a soothing motion.

"I wasn't sure whether to wake you or not. You were thrashing about and you screamed in your sleep," he murmured, my eyes closing as shame washed through me.

How fucking embarrassing, freaking out like that in front of him?

He must have felt my body go rigid, because his calm voice reached my ears again as I tried to get my shit together.

"I know you don't want to talk about it, but you need to, Rory. It's eating away at you more than you realize."

"I can't," I choked out, his hand still stroking my hair as he spoke carefully.

"Can't or won't? It doesn't make you weak for admitting it's too much. Think about it, okay?"

I nodded, finally feeling like I was able to breathe properly, and I eventually went back to sleep, snuggled up against his chest.

It didn't seem like much later that I was woken by chatting close by, and I knew it was Jensen and Tyler gossiping.

"Seriously, I don't get it. Maybe they dated?" Tyler mumbled, making Jensen snort.

"Maybe, but I doubt it. She's not just cut up at him for breaking up with her. She was way too freaked out by the shit he was saying last night."

"Maybe Caden's right and we should keep him away from her? What if he did something to her?"

Caden's voice rumbled in my ear as he spoke up without moving from his hold on me.

"You know we're awake, right? Stop gossiping like a bunch of fucking old ladies."

They were quiet for a moment before Jensen cleared his throat.

"Ah, sorry."

I went to sit up but Caden pulled me back down so that I was lying half on top of him, making me tense slightly.

What the fuck?

I stared at him, a small smirk hitting his face as he spoke quietly.

"Kiss me."

I heard Jensen snort with amusement, but I ignored him and stared into Caden's green eyes with confused.

"Why?"

"I can hear Max stomping our way. Live a little," he replied, making sure to move slowly as he ran his fingers through the back of my messy black hair, pulling my lips down to his.

My arm held me back from him at the unfamiliar closeness, but when he kept the kiss slow at my pace, I relaxed against him a little.

My hand rested on his chest as his hands went to my waist to hold me, and it actually felt nice.

I didn't even realize I'd climbed on him properly, until he smiled against my lips just as the door opened and Max's voice shouted from close by.

"Aurora Donovan!"

I went to sit up but Caden held me in place, his thumbs rubbing on my hips affectionately as he spoke to my father.

"No need to yell, Max. She can hear you."

"Caden, you listen to me...," he bit out, but Caden chuckled and cut him off.

"Nope."

"Aurora, get your ass up to your room. Now."

When I didn't move, Max stalked over and grabbed my arm tightly, yanking me off Caden more roughly than necessary.

I gritted my teeth as pain shot through my arm, but I refused to give him the satisfaction of hurting me.

Caden got to his feet and gave Max a glare, but he didn't seem to notice as he yanked me out of the room and up the hallway.

Once in my room, he slammed the door behind us and locked it, shoving me to the floor hard.

Uh oh, I'd poked the bear.

"Think you're funny for fucking your stepbrother? I didn't raise you to be such a dirty little whore. You can stay in here all fucking day and I don't want to see you until breakfast tomorrow, you got that?"

I scowled, standing up and stumbling as he backhanded me.

I blocked out the sting as I kept angry eyes on him and growled.

"Fuck you."

Wrong words, apparently.

I fell on my ass as his fist connected with my eye, but this time I rubbed it and winced, a snort of annoyance leaving him.

"Enough of the attitude, Aurora. I mean it," then he left the room, slamming the door behind him.

I stood back up on unsteady feet, wandering across the room and into my bathroom to stare at myself in the mirror.

My eye was already bruising, and his ring had left a cut on my cheek.

I quickly had a shower and had just climbed into bed to watch a movie, when there was a soft knock at the door.

Caden poked his head in, his gaze instantly zoning in on my face.

"Go away," I mumbled, but he ignored me and walked in, closing the door quietly behind him and moving towards me to sit on the side of my bed.

He slowly reached out and cupped my chin, turning my face towards him so he could look at the damage.

A nasty scowl hit his face, and I could hear the rage burning in his voice.

"He fucking hit you?"

I tried to jerk from his hold with frustration.

"Back off."

"No. Let me look," he replied softly, holding my gaze as my body calmed.

His fingertips trailed gently over my tender skin and he sighed.

"Let me talk to Mom about it. Maybe..."

Fuck no.

I yanked back from his grip and scowled.

"Leave it, Caden. Seriously."

His face hardened as he took one of my hands in his.

"Rory..."

The door opened and Max and Josie walked in, Max's face instantly becoming upset and distraught.

I knew it was fake and so did Caden, but that didn't stop him from having his fake meltdown to make it look like he gave a shit about me in front of Josie.

"What the hell did you do to her?"

Hold up, what?

Caden's eyes shot daggers at him, his voice lethal.

"The hell are you talking about? I didn't do shit, you fucking prick."

Josie gasped, horrified at her son's attitude.

"Caden!"

"Look at what he did to her face!" Caden shouted suddenly, my hand tightening in his as the anxiety started racing inside me.

I was frozen, which made me feel weak.

Caden shuffled closer to try and comfort me, but Max threw his hands in our direction with anger.

"I find you in here, trying to apologize for hurting her, and you blame me? I'd never hit my own child!"

"You lying piece of shit!" Caden bellowed, causing me to jump at the volume.

Josie watched as her son pulled me under his arm despite how tense I was, and when I winced slightly as he kissed the top of my head, she sighed.

"Caden Holloway, kitchen now."

"But Mom, she..."

"Kitchen. *Now*," she repeated, waiting for him to give in and follow her without further argument.

Max smirked before leaving the room, and I knew it would only be the beginning of trouble.

Caden didn't come back that night, and for once I craved to be held.

I just hoped Josie didn't believe my father's lies about her own son.

CHAPTER THREE

RORY

"The hell happened to you?" Lukas asked at school on Monday morning as he reached my locker, making me roll my eyes.

The bruises were throbbing, but I ignored them and opened my locker to grab my books.

"None of your business."

"Like, how it's not my business that you and Caden are messing around?" He asked dryly, a snort of irritation leaving me.

"Yep. Exactly like that."

He watched me silently as I closed my locker and turned to him, keeping my voice low.

"You and I aren't friends, Lukas, and I don't have to tell you shit. Stop trying to make it seem like you actually give a fuck about me."

He followed me as I turned and walked to class, his voice gentle.

"Aurora, I do care. You don't understand…"

Rage coursed through me as I shoved him hard into the

lockers beside us, ignoring everyone gawking at me as I got in his face.

I assumed no one got to push the kings of the school around, verbally or physically, but I wasn't going to take anyone's shit.

Fuck the system that they had in place.

"I don't have to understand shit. I fucking hate you, so stop trying to play nice with me."

Asshole.

I'd never forgive him.

He genuinely looked upset but sighed, putting his hands up in defeat.

"Okay, I'm sorry."

I snorted as I turned and walked away from him.

"So you keep saying."

I'd just sat down in class when Claire sat her prissy ass beside me with a grin.

"Where's your guard dogs today? I see you and Lukas are on the outs, so have they already lost interest in the pathetic charity case?"

A shadow fell over us, and Jensen's voice calmed me as he spoke.

"How about you try swinging a punch at her and fucking see?"

She gritted her teeth and glared up at him with irritation.

"Are you taking Caden's place while he's absent today?"

He chuckled, but there was nothing nice about it.

"Rory would kick your ass in a fight, and you know it. She's got more fucking mean in her than you do, so I wouldn't even try it. Now, get the fuck out of my chair."

Claire was fuming, and that made me smile a little as she snapped.

"How the fuck is this…"

"I'll let Rory remove you if you really want?" He cut her

off, waiting for her to growl and stomp across the room to her regular table before he sat down in the vacated seat and leaned back to get comfortable.

I raised an eyebrow, grateful that he'd gotten rid of her.

"Thanks, but I can take her on, Jense."

He gave me an amused smile before putting his arms behind his head lazily.

"You thought I was saving you? I was saving *her*, Rory. I know you'd beat her to a fucking pulp."

I grinned as I opened my book and read over my notes, but after a while I noticed him still watching me out of the corner of my eye.

I put my pen down and turned in my chair to look at him, my voice sarcastic.

"Something you wanna ask, Gilbert?"

He chuckled, leaning forward and resting his arms on the desk.

"It's not some tough girl act you've got going on, is it. You literally don't give a fuck about anything, and you'll throw punches whenever the fuck you think you need to."

I shrugged one shoulder and smiled slightly.

"I like to fight. You guys thought I was all bark and no bite? Cute."

"Yeah, you are," he grinned, making me snort.

"Oh, fuck off. You know I can hold my own."

"I mean you're cute," he replied more quietly, my body warming at his tone.

My face heated at his words, but I managed to speak through my embarrassment.

"Ah, thanks. I guess."

"So, since you live with Holloway, where the hell is he today?" He continued as if the conversation hadn't turned awkward a second ago.

Boys were weird.

Hang on, what?

I frowned, cocking my head slightly.

"You mean you haven't spoken to him?"

"Not since Saturday morning. We left after your dad dragged you out," he replied, looking right at the bruise I was still sporting, question in his eyes that he thankfully kept to himself.

"I haven't seen him since he came and checked on me after that," I mumbled, his eyes narrowing on me as he sat up straight.

"The hell do you mean you haven't seen him? You live in his fucking house."

People were listening in on our conversation now, so I leaned closer to talk.

"We had a problem after you guys left, okay? Can we talk after class?"

"No, let's go and talk now," he replied bluntly, casually standing up as if we weren't in the middle of class, giving me a frown when I didn't move. "Coming?"

Was he fucking serious?

I gave him an unimpressed look, speaking in a hushed voice to avoid getting into trouble.

"It's class time, and unlike some, I need to pass because I don't have money to bail my ass out."

"You'll pass, promise. C'mon, don't make me drag you. I know you don't like being manhandled," he sighed impatiently, causing me to hesitate before deciding he would definitely throw me over his shoulder and drag me out if I didn't.

I grabbed my books and followed him towards the door, causing the teacher to frown.

"And where are you off to, Aurora?"

Before I could reply, Jensen raised an eyebrow at him and cocked his head.

"Doesn't really matter. Does it, sir?"

The teacher appeared nervous but glanced at me with annoyance.

"Miss Donovan..."

"She's leaving with me. She's one of us, and don't you fucking forget it," then he shooed me from the room as people started gossiping.

Great way to lay low, right?

Once outside, I gave his shoulder a solid punch.

"The fuck was that? You can't just talk to..."

"Holloway says you're one of us, so I'll give you the rundown about how it works around here, okay? Our dads all pay a hell of a lot of money to this school to get them to turn a blind eye on a lot of shit. Lukas's mom pays a nice chunk as well now he's here, but that's just to keep up appearances. You'd know what she can be like when it comes to social standings. Our great, great grandfathers built this school, so we're basically school royalty or some shit. Lukas's mom can't stand the thought of him coming across as lower class, so that's her reason to throw money around. We could murder someone and it would get swept under the rug. You following?"

"Sure. You guys are the kings and we are your servants," I snorted, his lip twitching into a sly smirk.

"Servants? I like that, but you're far from a servant, Rory."

So full of shit.

"Are you blind? I'm the poor girl who..."

"You're the girl who managed to get in with the kings. Pretty sure that makes you a queen, babe," he winked, heading into an empty classroom and plonking down at a desk, waiting for me to do the same before his smile faded. "Now, tell me what the fuck happened after Ty and I left on Saturday."

I fiddled with my hands for a moment before meeting his serious gaze.

"Caden got the blame for my face. We were in my room and Max and Josie came in. Max went off at him for hurting me, and I'm pretty sure Josie believed it because she asked him to go out and talk to her. I haven't seen him since."

"Your dad's the one who hit you, yeah?"

I gave him a tiny nod, and he muttered a curse before replying.

"He's probably at his dad's. Josie sends him there when she doesn't know what to do with him, which isn't very often."

I leaned back in my chair, looking surprised.

"His dad's actually in his life? He's never mentioned him."

"No offense, but he's only known you for a few days, so he wouldn't have wanted to. His dad's a touchy subject at the best of times, so for him to tell you, he'd need to know you better. His dad's a mean son of a bitch when he wants to be, so Caden's never gotten along with him. He used to beat on Josie when Caden was younger, and he put Caden in the hospital when he was a kid because he tried to protect her. He was best friends with my dad when they were younger, but I've always been told to stay away from him. Caden hates him and he has good judgement, so I keep my distance. Tyler's the same, and Lukas hasn't even met him. You know, if you want to hang out without Caden on weekends and stuff, you can come see us, yeah? Like Sunday you could have…"

"I was locked in my room until this morning, and besides, I have no way of talking to you guys to find out where you are," I shrugged, still thinking about Caden's childhood, but he just rolled his eyes and smiled like a smug fucking asshole.

"Give me your phone."

"What?"

"Trust me?"

"Fuck no," I growled, earning an amused chuckle from him.

"Good girl," then he snatched my phone before I could react.

Fucker.

I went to snatch it back, but he held his other hand out to stop me with a grin.

"Calm down, I'm only putting my number in for you. I'll put Caden's and Ty's in too, in case you need them."

I was confused at him wanting to spend time with me without Caden, and it put me on edge a little.

From what I'd gathered, the guys didn't let outsiders in, so why would they want to bring me in to their group?

I relaxed slightly as he handed my phone back, before he pulled his own from his pocket and started texting casually, my voice sounding confused as I spoke.

I wasn't used to people just being nice, and it felt strange.

"Thanks, Jense."

Within five minutes, Tyler waltzed into the room with a smirk as he plopped down in a chair in front of us.

"You sure like to make a scene, Jense. Claire's posse have already spread it around that you and Caden are both banging her."

I snorted and gave Jensen an overly sweet smile.

"They *wish* I was fucking them."

Jensen raised an eyebrow, looking confused as fuck.

"Hang on, you aren't fucking Holloway?"

"No."

"Looks that way to me," he chuckled, not believing me for a second, not that I really blamed him.

"We like to upset my dad. Guess the jokes on us now that he's actually mad," I muttered under my breath, but Tyler looked at me sternly, his voice rumbling with anger.

"Doesn't matter how much you piss him off. No man,

especially your own fucking father, should lay a hand on you. Jense texted me about Holloway, and to be honest, he probably swung a punch at your dad and that's why he's in trouble. After school we'll drop you home and I'll ask Josie myself where he is. No biggie."

We stayed in the empty room until lunchtime, and by the time we got to the parking lot, Lukas was already there waiting for us.

He seemed surprised to see me with them without Caden, but he didn't voice it.

Wise boy.

"What's the afternoon plan, guys?" He asked as Jensen unlocked his car and shrugged.

"Gonna hang out with Rory at Holloway's for a bit. Might have a swim or something."

I was too busy checking his car out to be listening.

Why did all these rich fuckers have flashy cars?

He had a similar taste to Caden, and I shamelessly checked out the new model black Chevrolet Camaro coupe, trying hard not to drool.

I felt Lukas's eyes on me, and I glanced up to find him watching me cautiously.

I sighed. "Did you want to come with us to hang out?"

"You're cool with that?" He asked with surprise.

Don't take it to fucking heart, idiot.

"I personally don't give a shit," I smiled sweetly, waiting for the other two to jump in the back before I climbed into the passenger seat, and Tyler chuckled at Lukas who was scowling at me.

Fuck him.

I ignored him and turned to Jensen as he climbed into the driver's seat.

"Back to our talk before, why the fuck do people think

you're all kings of the fucking school? I mean, I get it, but how does everyone just follow that rule?"

"Easy. They're shit scared of us. We're hot and rich, and we fuck good," he winked, earning a disgusted swat to the arm from me.

The other two buckled up silently, but once on the road, Lukas leaned forward with a scowl again.

"The fuck are you telling her all that shit for? It's not just your shit to tell, Jense."

Jensen shrugged. "It's common knowledge, so it's fine. Besides, all kings need a queen, right?"

"Right?" He replied slowly, making Jensen smirk.

"Well, you're welcome. I made her ours."

Lukas looked annoyed as fuck now.

Well, good.

Asshole.

"What the hell does *that* mean?"

"It means, between Caden sticking up for her and me telling our teacher in class this morning that she's one of us, she is officially part of our group," he exclaimed proudly to Lukas's horror.

"Bad idea, Jense," he hissed, but Tyler laughed like a hyena, smacking his knee as he hooted.

"Claire's gonna blow a fucking gasket! Do you think people will just bow down to Rory?"

I listened to them talk it over, only half paying attention, but I perked up instantly when we arrived at the house to find Caden's Challenger parked in the driveway.

We all walked inside together, and Caden looked up as he leaned against the bench with a teasing smirk on his face.

"I know you guys can't handle it when I'm not around, but a welcome home party?"

Jensen rolled his eyes playfully.

"As if. We were coming over to swim in your pool and hang out with Rory."

Caden's eyes landed on mine and his expression softened instantly.

"Hey, how's the face?"

"It's okay," I shrugged, not knowing how to act in case he got into trouble, but he raised an eyebrow and smiled at me.

"Well, are you gonna just stand there, or give me a hug?"

I hesitated before walking across the room, a strange sense of relief washing over me as he pulled me against his chest and held me tightly, kissing the top of my head. "You sure you're okay? I would have checked on you, but Mom kept my phone here."

"Did she send you to your dad's?" I asked softly, his body tensing before he replied with bluntness in his tone.

"You know about my dad?"

"Only that he exists and you stay there sometimes," I mumbled, feeling bad for upsetting him, but he just chuckled.

"Liar. What have the guys been telling you?"

Jensen leaned against the wall and crossed his arms.

"Basic shit. You get sent there when you're naughty, and your dad's mean."

"When I'm fucking naughty, huh?" He asked with amusement plastered on his face.

"Yep."

"So, what did I miss at school today?" He asked, not moving back from his hold on me.

Tyler laughed like a maniac, waving his arms around with sudden enthusiasm.

"Oh, you should have been there, man! Jensen stood up for Rory in class, so you can imagine the gossip around that, but he took her from class with this big speech to the teacher that she's one of us. Guess the school just got themselves a you're all kings of the fucking school? I mean, I get it, but how does everyone just follow that rule?"

"Easy. They're shit scared of us. We're hot and rich, and we fuck good," he winked, earning a disgusted swat to the arm from me.

The other two buckled up silently, but once on the road, Lukas leaned forward with a scowl again.

"The fuck are you telling her all that shit for? It's not just your shit to tell, Jense."

Jensen shrugged. "It's common knowledge, so it's fine. Besides, all kings need a queen, right?"

"Right?" He replied slowly, making Jensen smirk.

"Well, you're welcome. I made her ours."

Lukas looked annoyed as fuck now.

Well, good.

Asshole.

"What the hell does *that* mean?"

"It means, between Caden sticking up for her and me telling our teacher in class this morning that she's one of us, she is officially part of our group," he exclaimed proudly to Lukas's horror.

"Bad idea, Jense," he hissed, but Tyler laughed like a hyena, smacking his knee as he hooted.

"Claire's gonna blow a fucking gasket! Do you think people will just bow down to Rory?"

I listened to them talk it over, only half paying attention, but I perked up instantly when we arrived at the house to find Caden's Challenger parked in the driveway.

We all walked inside together, and Caden looked up as he leaned against the bench with a teasing smirk on his face.

"I know you guys can't handle it when I'm not around, but a welcome home party?"

Jensen rolled his eyes playfully.

"As if. We were coming over to swim in your pool and hang out with Rory."

Caden's eyes landed on mine and his expression softened instantly.

"Hey, how's the face?"

"It's okay," I shrugged, not knowing how to act in case he got into trouble, but he raised an eyebrow and smiled at me.

"Well, are you gonna just stand there, or give me a hug?"

I hesitated before walking across the room, a strange sense of relief washing over me as he pulled me against his chest and held me tightly, kissing the top of my head. "You sure you're okay? I would have checked on you, but Mom kept my phone here."

"Did she send you to your dad's?" I asked softly, his body tensing before he replied with bluntness in his tone.

"You know about my dad?"

"Only that he exists and you stay there sometimes," I mumbled, feeling bad for upsetting him, but he just chuckled.

"Liar. What have the guys been telling you?"

Jensen leaned against the wall and crossed his arms.

"Basic shit. You get sent there when you're naughty, and your dad's mean."

"When I'm fucking naughty, huh?" He asked with amusement plastered on his face.

"Yep."

"So, what did I miss at school today?" He asked, not moving back from his hold on me.

Tyler laughed like a maniac, waving his arms around with sudden enthusiasm.

"Oh, you should have been there, man! Jensen stood up for Rory in class, so you can imagine the gossip around that, but he took her from class with this big speech to the teacher that she's one of us. Guess the school just got themselves a queen. Lukas and I weren't even in their class and we heard about it within minutes of it happening."

Caden finally moved back from me, giving me a frown.

"Why did Jensen need to save you today? Everyone knows to leave you alone."

Tyler kept fucking laughing.

"Save her? Fuck no! He told Claire to fuck off for her own safety, or he was going to let Rory kick the crap out of her. Kind of wish he'd just let her to be honest. I love a fucking girl fight."

Caden scowled, ignoring his friend's opinion as he turned to me.

"Claire started her shit on you?"

I rolled my eyes.

He was acting like I'd had the shit kicked out of me, not a little girl tiff.

"She just figured without you there to protect me, that she should see how far she could push me. She didn't do anything other than sit next to me. Jensen told her to get out of his seat before she could say much, though. It wasn't a big deal."

"His seat, huh?" Caden asked, a hint of sarcasm in his voice that I didn't understand.

I gave him a casual shrug that he didn't seem to really like.

"Yeah, he decided to sit with me so people backed off."

Caden and Jensen shared a silent conversation for a moment before Tyler spoke up, breaking their standoff.

"Let's all go swimming, yeah? Good to see you, Holloway," then he took off outside with Jensen and Lukas behind him.

Caden sighed before looking at me again with curiosity.

"So, they looked out for you today? No other problems?"

I fiddled with my hands and shook my head.

"No problems, but we left morning class and hung out till

lunch before coming home, so I guess no one got the chance. I still find it weird that we get out at lunch most of the week."

Seriously, study period wasn't compulsory, so unless we had a scheduled assignment or extra lesson, we never had to stick around once lunch was over.

He seemed confused for a moment before raising an eyebrow.

"They've seriously brought you into the crew, huh? Never thought I'd see the day."

I frowned, not following what he was implying.

"What day?"

"The day that a fucking girl brought them to their knees," he stated casually, taking my hand and leading me out to the pool to join the others as if he hadn't just dropped that little fucking bombshell.

Fuck me.

"Want a beer?" Tyler asked as he climbed out of the pool hours later, glancing around the group.

The other three nodded, but I hesitated, not particularly wanting Max to bust me drinking.

"Max would kill me."

Caden grinned, pulling me firmly against him and causing the cool water to splash around us.

"Mom and Max took off for a week. Mom's got some business stuff to do, and Max wanted to go with her."

"They left us alone?" I asked, anger lacing my tone.

I hardly knew these guys, and Dad had just left me there?

He was lucky that I was actually getting along with them, or I'd have blown a fucking fuse right about now.

He looked amused for a moment before winking at me.

"Well, they think I'm still at Dad's. Dad doesn't give a fuck what I get up to, so I came home when I heard they were going away for a bit. Figured you'd want company."

Jensen smirked, giving Caden a tormenting waggle of the eyebrows.

"Hey, I would've kept her company for you."

"I bet you fucking would've," he snorted, but gave me a small smile and continued, "Anyways, have a beer. It's fine."

I finally nodded and Tyler wandered inside to get everyone a drink, but Lukas watched Caden with a frown.

"What's the deal? Her dad isn't here for you to upset but you haven't kept your hands off her."

Great way to freak me out.

Thanks, Lukas.

My body tensed and I swam back from Caden slightly, but he rolled his eyes and gave me space as he replied.

"C'mon, I've got a hot stepsister. Why would I keep my hands to myself?"

"Oh, I dunno, because maybe if you knew what really happened to her, you wouldn't…"

For fuck's sake, was he ever going to shut his goddamn mouth?

I angrily threw a tennis ball at him as it bobbed past me, socking him in the eye with it.

"Mind your own fucking business, asshole."

He rubbed his tender eye and scowled at me.

"Damnit, Aurora. You are my business."

"Like hell. I haven't been your business in a long fucking time. It was all an act anyways, so stop acting so heartbroken by me," I bit out, his hands splashing water everywhere as he smacked them against the surface with frustration.

"It isn't an act and it never has been! I fucking loved you, Rory, and you won't even hear me out as to what actually happened!"

Tyler stood by the pool silently, glancing between us with

confusion, but Caden and Jensen paid close attention as we kept arguing.

Lukas was lucky I wasn't completely crazy, or I'd have drowned him where he stood.

I flung my hands in the air with annoyance, flicking water across the water's surface.

"You don't know what fucking love is, so don't give me that shit. I'm not doing this with you, back the fuck off."

"Why won't you let me explain?!" He shouted, but I was fucking done.

"Because, you can't fix it, so why bother? You have no idea what you did when you walked away from me that day. No fucking clue," then I swam to the edge of the pool and hauled myself out, snatching a beer from Tyler on the way past.

I made sure to slam the door on my way inside, and I didn't care if I looked like a spoiled fucking brat.

I was only alone for ten minutes before Caden found me in the kitchen.

He kept his distance as he spoke gently, waiting for me to go to him if I wanted the comfort.

"Hey, you okay?"

"I don't want to talk about it," I said bitterly, but he just shrugged.

"That's fine, just wanted to check on you."

"Well stop it!" I shouted, his eyes narrowing at my outburst.

I pushed myself off the bench and finished my beer as I chugged it down, glaring at him with frustration.

I knew I was alienating the one person who appeared to have my back at this point in my life, but I couldn't stop myself even if I wanted to.

"Stop pretending to care about me! You don't give a shit about anyone but yourself, so…"

He moved faster than I expected as my back hit the wall

and he got in my face, his hand wrapping around my throat before I could shove him back.

Panic surged through me as he became nose to nose with me and growled.

"You hardly know me, so don't you *dare* tell me who I give a shit about. Why the fuck wouldn't I want to check on you?"

"Don't fucking touch me!" I screamed, desperately clawing at his hands, needing distance from him.

He was scaring me.

"Why? You like it," he sneered, his words digging deep inside me until I couldn't fucking breathe.

My eyes watered as I tried to block the memories out, but I refused to let tears fall.

"Holloway, let her go!" Jensen snapped as he walked into the room, but Caden glared at him over his shoulder without doing as he'd asked.

"Fuck off, Gilbert. This has nothing to do with you."

"Bro, she isn't breathing."

"That's because my fucking hand's around her throat," he replied sarcastically, making Jensen glare daggers at him.

"Holloway!"

He snorted, letting go and shoving me hard in Jensen's direction.

"Fucking have her then. You only want to fuck her anyways."

I tensed up as Jensen's arms went around my middle to catch me as Caden stormed off, but he let go instantly as I yanked back from him, keeping his concerned gaze on me.

"Hey, breathe. I won't touch you, okay? But you need to work with me to help you breathe properly. Look at me."

I peered into his piercing blue eyes, and the look on his face told me to do as I was told.

There was something about him that made me want to

trust him in that moment, and I reached a hand out to him, needing the contact.

He hesitated before taking it, pulling me closer so he could hold my face gently in his hands.

"C'mon, it's just you and me, babe. Take a breath in with me, okay?"

I struggled, but after a few attempts I choked on fresh air, earning a small smile from him.

"There you go. Better?"

I choked again as more cool air filled my lungs, closing my eyes and leaning my forehead on his shoulder for comfort.

I wasn't going to lie, Caden had managed to scare the shit out of me.

"Caden…"

"Meet the *real* Caden Holloway. See why people are so surprised that he took you in so easily? He's not a nice guy unless you're me, his mother, Ty, or Lukas. What did you say to upset him like that?" He asked gently, his fingers stroking my back in a calming motion.

Shame burned inside me, but I shrugged.

"Nothing."

"*Sure* you didn't. You going to come back out to the pool to hang out or…"

I took a step back, shaking my head.

"Nah, I might head out for the night and stay somewhere else. I don't want to be here."

Not with the asshole still roaming around.

He sighed but gave me a small smile as if we were sharing secrets.

I guessed we were since Caden was such a private person.

"Word of advice? Holloway won't get violent with you. Ever. He didn't hurt you right now, he just scared you. It's how he works, babe. He just wants you to think he's capable of physically hurting you so you fall in line. I promise you're safe to stay here."

I hesitated before nodding, my anxiety calming a tiny amount.

"Okay. Thanks, Jense."

He looked uncomfortable, but he shrugged.

"It's okay. I'll see you later, call me if you need me."

I thanked him again before heading up to my room and shutting myself inside.

I curled up in bed and finally let the tears I'd been holding onto fall.

It was going to be a long fucking night.

I woke in the middle of the night, jumping when I noticed Caden leaning against the doorframe with his arms crossed and a hard expression on his face.

It was only just visible in the moonlight, but I could tell he was frustrated.

I scrambled back against the headboard, and he finally spoke in a low voice.

"Never tell me who I care for. You drove me insane this afternoon when you said that shit. You pissed me the fuck off if I'm being honest with you."

"Why didn't you hurt me then?" I asked softly, and he snorted as his expression hardened more.

"Hurt you? I wanted to do more than fucking hurt you, Aurora. I wanted to fuck some goddamn sense into you and make you scream from under me until you didn't even know your own goddamn *name* anymore."

A shiver ran through me at his tone, and when I didn't say anything, he stalked towards the bed and ripped the covers back.

His eyes scanned my face as he growled, "Tell me right now if I'm not allowed to fucking touch you, Rory. You got two seconds."

Ah, fuck.

I knew it was stupid, but I wanted him to touch me.

Deep down, I fucking needed him to.

Since he was one of the only people to be able to touch me and actually make me feel good about it, I was basically craving him.

I finally answered, no louder than a whisper.

"Touch me."

A growl ripped from him as he dove down to kiss me hard, a gasp of surprise leaving me at how sudden it was.

He ran his tongue along mine angrily, a groan leaving him as he took my lower lip between his teeth.

"You drive me insane all the fucking time, Rory."

I flattened my hands against his abs as his shirt rode up, and he gritted his teeth at my touch, giving me a small amount of confidence as he forced out, "You're making it worse. I just want to jam myself so deep inside you that you forget every other man who's ever fucking been there."

It was a nice thought if I was being honest, and the more confident I became, the more I knew I was asking for fucking trouble.

My hands ran further up his shirt as I absently kissed across his pecs and up his neck as I sat up and leaned over him.

Forgetting the memories would be nice.

"You think it would be that good? That I'd forget the rest?"

He smirked with a sense of cockiness that would look arrogant on anyone else, but it just made me hotter for him.

I was fucking melting.

"I *know* it would be that good."

"Promise?" I asked softly, and he hesitated as an unsure look crossed his face, mixed with confusion.

"Yeah, sure."

"Okay," I whispered, reaching for the waistband of his sweats, hoping he didn't see my hands shaking slightly.

He flipped me onto my back, a feral grin on his face.

"You sure? Because I'll be *devastated* if you're fucking with me right now."

I ignored the anxiety in my head that screamed at me to stop as I shuffled out of my own sleep shorts and shirt, a small boost of confidence hitting me as his green eyes greedily trailed over my naked body with appreciation.

"Caden, I trust you. I mean it," I added, something crossing his expression that almost looked like regret, but he masked it quickly and gave me his panty-dropping smile.

"In that case, lay there and let me make you feel good."

I knew I was tense as he moved down my body, but once his mouth moved over my pussy, I relaxed.

A complete calm washed over me as he worked me up until I was a gasping, shaking mess in front of him, my limbs feeling like jelly as I went to move in the aftermath.

He cockily crawled up my body, stripping himself off and moving his hand between us to stroke himself.

"We don't have to fuck if you don't want to."

"I do," I replied quickly, making him chuckle, oblivious to my desperate reason of wanting his touch.

"Alright. I'm rough in bed but I'll start off a little nicer on you. You on the pill?"

"Yeah, why?"

"Thank fuck," he groaned, startling me as he finally pushed inside me.

It fucking burned, and my entire body tensed up with discomfort.

He stilled, looking down at me in the moonlight with

confusion in his eyes.

"Hey, you okay?"

I nodded, trying hard to fight off the fear that threatened to spill out of me, but his face softened completely, and he lay over me more so he could stroke my cheek, taking my nerves as inexperience.

I mean, I guessed it was that too.

"I've got you, okay? I'll be gentle, I promise. I won't pick up the pace until you want me to."

Thank fuck.

I seriously needed a minute.

When I relaxed, he started moving again, and I had to admit that he knew what he was doing.

My nails dug into his back as the panic slowly left me, and he groaned the harder I dug them in.

He buried his face in my neck and sucked hard on the sensitive skin, causing me to let out a little moan that seemed to rev him up more.

His hips picked up the pace, and when he knew I was okay with it, he went even harder, lifting one of my legs over his shoulder to get deeper somehow.

I didn't know sex could be so good as he fucked me into the mattress, his fingers digging into my thigh and surprising me when an orgasm started to build so soon.

The angle of his thrusts changed and his pubic bone rubbed against my clit, sending me over the edge so suddenly that it startled me.

I clung to him as he hammered into me, my nails tearing his back up in the process which just seemed to turn him on even more.

I panicked as he moved back and flipped me onto my stomach, his arm going around my middle to lift my ass up as he moved back inside me.

I felt caged in and exposed, the panic rolling through me

like a wave.

His sweaty chest slid over my back as he kissed down the side of my neck, and just as I started to relax again, his hand came around the front of my throat and he squeezed, causing me to buck against him.

I was officially fucking panicking.

"Caden..."

"I warned you I like it rough, but I won't hurt you. Trust me, remember?" He murmured in my ear without moving his hand, and I shivered as he licked down the cord of my neck and bit into my shoulder firmly.

I'd never really understood why people liked the position, but the rougher he became the more I wanted to let him have his way with me completely.

There was something fucking wrong with me.

The arm he had around my middle moved slightly so his hand was between my legs, and I gasped as his fingertips rubbed my sensitive clit, making him growl.

"Fuck you feel good."

Oh, fuck.

My back arched and he groaned, moving his hand from around my throat to push my chest down into the mattress more to fuck me harder again.

I let out a loud scream as an orgasm ripped through me and he finally buried deep, coming inside me before slumping over my back to catch his breath.

When he finally rolled off me, he gently pulled me into his arms and placed soft kisses down my throat.

I knew I'd be bruised and sore in the morning, but I didn't mind.

It was worth it.

When I stayed quiet, he chuckled softly in my ear.

"What's on your mind? I can hear the wheels turning."

I fidgeted for a moment before speaking, my anxiety

fighting itself.

I wanted to be left alone to deal with my emotions, but also be held by him to deal with them.

"Can you stay in here with me tonight, or does that break your rules?"

He tucked me even tighter against him and kissed the top of my head, his voice a whisper.

"Of course I can stay. For future reference, you can't break the rules if there are no rules, baby."

I smiled against his chest, feeling safe despite the anxiety bubbling below the surface as I drifted off to sleep in his arms with a false sense of security.

Caden

I lied.

It totally broke my fucking rules.

I never cuddled.

Ever.

I should have gone back to my room, but something kept me there.

She annoyed the fuck out of me and I wanted her gone, but I'd let her get close, just for one night.

After all, I was the reason her father hurt her.

She was meant to just be a bit of fun until I got her and Max to fucking leave, but I found myself enjoying the company.

Usually, I spent most nights alone in my massive house, but now I at least had her noise in the background to make me feel less lonely.

Mom worked her ass off, so it's not like she was running off to party.

I had a good life because Mom made it for me.

I was lucky, I guessed.

Tyler was always alone because his parents were shit, and Jensen's dad was the only parent around in his life, but even that was a rare occasion.

Lukas's mom was basically always home, but she was fucking weird.

We didn't spend a lot of time at his, mainly because she wouldn't fuck off and leave us alone.

I knew everyone noticed me move to Rory's other side at school to stop Claire from tripping her in the cafeteria the other day, but I didn't give a shit.

I had to play my cards right.

Rory jerked in her sleep, making me frown.

She seemed to have nightmares whenever she slept, but she obviously wasn't going to tell me why.

Jensen offered to tie her up and scare it out of her, but Lukas had a few things to say about that plan.

I didn't see the problem.

It's not like we were going to actually *torture* her.

I was an asshole, not a thug.

Lukas claimed he couldn't tell us what demons she was trying to hide behind that tough girl mask, but I called bullshit.

He says the shit between them was old news, but it was definitely the reason she fucking hated him so much.

The moment one of us mentioned trying to get it out of her, he either changed the subject or flat out told us we were imagining shit.

I couldn't wait for her to finally break, because she was going to.

One way or another.

CHAPTER FOUR

RORY

"Hey, you okay today?" Jensen asked quietly as he leaned against my locker lazily the next morning.

I smiled, seeming to surprise him as I patted his arm.

"Yeah, I'm okay. Thanks, Jense."

"You sure? You seem different," he frowned, peering at me more closely as he studied me.

I didn't feel different, so I had no idea what he was talking about.

"Do I?" I asked with confusion, making him nod.

When I didn't flinch back from him as he moved closer, he carefully placed an arm around my shoulders and smiled as if we were buddies.

"Yeah. What happened? Did you bury Holloway somewhere?"

"I was buried somewhere alright," Caden's voice said from behind us, and we both glanced over to see him watching us closely with his arms crossed.

He looked pissed off, his eyes narrowing into a small glare which confused the fuck out of me.

Jensen raised an eyebrow, seeming amused by his mood.

"Well, good morning to you too. What's up your ass this morning?"

"You," he muttered, his eyes watching me intensely until I started to feel nervous.

Jensen took my tense body as a sign that he was making me uncomfortable, so he moved back from me as he replied to Caden.

"I didn't do shit. Look, don't give Rory any crap, okay? You…"

"Rory and I are good, don't you worry," Caden suddenly smirked, hooking a finger through the belt loops on my denim shorts and yanking me flush against him.

Jensen didn't look convinced until Caden ran his fingers through my hair and I gave him a small smile, the nerves melting away with the motion.

I didn't understand why I'd become so comfortable around him, but I felt like he understood me, and that took a lot for me to admit to myself.

Tyler and Lukas walked towards us, but before I could wave at them Caden dipped down and kissed me, backing me into the lockers with a solid thud.

People would gossip even more, but I was beyond caring as he planted his hands on my waist and deepened the kiss, pressing his front firmly against mine.

Holy fuck, I could do that with him all day.

"What the fuck did we miss?" Tyler's hyena laugh asked from close by, but Jensen shrugged.

"Fuck knows. I'm completely and utterly confused."

Caden was practically fucking me against the lockers with his clothes on, and I had to admit, I liked that all of his attention was on me in that moment.

When he finally moved back, he tucked my loose hair behind my ear and smiled at me cheekily.

"We should have just stayed in bed. Right, baby?"

Lukas tensed up, but Tyler cackled with laughter.

"Holy fuck, you two are banging? C'mon Holloway, she's your sister!"

People were gawking at us, but Caden just smirked and swatted my butt with a sharp crack.

"No, she's my hot sister, dude."

Oh my god.

He did not just fucking say that.

"Caden!" I exclaimed with horror, both he and Tyler cracking up with laughter, but Jensen rolled his eyes as if he were bored, while Lukas appeared genuinely worried for me.

Eventually, Caden simmered down and headed off to class with Tyler and Lukas, leaving Jensen to walk to class with me.

Once in the classroom, he gave me a sideways glance, speaking quietly.

"So, you and Caden, huh? You two hated each other yesterday afternoon, so how did it turn around to make-up sex?"

I shrugged, my face heating with embarrassment.

"It just did, okay? Now shut up."

"Aurora," he said gently as concern filled his tone, making me look over at him.

"What?"

He hesitated, a strange look crossing his eyes before he blocked it, shrugging it off as he glanced away from me.

"Never mind."

What was with him?

He acted strangely for the rest of class, and he kept glancing at me during lunchtime as I sat on Caden's lap at our table.

I'd fucking had enough of his attitude by the end of that,

and the moment the others had headed off to the gym for a workout, I cornered him by his locker.

"What the *fuck* is your problem?" I snapped, a snort coming from him without looking up at me.

"I don't have a problem."

"You've been weird all day, so start talking before I make you," I growled, fisting my hands by my side.

He raised an eyebrow and smirked at me with amusement.

"I seriously don't have a problem. I just don't want the girls having more ammo to throw at you. Banging your stepbrother is serious fucking ammo. You're hot when you're mad, Donovan."

"Jensen!"

"What? It's true," he shrugged, turning to close his locker but I shoved him hard, getting in his face as his back hit the lockers with a bang.

"Stop it! You're being a fucking..."

"You're turning me on, babe," he replied with a slow sarcastic groan, pissing me off more.

What an ass.

"Cut it out."

"Nope. I can't touch you, but I sure as shit can tell you all about how I'd like to," he grinned, his expression faltering when I frowned at him with confusion.

"Why can't you touch me?"

"Well for starters, you don't like to be touched by anyone except Caden, but you two are dating, so..."

"We aren't dating!" I squeaked out with alarm, and he blinked at me as if he was trying to figure me out.

"You sure?"

"We fucked once, and everyone knows Caden doesn't date," I snorted, my breath catching as he reached up and cupped my chin gently in his hand.

"I can't touch you, Rory. I won't do that to you."

"What do you mean by that?" I whispered, watching the fight in his eyes.

I wouldn't have stopped him if he wanted to touch me.

I was starting to think maybe I actually trusted him.

"I just... fuck," he muttered, his hand moving to play with the tips of my black hair as he argued internally with himself.

"What's going on?" I asked softly, his chocolate hair flopping over his eyes as he shook his head.

"Nothing. I just won't hurt you like that."

Huh?

"You won't hurt me."

"Yes, I will," he said sternly, a shiver going through his body as my hand lifted to rest on his tense chest.

"I trust you not to."

He let out a growl, swooping down and kissing me hard for what felt like an eternity before he pushed himself back and shot me a hard look, ignoring the surprise on my face from the kiss that wasn't at *all* unwanted.

"Then you're stupid. Don't trust anyone, Rory. I fucking mean it," then he stalked off after the others, leaving me alone in the empty hallway.

What the fuck was that about?

I headed to the library to finish my homework, not at all surprised to find the guys still in the gym when I'd finished.

I leaned against the wall, watching as Caden and Jensen appeared to be racing each other on the treadmills at high speed, sweat drenching their toned bodies as their arms kept pumping.

Tyler on the other hand gave me a strange glance as he lifted his weights, but he didn't say anything, and neither did Lukas, who was using an exercise bike.

When Caden finally noticed me standing there, he slowed his machine down and gave me a naughty wink.

"Hey, baby. You ready to head home?"

"I can bus it if you guys aren't done?" I offered, but Lukas rolled his eyes dramatically.

"Trust me, we're done here. I'll see you guys tomorrow," then he bailed off the bike and stalked off, causing me to frown with confusion.

Caden noticed the expression on my face and smiled.

"Don't worry about him, he's just pissy about you and Jensen locking tonsils."

Wait, what?

My entire body tensed up, and he gave me an amused smile as he grabbed his sweat towel.

"Did you think Jense would just keep it to himself? He's my best friend, Rory. We don't keep secrets."

"No, I just wanted to tell you myself," I grumbled curtly, making him frown at my discomfort.

"Hey, relax. We aren't together, like you told Jense, so it's okay. Maybe don't parade it around in front of people though. Save yourself some drama."

Jensen finally climbed off his machine and snatched his towel off the bench before stalking right past me with his jaw clenched.

Fuck that.

His body went completely rigid as I reached out and rested a hand on his arm, a slight snarky tone in my voice.

"Why are you mad at me?"

He swung his gaze to mine, his expression softening as his blue eyes clashed with mine.

"I'm not, babe. I just can't do this shit with you, okay?"

"Okay," I replied softly, watching in confusion as he gave me a sad smile and left without another word.

Tyler followed silently, leaving Caden and I to walk out to his Challenger alone.

Once we were inside it and ready to go, he sighed.

"Give Jense some time. He'll come around."

I gave him a look of surprise, a bit confused about him not being mad.

"You want him to come around? Do you guys normally mess around with the same girl?"

He shrugged, starting the car and causing the engine to roar to life, Pull Up by L.A Leakers blasting instantly and almost deafening me.

He reached over and turned it down a bit as he drove out of the parking lot and towards home.

"There's nothing wrong with it. Ty would climb you like a tree too if you let him."

"Really?" I was confused about everything now.

Tyler was always fucking around about shit, but he'd never actually shown any real interest.

Had he?

Caden was quiet for a moment before glancing up at me, his green eyes suddenly serious.

"What happened between you and Lukas?"

I looked out the window and clammed up instantly.

I wasn't ready to talk about that.

It was still too raw, and it had nothing to do with him.

"Nothing that matters."

"Well, it does fucking matter because it's causing a rift between the guys. You and Lukas can't be in the same fucking house together without starting a fight, and the guys are starting to think the worst. Do us all a favour and start talking, Aurora."

I glared at him, becoming defensive at the tone he was using on me.

"Excuse me? It's none of your goddamn *business*, Holloway."

A nasty smirk hit his face as he turned a corner, not looking over at me.

"*Everything* is my business, babe, so tell me what happened. You two dated and he cheated on you? He broke your heart? He…"

"Stop the car," I forced out at a whisper, making him snort.

"No."

"Stop the fucking car, Caden!" I shouted as panic and rage overtook me.

I unbuckled my seat belt and threw myself out of the car the moment he slammed on the brakes, the door slamming behind me.

He followed, angrily grabbing my bicep and yanking me back sharply.

"You want a repeat of the other night? Get back in the car and talk, for fuck's sake."

"Let me go, asshole!" I shouted, but his hand clamped over my mouth and he shoved me against the side of his car.

He didn't flinch, but I cringed and hoped it didn't put a dent in it.

"No. You listen to me, okay? No one gets between me and my guys. The fact that you're making everyone turn on each other is starting to piss me off. Just do as you're fucking told and everything will be peachy. So…"

I bit his hand hard as a last resort in my panic, an angry growl ripping from him.

When he pulled his fist back, I closed my eyes and waited for the impact, but it never came.

I finally braved a peek at him to find him watching me, his hand by his side again as if it had never happened.

Maybe it hadn't and I was finally fucking losing it.

"Are you going to get back in the car and talk, or do I fucking leave you here?" He asked in a low voice, frustration in his intense gaze.

"I'm not getting back in that car with you," I snapped,

feeling proud that my voice didn't shake, despite feeling like a panic attack was forming.

He wasn't going to shove me in there and kidnap me, was he?

"Suit yourself. Enjoy your walk," he shrugged to my relief, climbing back into the driver's seat and revving the engine, taking off with a screech of tires like the asshole he was.

I flipped him off as I snatched my phone from my pocket, texting Jensen to pick me up and hoping he was over his tantrum.

Rory: Hey, can you pick me up from the old tree just down from the school? Had a fight with Caden.

I only had to wait a second before he replied, my panic attack slipping away as my body relaxed.

Jensen: Sure thing, babe. Be there in a few.

I leaned against the tree and scrolled through Facebook until the crunching of tires on gravel made me look up to see the Camaro pull over on the side of the road.

Jensen rolled the window down and jerked his head towards the passenger seat, and I silently walked around the car and climbed in, waiting for him to speak.

He drove for a minute or two before glancing over at me.

"What did you fight about, and where is he?"

I laced my fingers together on my lap with a sigh.

"Lukas and other stuff. He manhandled me and went to hit me, so I wasn't about to get back in his car. He took off towards home."

He looked sad for a moment as his voice turned gentle, soothing me slightly.

"Babe, trust me when I say he'd never actually hurt you. He just likes to scare people into doing as they're told."

"I don't care if he physically hurts me or not, I'm not some lapdog that sits when I'm told. He doesn't own me, and the sooner he figures that out, the better off he'll be," I bit out without looking at him, my hands fisting into balls.

"Is the shit with Lukas really that bad? Why can't you just tell him to shut him up?"

My gaze finally slid over to him, and I hesitated before speaking.

"It's fucking personal, so no, I won't tell him shit."

He was quiet for a while, making me sigh.

This conversation was going fucking nowhere.

"Can I stay with you tonight?"

"Like, on my couch?" He asked slowly, his pretty blue eyes glancing at me with uncertainty from behind his chocolate hair.

I shrugged. "I don't care where, I just don't want to be near Caden. He's been so nice since I moved in, but ever since he got back from his dad's, he's been a moody asshole."

"Yeah, alright. But on one condition?"

"What's that?"

"You talk to me. Doesn't have to be everything, but I just need something. I can see everything in your mind is still hurting you, and I think opening up a little might ease your mind slightly," he said softly, making me meet his gaze again.

My chest tightened with anxiety, telling me I was probably going to have a fucking panic attack after all.

He slowly took my hand, giving me an understanding smile.

"Not right now, later. First, I think we need a beer."

"Caden's pissed that you're staying here," Jensen stated later that night as he glanced up from his phone, making me snort from my spot on the couch.

"Good. Hope his shitty mood keeps him awake all fucking night, too."

He chuckled, stretching out on the couch and putting his

phone back in his pocket, glancing over at me again and catching me checking out his yummy abs where his shirt had ridden up.

He smirked, amusement in his voice.

"See something you like, babe?"

I snapped out of it, giving him the middle finger and lying back on my part of the couch to sip my beer, hoping my face wasn't too red.

When his gaze remained on me, I looked back at him with irritation.

"What?"

"We've had a few beers now, so it's time you start talking, don't you think?"

I hesitated before sitting up, wrapping my arms around my legs to rest my chin on my knees.

I pushed the panic down, convincing myself I could trust him, despite not wanting to.

Doubt nagged at me, but Jensen wouldn't hurt me.

I felt it deep in my bones that he had my back, even if the others didn't.

"Where do I start then? I don't think I can talk about all of it, and…"

"Hey, just start wherever you want. I won't make you talk about things you really don't want to talk about, okay? I just need you to open up a little bit."

His blue eyes were gentle, and it gave me the courage to nod, deciding to confide in him.

"Lukas and I were best friends since the first day at preschool. We lived in each other's pockets from day one, but shit got complicated at the end of middle school. He got weird around me and seemed to find excuses to bail on our plans and shit. We slowly became more distant, until the one time I needed him the most and he completely turned his back on me."

Hot tears stung my eyes, but I took a deep breath and looked him right in the eye, ignoring my voice as it cracked with emotion.

"My dad's always getting into debt with people a lot richer and more important than he ever was. He lost a bet to some rich guy at one of his parties a few years after we lost basically all of our money, and we had *heaps*. He tried to win the money back at poker but lost all over again. He was already in debt to this guy and was well over his head before that night, so Max threw me under the bus to save himself like he has many times before. This time was different though. I'll never forgive my dad for it, and when he dies, he'll be lucky if I show up to spit on his fucking grave."

I knew I was crying and probably looked a mess.

All I wanted was to reach for him, but at the same time, I couldn't bear the thought of having someone touching me.

I closed my eyes and took a shaky breath to continue, the panic and anxiety clawing at my insides, threatening to tear me apart.

"The creep made a bargain with Max that all his debts to him would be cleared if he gave me to him for the night."

Jensen's body stiffened, and he went to reach for my hand but stopped last minute when I flinched back as if it were a snake.

"Fuck, Rory…"

Sobs wracked my body as I curled into myself, as if to protect what was left of me, but I kept speaking from behind my shield.

"Dad knew he'd rape me. He knew how horrible the man was, but he still tossed me at him because he only gives a shit about himself. Lukas came over the same night, and I saw him at my fucking bedroom window before he ran away. He didn't even call for help, he just…," I choked out before completely breaking down at that memory.

That always hurt more than the memory of the rape.

Lukas had fucking *abandoned* me.

When I didn't flinch back as Jensen took my hand, he gently hauled me into his lap and cradled me against his chest, hiding my face in his shirt to let me cry it out.

I didn't know why I'd told him so much of the truth, considering I was going to just work around the worst of it to shut him up.

I'd needed to tell him though, and I was relieved to finally talk about it as some of my demons went silent inside me.

I trusted him.

"He never told you why he didn't help you? Or why he went to a different high school?" He finally asked, making me sniff and look up at him through my broken blue eyes.

"I basically didn't see him again until I came to your school. It's too late now, and I don't want to hear his excuses. He gutted me that night, and I won't ever forgive him for it. He has no idea how bad it was."

"Who knows about this? Have you ever spoken to a counsellor or…"

"No, and I don't want anyone else to know," I warned, watching his eyes as shame and regret washed through him before he covered it up and gave me a small smile, making me forget about it.

"Hey, it's okay. How about I put a movie on and we can just stay curled up here for a few hours, yeah?"

I nodded, moving off his lap so he could set the movie up and grab more beer.

When he was done, he got comfortable on the couch and pulled me onto his lap again, hesitating before placing a soft kiss on top of my head.

"You're safe here, baby. I promise."

I wasn't sure when I managed to fall asleep, but I woke up to Jensen carrying me up to his room and tucking me into his bed, sliding in beside me and putting his arms around my middle to snuggle up to me.

I fell back to sleep not long after.

Jensen

Fuck.

Holy fucking shit.

Caden couldn't use that shit against Rory.

No way in fucking hell.

I mean, even if she hadn't grown on me, I couldn't make a joke out of being raped.

No wonder Lukas freaked out every time we started talking about basically beating it out of her.

It explained her nightmares, but it also explained her being so wary.

I felt like a piece of shit, actually.

I'd wanted to fuck her, then break her the good old-fashioned way by leaking gossip around school or locking her in an abandoned house all night to scare her.

I got the feeling that she wasn't the type of girl that scared easily though.

If I was being honest, it was hard to stick to the plan after finding out the truth.

I mean, after finding out all the shit about her past, I felt bad.

She was a pretty cool chick, and I didn't say that about many girls.

Sure, I'd fuck her if I got the chance because she was crazy hot, but I'd probably go back for seconds with her, maybe thirds.

That's how cool she was.

She slept pretty peacefully apart from a few violent twitches through the night, but she relaxed again the moment I'd tightened my hold on her, making me feel like fucking shit all over again.

She shouldn't trust me, but she'd contently fallen asleep in my arms as if it were normal for us to do.

I needed to keep my distance from her, or I was going to be in fucking trouble.

I hoped she'd head home when she woke up, because I needed to go and fuck some other bitch to get her out of my head.

Might see if Lukas wanted to join me and make it a fucking party.

Get it? Fucking party?

Like, literally?

Ah, fuck. Forget about it.

CHAPTER FIVE

RORY

*L*oud banging woke me the next morning, but my sudden panic was instantly calmed as Jensen's sleepy voice rumbled from behind me, his arms pulling me against him more.

"It's okay, it'll be Ty. He said yesterday he might stop in this morning on the way to school. He can use the spare key to get in."

I went to speak, but footsteps stomped up the hallway and the bedroom door slammed open, Caden glaring straight at me as he leaned against the doorframe like the king that he knew he was.

"Now he's fucked the angry out of you, you going to come back home and talk?"

"Caden…," Jensen warned in a low voice, but Caden wasn't having it, as usual.

"Shut it!" He snapped, keeping his angry green eyes on me.

I snorted, flipping him the bird without moving from my safety net of Jensen's arms.

"Fuck off, Holloway."

He looked ready to strangle me as he moved around to my side of the bed and gripped my throat firmly, but not painfully.

"Still got attitude, huh? How about Jense and I fuck it out of you together then?"

My entire body went rigid as his other hand went to grab the top of my pants, panic filling me as the air in my lungs went tight.

Jensen suddenly gave him a solid shove, surprising him with his outburst.

"Back off, Holloway!"

"The fuck, man? She's fucking us anyways, so why the fuck…"

"She fucked you once, doesn't mean shit," he gritted out, and I knew he felt me jump at the angry tone in his voice because his hand carefully rested on my waist for comfort.

"But you…," Caden managed to get out before Jensen cut him off again.

"I let her stay here, I didn't fuck her. Get the fuck out and I'll meet you in the kitchen," he growled, pulling me close to calm me more.

Caden glanced at my shaking body and frowned before leaving us in peace, and Jensen instantly rolled me over to face him, cupping my cheek as he met my gaze.

"Want me to throw him out? Are you okay?"

"I might go and jump on a bus to school. You guys take your time," I mumbled, intending on bailing from the bed, but the hand on my waist gave me a small squeeze, causing me to hesitate.

"Hey, I've got plenty of cars so you can take one of mine. Meet me at your locker?"

I nodded, climbing out of bed and having a quick shower to clear my head before padding down to the kitchen.

I slowed when I noticed Caden and Jensen talking, but

Jensen looked up and gave me a genuine smile, tossing me a set of keys.

I snatched them from the air with a frown.

"Which one?"

"Camaro, babe," he winked, making me roll my eyes as I thanked him, but inside I was having a fucking *orgasm* and singing a prayer to Jesus.

I headed down to the garage, running my hand over the Camaro's hood with admiration before unlocking it and sliding into the driver's seat, letting out a loud moan as I turned the key and the engine roared to life.

I'd never driven a v8 before, but now I understood why most guys would cut off their left nut for one.

I always thought cars like this were sex on wheels, but holy hell, I had a whole new respect for them now.

I gently eased it out of the garage and moaned again as it rumbled with power, cranking the music up until the bass shook the whole car.

I drove towards the school, finding Tyler and Lukas leaning against Tyler's burnt orange BMW i8 Roadster coupe when I arrived.

I parked beside them and turned the music down, ignoring everyone looking at me with wide eyes as the whispering started.

I made sure to lock the Camaro once I'd climbed out, making my way over to the other two confidently.

Tyler grinned, his arms crossed against his chest loosely.

"No way, Jense let you drive the Camaro? He's just out to piss Holloway off now, isn't he? Caden knows that it's one car that Jensen doesn't let anyone else drive. Seeing you driving it will make him crazy mad."

I shrugged, already guessing that not just anyone got to drive it.

"He's already crazy mad. Woke me and Jense up and basically tried to drag me out of bed. I left him at Jensen's because they were fighting or some shit, I dunno. Jensen just tossed me the keys and said he'd meet me at my locker."

"You stayed at Jensen's?" Tyler asked with surprise, and I nodded once in response.

"Yep. Caden can kiss my fucking ass," I retorted, Tyler smirking at me crudely.

"He's more likely to *eat* your ass, babe, but whatever. If he won't, come knock on my door and I'll eat it for you."

"Charming," I replied dryly, intending on walking off, but he waved a cigarette at me with a friendly smile on his face.

"Ignore me, I'm a fucking asshole. Come lean on my car and look cool with me. We were just talking about the party I'm throwing at mine on Friday night. You're coming, right?"

I cringed as I took the cigarette and lit it.

I didn't do big parties, and I assumed these rich pricks knew how to throw a fucking big one.

Don't get me wrong, I liked to party as much as the next bitch, but crowds of strangers made me nervous.

"How many people are going?"

"Everyone, but you're our queen, so you get to hang out in the cool kid's corner with us and avoid people, if you like."

"I do like to party," I finally mumbled, causing Lukas to frown.

"You do?"

I met his gaze and raised an eyebrow.

"Well, I like being drunk or high. So yeah, I guess."

"You smoke weed now?" He choked out with surprise, earning a snort in return.

"Who said I just get high on weed?"

I had a drag of my cigarette before glancing over my shoulder as the sound of power rumbled into the parking lot and a blood-red Lamborghini came into view that I'd seen in Jensen's garage that morning.

Caden's Challenger drove in behind him and they parked next to the Camaro, Jensen climbing out and making a show of checking the Camaro over for damage as if he thought I'd take it off roading or something.

"Looks like you handled her okay then?"

I smirked, flicking the ash from my cigarette.

"C'mon, I'm a good driver, and I have a high respect for muscle cars and V8's. Why be so surprised that it's in one piece?"

"I'm more impressed than surprised, babe," he grinned, jerking a thumb in Caden's direction and turning serious. "Someone has something to say to you."

I glanced over at Caden, noticing the awkward expression on his face, and my eyes instantly jerked back to Jensen accusingly.

"You fucking told him, didn't you?" I hissed, a sigh leaving him.

"No, but I told him to fucking apologize for making it seem like we were going to rape you tag-team style."

Lukas choked on his cigarette, staring at me with wide eyes.

"You told Jensen?"

Before I could take more than two angry steps in his direction, Jensen's arm went around my waist and pulled me back against his chest, his lips tickling my ear as he spoke loud enough for only me to hear him.

"Please let Caden speak, and I'll tell Lukas to back off, okay?"

I relaxed against him slightly, taking a deep breath as I nodded, but he didn't move back from me as he leaned against the BMW beside Tyler, pulling me back with him as his eyes met Lukas's.

"Dude, shut your mouth, okay? It's not your business."

"What the fuck did she tell you?" He growled, and Jensen narrowed his eyes with irritation.

"The truth. Fuck off and leave her alone."

Caden watched us suspiciously for a moment before he set his jaw hard, speaking firmly.

"I'm sorry, okay? I didn't think it would scare you like that. I'd never force myself on someone. I figured you'd be down since I thought you were fucking Jense too."

I glanced at him before looking away, shrugging slightly as I tried to look like it wasn't a big deal.

"Okay."

"Okay?" He asked with a frown of confusion, and I looked up and met his gaze again.

"Yeah, okay. I heard your apology."

He seemed torn for a moment before giving Jensen a silent conversation and heading off to class, jerking his head at Tyler to follow, leaving Jensen and Lukas with me.

Lukas's expression became soft suddenly, and he took a small step in my direction without getting too close.

"I'm worried about you, I really am. Did you seriously talk to Jense about it?"

I was tense but nodded.

"Yeah, I did."

"All of it?"

When I was quiet, Jensen spoke gently but sternly, proving I was right about him having my back.

"She doesn't have to tell me all of it if she doesn't want to. Jesus Christ, Lukas. Let her deal with it in her own fucking time. Stop bringing it up in front of the others, too."

Lukas seemed to be processing it for a moment before finally sighing, defeat filling his almond eyes.

"You think I turned my back on you, but I didn't know what else to do, Rory. You didn't know about the other players in his game."

That made me frown, uneasiness washing over me.

"Other players? There weren't any?"

"Yeah, there were. Like I told you, you never let me explain it all to you."

Jensen moved past me and scruffed him firmly by the front of his shirt, anger rolling off him in waves.

"Explain how you could walk away after what you saw? Give it a fucking crack Lukas, we're all ears."

"Max's debts went way past that one filthy piece of shit. She was promised to more than just him, but I'd managed to pay most of them off myself behind Max's back. That one guy didn't want the money though, and he refused to meet up with me. He wasn't the original deal either," he explained with venom in his voice, a shiver rolling through me.

His eyes were full of pain and apology as he kept speaking, my heart tearing open in the process.

"Max tried cutting me a deal to help with some of my mom's debts to him that weren't even that fucking bad, he just claimed he didn't want the money. He thought if I roughed you up a little and some other shit, that you wouldn't be such a bratty fucking child, then Mom would be square with him."

"What do you mean, roughen her up?" Jensen growled, the pain spreading across Lukas's face as he continued.

"I was meant to do to her, what that piece of shit did. He even threatened to kill Mom if I didn't. Obviously, I told him to fuck off. I loved you, Rory. I didn't think he'd actually let anyone else hurt you like that. When he called and told me to go peek in your window, I did. I had to make sure you were alright, and when I turned away from the window, I was heading inside to fucking kill whoever that prick was, but your father stopped me on the way in. He told me he had someone at my house watching my mom, and all he had to do was give the word and they'd kill her. When I got in his face and tried to get past him still, he told me if I helped you in any way, he'd get someone new to visit you every night instead of the once, and that's what stopped me. I couldn't face you after that, knowing what you thought of me. I was a kid, Rory. Max was super powerful at the time, and…"

I couldn't listen to it anymore as I flung myself at him, wrapping my arms around him tightly and burying my face in his neck as I tried to hold my emotions in.

I wasn't going to fucking cry in the school parking lot.

Fuck no.

After a moment, his shock seemed to wear off, his arms going around me tightly.

"I'm so sorry I couldn't stop any of the hurt. I'm so fucking sorry."

I finally looked up at him and gazed into his eyes.

I'd never noticed the guilt he'd been carrying over the last few years, but now I saw it all.

It had broken his heart knowing he couldn't stop it all for me.

I didn't have the heart to tell him it had basically been for nothing.

"Don't be sorry. There's nothing to be sorry for, Luke."

His body seemed to sag in relief when I called him by his nickname, and he kissed the top of my head affectionately like he always had when we were kids when he wanted to comfort me.

"We can talk later, okay? C'mon, we're going to be late for class."

Jensen muttered something under his breath, but he seemed to perk up slightly as I moved back under his arm as we walked into the school together.

I knew it would happen, but not like this.

Girls usually stole the new girl's clothes in the shower block or made up nasty rumours, but these rich girls were beyond petty crap.

They grabbed me from under the shower spray after gym class, dragging me towards the main door, completely butt naked.

I struggled against their hold on me, but Claire's posse didn't let go until we were out in the main hallway, where they pushed me to the ground and locked me out without even a towel to cover myself.

Familiar panic set in as I noticed eyes on me everywhere as people whispered and giggled, and I scooted back into the corner, trying hard to shield myself from everyone's stares and jokes.

No one moved towards me to help, and tears formed as the anxiety started to race through me.

I never cried in front of people and let them see my weakness, and I was only just managing to hold myself together as a familiar voice cut through the growing crowd.

"C'mon guys, move along. What the fuck are you even looking…"

I peered up from behind my wet tangled hair, finding Caden and the guys in front of me.

For a moment it didn't look like they were going to help me, until Lukas suddenly yanked his hoodie over his head and moved towards me.

Jensen followed, blocking me from everyone's view as Lukas helped me into the hoodie that luckily went halfway down my thighs.

I still felt too exposed, but at least I was covered.

Once they helped me to my feet and I was safely tucked under Lukas's arm, Jensen glared at the crowd of students that had gathered, with complete rage.

"Who the fuck did this, huh? You all know what happens to people who fuck with us, so speak up!"

Caden lazily walked past us, glancing over at me through hooded eyes, his voice quiet.

"They still in the showers?"

I nodded, watching as he kicked the door hard, hearing wood splinter as the door swung wide to see Claire and the girls stop their gossiping, some having the decency to look fucking scared.

Claire was only in her panties and bra, but she smiled as if he was about to sell her a fucking puppy with a bow on it.

"Problem, Holloway? If you wanted a good time, you didn't have to kick the door in. You know I'd let you in."

No one moved as Caden's hand shot out and grabbed her throat, fear flashing across her gaze as he shoved her back hard into the wall with a scowl on his face.

"What did I say, Claire?" He asked in a low voice, the other girls scattering, their leader forgotten.

I'd call them pussies, but I didn't blame them.

He was mad as *fuck*.

"Oh, come on, she...," Claire started, but he just shouted over the top of her.

"She's one of us!" Then he slammed her hard into the wall again to get his point across.

She just chuckled, looking over at me with a nasty glint in her eye.

"It's just one big game to them, you know? Girls don't join their group. They'll fuck you until they're bored, then all of a sudden you'll be dropped like a sack of shit. You think they're actually your friends? You're just a way for them to be amused for a while. Just you wait, Aurora. They're making a joke out of you and you don't even know it."

Caden muttered under his breath at her, making her

sneer before he released his grip and stalked off without a backwards glance.

Tyler got everyone to move along, while Jensen and Lukas guided me into the bathroom to collect my things.

Everything was a soaking pile of fabric in one of the showers, so I sighed as I grabbed my bag, leaving the clothes there in the splattered heap.

I moved against Jensen, hiding my face in his chest as his arms went around me protectively, my anxiety pushing and pulling inside of me as I tried to calm myself.

He kissed the top of my head before brushing the damp hair off my face, meeting my gaze.

"Let me take you home, okay? Lukas can drop the Lambo off at mine later."

I nodded silently, letting him lead me out of the room and through the school until we reached the parking lot, not speaking as we climbed into the Camaro and drove off.

Once he'd gotten me home to the Holloway's, he helped me into my room, pulling me against him for comfort.

"Are you okay?"

"No," I mumbled honestly, his hand cupping my cheek as he gave me a small smile.

I nearly melted at how cute he looked when he did that.

"You want me to stick around for a little?" He offered, and I let out a nervous bubble of laughter.

"Should I at least put pants on?"

That earned me a cheeky smirk from him as his thumb ran across my lower lip.

"Only if you really have to. Kind of wish it was my hoodie you were naked in."

I peered up at his bright blue eyes, my lip twitching into a tiny smile.

"Make up your mind, Gilbert. Do you want me naked, or in your hoodie?"

"Trust me, you'd look better naked," he murmured, his hands resting on my waist as if to stop them roaming my body.

"Jense?"

"Hmm?" He hummed, his thumbs rubbing along my hips.

"Take my mind off today," I whispered, an unsure expression suddenly crossing his handsome face.

"Aurora…"

"Just kiss me, please," I asked, hating that I was practically begging him.

I just needed the comfort, and to forget about the shitty afternoon.

He groaned, his hand moving to the back of my neck, pulling me closer as he kissed me without another word, his other hand sliding down to squeeze one of my butt cheeks as the hoodie lifted slightly.

I rubbed against him as his kiss became more desperate, until he suddenly growled and grabbed my thighs, lifting me and carrying me across the room to plonk my ass down on top of the drawers.

I parted my legs and pulled him closer, letting out a breathy moan as one of his hands moved between us, his fingertips teasing my clit lightly.

He yanked me forwards, pushing a finger inside me and making both of us groan as he started pumping it faster.

My nails dug into his shoulder through his shirt as he added another finger, his lips moving to my neck before he nipped me sharply and took me by surprise.

My legs clamped around his waist as if to hold on when the tingling started, and the moment his thumb rubbed my clit I fucking detonated, pulling him closer if that were possible.

I bit his neck to silence myself until his fingers slowed

and I leaned back, his lips softly kissing over my tender skin where his teeth had nipped me.

"Holy fuck, Rory," he murmured, as if I'd been the one to rock his world instead.

My body was weak from the intensity of it, and I hardly remembered him tucking me into bed and closing the door on his way out as I drifted off to sleep.

He and Caden were going to kill me with orgasms one day, I just fucking knew it.

Caden

I don't even know why I'd helped Rory.

Claire had that shit planned since day one, but I'd told her to fucking hold off on it.

Tyler tracked me down after I'd taken off, a satisfied look on his face as he approached.

"You're starting to like her, aren't you?"

"Why do you say that?" I growled, leaning against the building and lighting a cigarette with irritation.

I watched Jensen lead her up to the parking lot, not realizing I'd made a noise of annoyance until Tyler moved in front of me with a smirk.

"You took off for starters, but you get shitty whenever Jense helps her out. Let him play with her for a while, you've had a turn."

She was fucking with Jensen's head, was I the only one who saw that?

I kept catching him watching her when she wasn't looking, and his attention usually *never* wandered, unless the bitch was at least fucking naked.

Then again, she was starting to fuck with my head too.

I caught myself wondering what she was doing whenever she wasn't with me.

Only for a split-second, but the thought was still there.

"Holloway, we can call this shit off if you want? Maybe we just stop and let Lukas fucking have her. You know he's got his hackles up about it all," Tyler stated, snapping me from my thoughts.

I shook my head, giving him a dirty look.

"Lukas doesn't fucking know what he wants. Leave it, I mean it."

"Alright, it's your call," he shrugged, but I could hear the irritation in his voice.

Fuck me, were they all getting soft?

Rory

"It reeks like pussy in here," Caden stated as he wandered into my room a few hours later.

I peeked out from under the covers and stretch out contently like a cat in the sun.

"Don't like it? Leave, Holloway."

A smirk hit his face and he winked.

"Didn't say I didn't like it. I happen to quite like your pussy."

I hesitated before moving over and patting the bed beside me.

"Jump in?"

He seemed surprised but nodded, pulling the covers back and climbing in, putting an arm out for me to cuddle up to him.

He groaned as I placed one of my legs over him, his hand resting high on my thigh.

"You're still only wearing Lukas's hoodie? C'mon, babe. Play fair."

I snorted with amusement.

"My lack of underwear suddenly a problem for you?"

He grinned, his hand running up and down my thigh, toying with the bottom of the fabric.

"It's not a problem, my lack of willpower might be though. You been playing with yourself in here, or has someone been doing it for you?"

Fucker.

My face heated, a low chuckle coming from him instantly.

"Jense help you relax, did he? I noticed today that you and Lukas's seem friendly again. You guys playing nice now?"

"We had a talk this morning after you left. I don't really want to talk about it, but…"

"But you talked to Jense, right?" He shrugged, hurt in his voice that had me peering up at him, speaking softly.

"I don't want to talk about it again, okay? Jense and Luke can tell you about it though, if you really wanna know."

"Hey, that stunt the girls pulled at school today will be dealt with, okay?" He stated, changing the subject.

I tensed, but his hand trailed right up my thigh and moved under the hoodie, resting on my bare hip.

"They seem to forget that we run the school, not them. It's time they were put back in their place."

He seemed startled when I leaned over and kissed him, but he recovered quickly and kissed me back, almost pulling me on top of him in his need to get closer.

His hands clamped onto my butt cheeks as he ground himself against me, and the moment I nibbled his lower lip, he growled in warning, flipping us over so that I was laying under him.

He yanked the hoodie over my head before he jammed two fingers inside me, a gasp leaving me at how aggressive it was.

Fuck yes.

"Do you want me to fuck you, Rory?" He bit out as his fingers worked harder and faster, a groan of surrender leaving me.

I was going to fucking hell.

"Yes."

"Yes, what?"

"Yes, I want you to fuck me," I breathed as he pulled his fingers out and quickly unzipped his pants, my back arching as he pushed himself inside me firmly without any other warning.

He fucked me like a crazed man, making me scream as he fucked me savagely through my orgasm once it peaked, and when he buried deep and came inside me, he collapsed on top of me with a groan.

We laid in silence for a while, which was surprisingly not awkward in the slightest.

His phone rang from down the hall, making him groan with annoyance as he gave me a kiss and rolled off my sweaty body.

"Come join me in the kitchen in a bit? I'll make some dinner."

I gave him a nod, watching him leave the room before pulling myself out of bed and padding into the bathroom to have a quick shower.

When I finally walked into the kitchen in my tank top

and shorts nearly twenty minutes later, I found Caden shirtless in front of the stove, cooking us steak and fries.

I'd never noticed it before, but all the guys seemed to have tattoos here and there, Caden and Jensen having the most.

I was a sucker for a bad boy with tattoos, apparently.

I was surprised to find Tyler sitting at the bench with a beer in his hand, his eyes running over my body before giving me a wink, causing tingles inside me.

"You've got the nicest fucking legs I've ever seen on a woman, Rory. They'd look better over my shoulders though. Come sit on my lap."

"That's a shit pick up line, and you know it," I snorted, despite it actually working as my traitorous body warmed at the thought.

I sat beside him, giving Caden a grateful smile as he slid a cold beer in front of me, while Tyler grinned as if he was saying the world's greatest fucking joke.

"You'd know if I was trying to pick you up, because you'd be on my lap, screaming my name, babe."

Bold assumption.

Also, probably true.

"Believe it or not, you aren't that irresistible, Johnson," I lied, popping the top on my beer and sipping it casually as I tried to control my hormones.

"Ouch, damn girl. That's cold," he laughed, taking a swig of his beer and giving me an amused expression.

Caden placed a plate in front of both of us before sitting down to eat his own.

Such a gentleman.

Tyler groaned as he watched me shovel fries into my mouth like the animal I was.

I was fucking starving, alright?

"I love a woman who can eat. Seriously, come sit on my lap."

"Nope."

"But you're the most beautiful woman I've ever seen, and it would be such an honour to…," he started with the fakest sweet smile I'd ever seen.

The fact that I was tempted pissed me off, so I stabbed my knife into his steak swiftly, causing him to jump as I smiled back with the same fake sweetness.

"I said no, Ty. And you're so full of fucking *shit*."

Caden cracked up laughing as I took my knife back, but Tyler shrugged.

"Well, it's kind of true. You're super fucking hot."

Wow, romantic bastard.

I took a big forkful of steak and rolled my eyes, letting the guys talk over the top of me for a while.

I jumped when a pair of hands suddenly landed on my waist and I looked over my shoulder to see Caden behind me, seeming apologetic.

"Didn't mean to startle you, baby. You wanna come for a swim with us? Ty skinny-dips most of the time, just a heads up."

I pushed my plate away with a nod and climbed off the seat to follow him outside, wondering if it was a good idea.

Tyler had thankfully jumped into the pool by the time we got outside, and when I subconsciously pulled my shirt over my head, Caden growled.

"You're swimming in your fucking bra and panties? You trying to kill me?"

I chuckled with fake confidence as a tug of anxiety moved through me, ruffling his hazel-brown hair playfully to hide it.

I wasn't sure if these guys were making me brave or fucking reckless.

"Well, I'm not swimming naked, now am I?"

"You totally could!" Tyler offered from the pool, Caden grinning with obvious agreement.

"Yeah, Rory. You could."

Pigs, the both of them.

I rolled my eyes and sat on the edge of the pool, sliding in and enjoying the cool water as it lapped at my warm skin, simmering my nerves slightly.

There was no fucking way I was going to get naked in front of Tyler.

Caden jumped in and swam up to me, backing me into the pool wall with a smirk.

"You make me so fucking horny."

"So I can feel," I smirked back, startled when he kissed me hard without warning, pressing his erection against my hip firmly.

Tyler mumbled something under his breath, but I ignored him as Caden's hands trailed across my bare waist, setting my skin on fire.

I tensed when his fingers dipped into my panties, but he didn't seem to notice how anxious I was.

As much as I loved his hands on me, it scared me at the same time.

I wasn't supposed to want this.

His voice was soft, calming me slightly.

"Relax, baby. Let me look after you."

"But, Ty…"

"You'll just give him blue balls, it's fine," he grinned, earning a splash from Tyler.

"Hey! Blue balls fucking suck, asshole!"

I ignored Tyler, giving Caden an uneasy glance.

He placed a kiss on my shoulder to reassure me, and I'll be damned, but it soothed my panic.

"You can trust him, you know? He'd never make fun of you for anything."

I relaxed more as his fingers brushed over my clit, my head dropping back as he moved them in a slow circle.

God, it felt so fucking good.

"Oh, fuck," Tyler murmured, shamelessly watching us as Caden worked me towards release.

I should have been ashamed of the public display Caden and I were giving Tyler, but I just didn't fucking care.

Somehow, these guys understood me, and I knew I was safe with them to explore if I wanted to.

Caden suddenly spoke up again, a small amount of panic rising in me.

"Let Ty in behind you."

Hell fucking no.

My head flew up, but he kept moving his hand, his voice remaining calm.

"Not to fuck you, don't panic. I just don't want your back scraped up from the pool, or for you to hit your damn head."

"Promise?" I whispered, fear seeping out of me as I spoke.

It was a big gamble to let them corner me like that.

I was comfortable with Caden, but I didn't know how much I trusted Tyler.

Caden kissed the tip of my nose affectionately, his voice quiet.

"I promise, he won't do anything without you allowing it."

Fuck it, they wouldn't hurt me.

When I finally nodded, he motioned for Tyler to swim towards us, and he moved behind me slowly so that he didn't startle me.

I still didn't like the feeling inside me that was growing.

It was something between joy and pure fucking fear.

"Ty's just going to hold your waist, okay?" Caden murmured, gently moving me back so I was pressed against Tyler's bare chest.

I was completely tense, slamming my eyes shut as Tyler's large hands moved to my waist.

I was boxed in and trapped, and as if he knew what I was thinking, he spoke in my ear in a gentle voice.

"You're in charge. I only touch you when you let me. Want me to move my hands off you?"

Caden watched my eyes as I opened them, darting them around nervously.

I tried hard to relax, letting a breath out before shaking my head slightly.

"It's okay, I just don't like being boxed in," I whispered, Caden giving me a small smile that made me feel safe somehow.

I hated looking weak when I'd taken pride in the hard exterior I'd accomplished over time.

"Trust me. Let me make you feel good. I won't fuck you, okay? This is only about getting you off."

Tyler's thumbs rubbed up and down my hips, and I nodded as I started to relax a little bit, Caden kissing me to soothe my panic even more.

After a while, it became nice being between them, and my head dropped back to Tyler's shoulder shamelessly, his breath on my neck becoming more noticeable as it set my senses on fire.

I tilted my head to the side, letting out a breathy moan as Caden slipped a finger inside me, Tyler's voice rumbling in my ear seductively.

"Can I kiss your neck?"

It seemed like an odd question, but I mumbled a yes, appreciating the fact that he'd asked.

His soft lips trailed across my skin, and I arched slightly as his fingers dug into my slender waist, holding me in place as Caden kept working me until I was shaking with need.

If he stopped, I was going to knock both of them the fuck out.

"Tell me what you need, baby," he murmured, pulling my

breast out of my bra and sucking my nipple into his mouth, a small whimper leaving me as I squirmed.

I was desperate to get off, and I suddenly blurted out, "Fuck me!"

Did I say that?

He lifted his head and raised an eyebrow, obviously liking the idea but not wanting to push me.

"You sure?"

"Yes!" I snapped, making him chuckle.

"Alright, turn around for me."

I gave him a confused look, but he simply grinned back.

"Trust me."

I nervously turned around, not feeling sure about it as my front pressed against Tyler's, my panties going flying onto the lawn close by, courtesy of Caden.

I knew Tyler felt me tense as my naked mound rubbed against his erection, but he spoke tenderly to calm me before I could let complete panic take over.

"Ignore it. Caden's fucking you, not me."

"But…," I choked out, earning a gentle expression from him that suddenly had me running my arms around his neck for comfort.

His voice was affectionate as he spoke, his steel-grey eyes piercing into mine and sending a blanket of calmness over me.

"Can I touch you?"

"Where?"

"Let me rub your clit while Caden fucks you," he whispered, a shiver running through me as Caden moved right up behind me as I nodded.

Tyler groaned, startling me with an unexpected kiss as his hand moved between us, and a sudden jolt went through me as Caden pushed inside my pussy.

I couldn't help it as I kissed Tyler back with just as much

desperation as he gave me, and when my orgasm raced through my body, I clung to him as Caden fucked me even harder.

I moaned loudly at the sensations running through me, not sure if I could handle it much longer, but Tyler's hands roaming my body also made me want to fuck him too.

They were turning me into a fucking sex maniac and I just wanted to keep going, which was weird, considering I wanted to have a complete break down at the thought of someone touching me usually.

I pressed myself more firmly against him with a sudden boost of confidence, and he groaned as Caden's thrusts pushed me forwards so that I was rubbing on his dick more.

"Rory, you'll make me bust a nut if you keep doing that."

"I know," I smiled, kissing him as Caden came with a grunt, gently moving back from me to make sure he didn't hurt me.

Tyler went to move too, but I ran a hand between us and wrapped my fingers around his hard length, his eyes going to mine instantly.

"You don't have to do…"

"Let me," I cut him off softly, my free hand running through his light brown hair, making him growl in a way that would have melted my panties off if I'd been fucking wearing any.

His lips crushed mine and his arms went right around my middle to hold me closer as I pumped my arm, confidence building inside me as he gritted his teeth and dropped his head forward onto my shoulder.

His hands tightened on my waist every so often, and I couldn't stop the small moan that escaped me as he lifted his head, nipping at the soft skin just below my ear.

I had no idea what I was doing, but his reactions told me that he liked it.

His hands gripped my waist hard as I jerked him faster, his length pulsing against my fingers as he suddenly groaned with relief, his forehead resting on mine as he gave his body a moment to recover.

I hesitated before putting my arms around him, curling myself against him with a content sigh as he tightened his around me in return.

Things sure were changing, and I wasn't sure why, but that worried me as anxiety bubbled below the surface.

Tyler

"I could kill you," I groaned later that night, causing Caden to smirk as we walked into my house.

As usual, no one else was home.

Shocker there, right?

"Why would you want to do something so dramatic?"

"You're actually banging that regularly? C'mon, that isn't fucking fair, I thought we shared things?" I joked, grabbing us a beer each before getting comfortable in the loungeroom.

He rolled his eyes and grabbed a cigarette from his pocket, leaning back on the couch as he lit it.

"She's timid as fuck, so I've got to get her to trust you first. Besides, why are you complaining? You got to fucking come, didn't you?"

"Yeah, in her fucking *hand*. Is she tight? I bet she is. Do you two call each other bro and sis while you fuck in private? She's a freak in bed, isn't she?" I complained, swigging on my beer as my best friend laughed at me.

He was an asshole, but he was my asshole.

In a non-homo way, obviously.

We'd been best friends for as long as I could remember, so I put up with his shit, and he put up with mine when I used to get drunk and set shit on fire.

I was a troubled kid.

"She's not too crazy in bed, but she's tight as fuck. If I didn't know any better, I'd assume she was a virgin, man. Jense was totally right, live-in pussy is fucking great," he replied, and I flipped him off.

He got all the luck.

I scrolled through Facebook, accepting all the friend requests, before glancing over the bucket load of messages.

I had three from Claire, one being a picture of her tits.

I flashed the screen at Caden and snorted.

"Did she send you this too?"

He grabbed his phone and scrolled for a few moments before grinning.

"Yep. You should've seen the photo she sent me last week of her fingers in her pussy."

"I saw it, she sent the same one to Jense. Hey, get your new sister to send you a snap of her tits. They're fucking nice, I won't lie."

He chuckled, finishing his beer and using the empty bottle as an ashtray.

"I don't need a photo of her tits, because I have the real thing whenever I want. Doubt she'd be into that shit anyways, she's too fucking shy. Seriously, get the kink fantasy out of your head, because it isn't like that."

"What's it like then?"

"She just seems to freak out easy. I try to keep shit simple so I get to fucking bust. She's hot when she comes though. It's like no one's ever made her come before, because she seems surprised as fuck by it."

I grinned, pointing my beer at him.

"She's probably just surprised that you even know how to get her off. I'm surprised too."

He flipped me off before standing and heading into the kitchen to grab us another beer each, and I texted my buddy Slash to remind him of the party I was hosting on Friday night at mine, knowing he'd hook me up with his supply of cocaine.

I wonder if Rory would let me do lines on her tits?

CHAPTER SIX

RORY

*F*riday night was bigger than I fucking expected.

I stepped into Tyler's house for the first time, finding it completely full of people.

The sound system was pumping through the neighborhood, and the back deck was covered in teenagers smoking and drinking.

Caden put a reassuring arm around my waist, leading me into the kitchen to find Jensen and Tyler doing shots, while Lukas stood close by with a bottle of whisky in his hand.

I smirked, snatching the bottle from him and chugged some down, needing a little liquid courage to keep my anxiety in check for the night.

"That's mine, you know?" He chuckled with amusement as he tongued his lip ring, taking the bottle back as I held it out with a grin.

"Oh, I know. I just wanted a sip."

Jensen was suddenly in front of me, his arm going around my waist as he pulled me in for a hug as if we had known each other forever.

It was nice.

"Hey, babe. You want your own bottle? I might have brought one with me for you."

"You're a sweetheart!" I beamed, but Tyler just snorted.

"He just wants you to go home with him and fuck his brains out. Forget that idea, dance with me?"

Jensen rolled his eyes but moved back from me with amusement.

"Go have fun with Ty, I'll find you with that bottle after."

I kissed his cheek with a smile before taking Tyler's hand, letting him lead me to the designated dance floor and pull me close.

I peered up at him shyly, earning a wink from him.

I hated how weak these guys were making me, and a wink shouldn't have made me wet like it did.

"You look super-hot, as usual," he exclaimed, his playboy smile firmly in place, earning a snort from me.

"I'm not getting naked for you."

"That's what you said last time," he whispered, shoving a leg between mine to dance as Striptease by Hinder blasted through the house.

I knew Jensen and Lukas were watching us with surprise as I basically humped his leg like a horny fucking dog, but Jensen suddenly looked pissed off when Tyler's fingers ran through my hair to yank me closer, kissing me hard, right there in the middle of the crowded dance floor.

I didn't realize we were in our own little world until someone pushed up behind me and Caden's voice rumbled in my ear, turning me to fucking jelly.

"You're making a scene and you're making me horny. Probably don't fuck Ty in the middle of the party, even though it looks hot as fuck."

Oops.

I leaned back, his hands dropping to my waist as he kissed the top of my head affectionately.

Tyler chuckled, drawing my attention back to him.

"Jense looks pissed, heads up."

Huh?

I didn't have time to glance over before Jensen's arm snaked around my waist and hoisted me against him, a sneer on his face that was aimed at the two guys who'd just soaked my panties.

"Back off guys, Jesus."

I relaxed, patting his chest gently, his concerned eyes looking down at me instantly.

"It's okay, Jense. They'd back off if I asked them to."

"Is that right?" He asked, receiving a firm nod in return.

"Yeah, I trust them."

He glared at both of his friends before shaking his head at me, sorrow and pity in his gaze that I'd seen before.

"Like I said, you're fucking *stupid* if you trust anyone," then he took off towards the backyard, my body becoming cold as his touch left me.

What the fuck?

Tyler grinned, not at all fazed by the mini meltdown.

"Wow, someone's panties are in a fucking twist. Want me to go see what his problem is?"

Bad idea.

I shook my head, not wanting him to make it worse.

We all knew he fucking would.

"It's okay, I'll find him. I'll be back in a minute."

Caden pulled me close and kissed my forehead, his voice warm.

"Be careful."

I nodded, giving him a quick kiss before heading outside after Jensen.

I found him by the fire pit with a beer in his hand and a scowl on his handsome face.

Some girl was trying to rub up against him, but he kept pushing her away, snapping angrily at her until she scuttled off like a frightened rabbit.

Girls around here had no fucking backbone.

I walked over, stopping directly in front of him and crossing my arms tightly, a no-nonsense expression on my face.

"What the fuck was that?"

"Fuck off, Aurora," he growled, my face hardening stubbornly.

"No. Tell me what the fuck that was."

He seemed to calm slightly, but he shook his head as he lifted his beer to his lips.

"Just go back to the others, okay?"

"No," I argued, scowling at him as he wrapped my black hair around his fist and yanked my head back to meet his gaze in the fire light.

"Aurora, seriously. Fuck off."

"Talk to me, for fuck's sake," I demanded, watching him hesitate before scowling right back at me.

"Why?"

"Because, I fucking care about you and I don't like you angry at me!" I finally snapped, his eyes darkening as he yanked me forwards and kissed me suddenly, dropping his beer in the process.

He grabbed my thighs and lifted me, waiting for me to wrap my legs around his waist to hold on to him, before pushing his tongue into my mouth with a groan, my arms tightening around his neck to make sure he didn't drop me.

Not that I thought he would, but I couldn't be too careful.

I was too brave for my own good as I let him manhandle

me so publicly, ignoring any nerves that lingered below the surface.

"Jensen Gilbert, who's your pretty friend?"

I stiffened at the unfamiliar voice, but Jensen kept hold of me, stroking my thigh to soothe my anxiety as he turned us to face a guy I'd only ever seen around town.

He was covered in tattoos from his neck all the way down to his fingertips, snakebite piercings in his lip, and a silver ring in his nose.

He honestly looked hot, as well as scary as fuck in my opinion, but Jensen smirked without hesitation.

"Evening, Skeet. This is Rory Donovan. Babe, this is Skeeter Maddox."

Skeeter reached a tattooed hand out towards me, but Jensen took a step back as my body tensed.

He was a little too scary for me, thank you very much.

"No offense, dude. Don't touch her, like ever."

Skeeter raised an eyebrow, dropping his hand with a shrug.

"All good. Isn't she with Holloway? That's what I heard, anyways."

I smacked Jensen's arm until he put me back on my feet, feeling Skeeter's amused gaze on me at my escape.

It was none of his fucking business who I was with, but the fact that he sounded so cocky about knowing who I was, just pissed me off.

I stalked off and headed around the corner of the house, my eyes instantly landing on Claire.

She was laughing at something a guy was saying to her, but Caden emerged out of nowhere and made his way towards her, instantly capturing her attention.

She smiled and placed a hand on his chest, moving against him so she was basically rubbing on him like a fucking cat in heat.

He looked bored with her swooning, but he didn't remove her either, which set off a bomb of jealous inside me.

I made a beeline over to them and tapped her shoulder, a sly smirk spreading across her face as she realized who was there.

I didn't give her time to speak before I swung my fist back and knocked her to the ground with one punch.

Oopsie?

She was instantly out cold, the anxiety from the party moving aside to make way for the adrenaline that was now pumping through my veins.

Caden's eyebrows shot up in surprise, but I turned and headed back into the house in search of some whisky, hoping no one bothered to follow me.

I was done dealing with bullshit for the night and I just wanted to get drunk and go to fucking bed.

"Hey, superwoman!" Tyler's hyena laugh hit my ears and he was suddenly in front of me, a bottle of whisky in his hand and an unlit cigarette in the other.

I glared at him but happily snatched the bottle, chugging into it before handing it back with a scowl.

I wasn't really mad at him, but he could have warned me that bitch was going to show up.

"What the fuck is she doing here, Ty?"

"C'mon, babe, it's a public party. Nice way to earn your hardcore street rep though. One hit wonder and all," he replied as he continued to laugh, handing me a lighter as I snatched the cigarette from his hand.

"How is it a public party? It's in *your* fucking house."

"It's private to a point because only particular schools can attend, but it's open to anyone at those schools," he shrugged, lighting another cigarette for himself and leaning back on his heels.

"Which school is Skeeter from then?" I asked casually as

the anger simmered down, honestly wanting to know how they all knew each other.

Skeeter and his friends looked like trouble.

People crossed to the other side of the road to avoid walking past them, I'd seen my own dad do it before, and he thought he was fucking invincible.

Tyler's eyes snapped to mine, narrowing as he spoke tensely.

"You met Skeet?"

"Yeah, he interrupted me and Jensen," I replied, dragging on my cigarette and trying hard not to took too interested in the conversation, despite wanting to know everything about the tattooed bad boy with the dangerous smile.

"What exactly did he interrupt, Miss Donovan?"

I shrugged. "None of your business."

He moved closer and spoke in my ear with a grin.

"You said you like to get high, yeah?"

I frowned at the change of subject but nodded, flicking my cigarette and watching the ash fall to the ground.

"Yeah, why?"

"You do coke?"

"Does a bear shit in the fucking woods?"

"C'mon then," he chuckled, taking my hand and leading me through the crowded house and into a room that only had a handful of people in it.

A few guys were perched on couches with skanky looking girls on their laps, but one guy grinned at us and spread his arms wide.

His short ash-blonde hair stuck up slightly where he must have run his hand through it recently.

I'd seen him in town with Skeeter before, but I'd never seen him look genuinely happy to see anyone.

"Ty, my man! Nice party as always, brother. Who's your

bitch?" He asked arrogantly, anger vibrating through me as I lunged at him.

Tyler snaked an arm around my waist and hoisted me back against his chest as he sat down, pulling me onto his lap as if it was normal for us to do.

"C'mon Slash, be nice. This is Rory."

The guy frowned, looking completely confused as he spoke.

"Holloway's piece?"

Asshole.

I struggled in Tyler's grip and glared, my usual anxiety staying away, probably thanks to all the whisky and beer I'd consumed.

"I'm no one's piece of ass, you fucking cunt!"

Slash's eyebrows shot up as Tyler chuckled, sounding nervous as he tightened his hold and kissed my cheek to try and calm me.

"Relax babe, let me talk."

I scowled, but Slash narrowed his dark grey eyes on Tyler with disapproval.

"You really let the girls talk like that now? Getting soft, Ty."

"I don't have to let her do shit. Besides, she isn't a piece of ass, she's with us, so leave her alone. She just knocked Claire Davidson the fuck out with one punch, so she's just a little mad right now. Apologies."

Slash's face broke into a smirk and he chuckled, all anger fading away.

"She knocked her out, huh? What for?"

I clenched my fists, speaking through my teeth.

"Being a whore. I came in here to get high, not chit chat."

I made sure to give Tyler a filthy look, but he rolled his eyes and nodded towards one of the others who pulled a bag of powder out and tipped it onto the table as if we were about to make some fucking scones.

Slash lined some up and handed me a rolled-up bill as he and Tyler went back to talking, leaving me to do a couple of lines, before passing the bill along to another one of his friends.

They were part of a gang, apparently.

They all had gang jackets on, not that my drunk vision let me read the club name.

I took the whisky from Tyler as he offered it to me, taking a long drink before noticing Slash watching me, my eyes narrowing defensively.

"The fuck are you staring at?"

He grinned like I was the most amusing person he'd ever fucking spoken to.

"I see why Holloway's boys like you. You've got fire, babe."

I angrily chewed on my tongue bar, calming when Tyler's lips moved across my neck as he nibbled my skin.

I should've been freaking out, not leaning into it.

"You want another line before we head back out? I wanna dance with you," he murmured in my ear, waiting for me to nod.

Slash lined up again before I could even ask, and once I'd snorted it, he gave me a nod.

"You run into trouble, you call me and my guys, okay? Unless it's a girl problem, but by the sounds of things you got that shit handled."

I thanked him before saying goodbye, allowing Tyler to lead me down the hallway and back towards the party.

I gave him a small frown of confusion once we were away from them.

"Who's his guys?"

"Slash Russo is the leader of the Bloody Psychos. Skeet's

his right-hand man," he said over his shoulder, making me snort.

"An actual gang, or what?"

"Most people call it a gang, but they're a street crew. They *hate* being referred to as a gang. You're lucky you're with us because Slash has killed people for calling him much less than a cunt before. Man's a little trigger happy if you ask me," he tsked as we reached the dance floor.

He pulled me close to dance, the high riding through me and boosting my confidence through the roof as Na Na by Trey Songz boomed through the speakers.

He groaned as I turned around to dance against him, grinding my butt against his groin in a way I never would have before.

That kind of behaviour was asking for trouble, but Tyler would keep me safe from anyone else, I just knew it.

His hands clamped onto my waist as he moved with me, my head dropping back as I put my arms up, running my fingers through his short light brown hair.

I could feel his erection digging into me the more I danced, and I grinned stupidly when Lukas's unamused face was suddenly in mine.

"Are you fucking high?" He snapped, a giggle breaking free as I grabbed the front of his shirt to pull him against me.

"*Super* fucking high, Lukas James."

"Damnit, Rory. I can't leave you alone for five fucking minutes?" He growled with frustration, but I closed my eyes and put my hands on his waist, moving against him as the music pulsed through me.

"I wasn't alone, I was with Ty. Dance with us?"

"No. Ty, what the fuck man?" He bit out angrily, but Tyler just groaned as he pulled me back against his chest firmly.

"She's having fun, leave her alone."

"Leave her alone? She's already punched Claire out cold,

gotten high on fuck knows what, and drank a lot more than I fucking gave her. You..."

"Cocaine," I laughed, making him frown with confusion.

"Huh?"

"I got high on cocaine," I repeated, grinding against Tyler who bit my neck firmly, nearly making me fucking come right there and then.

Lukas gave him a filthy look before stomping off, another giggle leaving me as one of my hands ran down Tyler's front until I reached the bulge in his pants.

His teeth bit into my neck hard as he grunted, one of his hands dipping into the front of my shorts to tease me.

I held my breath as I waited for the contact that my body was basically screaming for, but just as his fingers brushed against my clit they were yanked away, my eyes opening and meeting Caden's as he smirked in front of me.

"Hey, baby. You two just gonna fuck here in the middle of the dancefloor, or what?"

I scowled, stumbling as I pushed him back slightly.

I was more fucked up on alcohol and powder than I thought.

"Fuck off, Caden. Go back to Claire."

He raised an eyebrow before his hand moved to my throat, squeezing gently, somehow making me fucking horny in the process.

He pissed me off as he grinned almost cruelly.

"You jealous, Aurora?"

"She can keep her skanky fucking hands to herself," I growled, his grip tightening.

"You think I'd want her riding my fucking dick? You angry that you'd miss out?" He taunted.

I glared at him through the drug-induced haze, trying hard to focus on him.

"Fuck you. You can fuck who you want but you can stay the hell away from me."

His hand tightened until I struggled to breathe, pressing his forehead to mine.

His expression softened, along with his voice.

"You're an idiot if you think I'd want Claire on my dick instead of you, Aurora," then he kissed me with so much passion that I almost ended up on my fucking ass.

I wanted to push him away and remain angry, but I was beyond turned on and fucked up, so I went with it and pushed my tongue into his mouth.

My skin shivered as his hand moved from my throat and up under my shirt instead, his fingers fanning out across my warm skin as if he couldn't get enough of me.

When he moved back, he peered into my eyes with a smirk.

"Did Ty get you high?"

"I got me high, Ty just put me in the right room," I grinned, jumping when Tyler swatted my ass firmly with a chuckle.

"I'll get you high on me later, babe. Don't you worry."

I backed up to him to dance again, but as I started moving between the two of them, I looked up to find Jensen and Skeeter watching us from the kitchen.

I gave Jensen a playful wink before throwing my arms around Caden's neck, his mouth dipping down to kiss me hard, nibbling my lip ring before pulling back.

Why did that make me fucking horny?

Skeeter

"What's the deal with her? You all fucking her?" I asked as I watched Rory grind between Tyler and Caden.

Jensen watched her through hooded eyes beside me, not looking up as he replied.

"It's complicated."

"Then *uncomplicate* it. You're banging her, they're banging her, how about Lukas? He hitting that ass too?"

He finally glanced over at me with irritation all over his face.

"You have no fucking clue what's going on, Skeet. Stay out of it. Why do you give a shit, anyways?"

I didn't give a fucking shit, I just wanted to know because I knew everything that went on around town.

That was my story and I was sticking to it.

I peered back over at her, my eyes running over her entire body as she winked at Gilbert before kissing Caden all slow and sexy-like.

Was she even legal?

"She's seventeen, and she's only fucked Holloway. She's jacked Ty off, and I've fingered her, but that's it. Stay away from her, alright? She's our toy to play with," Jensen stated, not being able to stop my snort of disbelief.

Did I ask that shit out loud?

Did he actually believe that they were just playing with her?

I'd known the guys for a while, so I knew how they acted around girls.

They didn't keep them around long, and they sure as shit didn't get defensive about them.

Slash told me that Tyler got her high on the good shit, so I knew for a fucking fact that she wasn't a toy.

I saw her flinch when I went to shake her hand outside too, so I also knew that she wasn't one of those girls who got on her fucking back as a side hobby.

She was timid as fuck, so they must have taken their time to warm her up to the idea first.

She didn't seem too fucking shy as she palmed Holloway's dick through his pants, but our cocaine could make a fucking nun hump the wall, so I wasn't really surprised.

Jensen stood in front of me suddenly, a scowl on his face.

"What's your sudden interest in her? Seriously man, lay off this shit. She's ours."

Had he actually looked at me?

I wasn't full of myself or anything, but if I really wanted to take her, I could.

Whether it was by kidnapping or my charismatic charm, I wasn't really fussy.

Either way, I'd have her tied up at my place.

"If she's just a piece of ass, what's the problem, Gilbert? I think she'd look real pretty on her knees with my dick jammed down her fucking throat."

Totally true.

She was hiding a dark side behind those pretty baby blues, I could tell.

I scared her a little, but the rush of danger could tempt even the saintliest of angels.

"The problem is, she's *our* piece of ass. You've got plenty of your own down at the shed, so how about sticking your dick in them instead," he snapped back at me, but I could see the worry on his face.

He should be more worried about Rory finding out about him calling her a piece of ass from what I'd heard, but whatever.

That was none of my fucking business.

I chuckled, swigging my beer and looking back at Rory as the guys started dragging her out of the room.

"I don't know about you, Gilbert, but shouldn't you or

Lukas be keeping an eye on your boys? They're getting a bit frisky with the little lamb."

Easy distraction.

He cursed, blurting out a goodbye, before chasing after them.

He was totally going to save her from them.

Tell me she's just a piece of ass?

What fucking bullshit.

I didn't know what it was, but something was interesting about that girl, that was for sure.

CHAPTER SEVEN

RORY

My memory was shot to fucking shit.

I remembered stumbling up the hallway towards Tyler's bedroom with Tyler and Caden, but I'd woken up to find Jensen curled up behind me instead.

His eyes opened as if he felt my gaze on him, a smile slowly stretching across his face.

"Morning, babe."

I rolled onto my back and stretched out with a groan.

Fuck, I felt like shit.

"How'd I end up in here?"

"You don't remember? You *were* fucked up, huh? Ty and Caden got a little bit too full-on for you, so I brought you to bed with me instead."

I frowned, rolling over to face him, throwing a leg over his to curl up to him.

"What do you mean they got a little *full-on*? Last thing I remember, I was dancing with them? Then going to Ty's room?"

He cringed, not looking comfortable in saying it as if I was going to have a fucking meltdown.

"I wasn't sure how you'd feel this morning about having a threesome, and when I say threesome, I mean a full rough and rowdy one in the front and one in the back kind of threesome. They're both rough in bed, so I was worried you'd regret it or end up hurt and freaked out."

"I agreed to a threesome?" I spluttered, ignoring the thumping in my skull.

"You were coked out of your fucking brain on top of being drunk. I didn't think you'd agree to it sober, and until you do, I don't think doing it drunk and high is a good idea."

I peered at him, reaching a hand up to run my fingertips across his cheek affectionately.

"Did I climb all over you?"

He chuckled, resting a hand on my waist as he shuffled closer.

"Nope. By the time I got you away from them, you were basically passed out in my arms."

Well, fuck.

The door swung open and Caden walked in with a scowl etched across his face.

"Morning, baby. Morning, *cockblocker*."

Jensen snorted, tucking me against him and putting his arms around me as if Caden would yank me from the bed.

"Fuck off, Holloway. You guys would have been too much for her, and you fucking know it."

He shrugged before moving across the room and flopping down beside me, placing a kiss on my neck that sent tingles down my spine.

"You have a good night? You seemed to be enjoying yourself before cockblocker dragged you away to sleep."

I smiled, not at all bothered that Jensen had safely taken me to bed.

I wasn't sure if a drunk threesome would have been a good idea, so I was kind of thankful for him.

"Yeah, I had heaps of fun. Where's Ty?"

"Probably still crying in bed because he didn't get you to bounce on his dick last night," he replied crudely, making me roll my eyes, choosing not to comment on that.

"Which room's his? I'll go wake him up."

He looked amused but motioned towards the bedroom door.

"Turn left, and it's two doors up on the right."

I climbed over him and kissed his cheek, slipping from the bed and padding down the hallway to Tyler's room, finding him sprawled out in bed snoring.

I hesitated before sneaking in and climbing under the blankets, his eyes opening as he smiled at me sleepily.

"Well, good morning. What are you doing in here?"

"Waking you up."

"With a blow job?" He asked hopefully, an amused laugh leaving me.

"No," but I cuddled up to him anyways, despite him being filthy-minded.

I was starting to get used to them all being so fucking rude.

I squealed as he suddenly jumped on top of me, pressing his erection against my crotch with a gentle thrust.

"You made me so fucking horny last night. You're a lot of fun when you wanna be, Donovan."

"Get off me, you fat piece of shit," I laughed loudly, but I was surprised when he ran his thumb along my lower lip and held my gaze.

"You aren't freaked out this morning, are you? You know what nearly happened last night, right?"

"Apparently, I nearly had a threesome with you and Caden," I shrugged, watching him nod.

"Yeah. One night I'll get you into my bed for some fun

with Holloway. You'll love it," he murmured, a groan coming from me as he bent down to kiss me softly.

I wrapped my legs around him, pulling him completely down on top of me, a feral growl coming from him as he thrust against me while pulling my hair slightly.

Great, I was fucking wet again.

"Thought you were just coming in to wake him up?" Caden chuckled as he walked in, earning an amused smirk from Tyler as he glanced over his shoulder at him.

"Oh, trust me. I'm awake."

"So I can see," he snorted, giving me an amused smile.

I suddenly felt shy, and I went to push Tyler off of me but Caden shook his head and softened his gaze, noticing my discomfort.

"Stay in bed if you want. I'm heading back to Dad's anyways."

Fuck.

I frowned, anxiety bubbling up at the thought of being in that massive mansion by myself.

"Why?"

"Because, Max and Mom got back this morning, and I'm not meant to be there. Remember?" He stated before turning to leave, my heart thumping harder at his retreat.

"Wait."

I fumbled as I managed to shove Tyler off me and climb out of bed, jumping into Caden's arms and wrapping myself around him tightly.

He chuckled and gave me a kiss, but it sounded fake which put me on edge.

"I'll see you on Monday at school anyways, but maybe if you ask the guys real nicely, they might wanna hang at the house to keep you company?"

"I'll miss you," I mumbled into his neck nervously, and

sure enough, his body went tense before suddenly relaxing again.

"I'll miss you too. I'd better go."

I nodded, letting him put my feet back on the ground before he gave me a goodbye kiss and left the room, Tyler sighing dramatically.

"Guess that means we'd better get you home, huh party animal?"

Jensen wandered in with a frown on his face as he stared at his phone, making me nervous all over again.

What was wrong now?

"You didn't tell me you had a Facebook account?"

"Who doesn't?" I snorted, relaxing when I realized it wasn't anything serious, but he rolled his eyes as if I'd sassed him.

"Well, I added you and sent the profile link to the guys, so accept us or else. Oh, expect pictures to be plastered all over it all the time, okay? Some from last night are going up today, so I'll tag you in them."

Dread rolled through me as I stared at him.

Did I flash my tits or something equally stupid?

"What do you mean? Pictures of what?"

He pulled me against him and laughed.

"All of us, silly!"

My phone rang and I frowned as I looked around the room until I noticed my bag in the corner.

I walked over to it and rummage inside, snatching the phone and answering it before it could ring out, ignoring how it hurt my head.

"Yes?"

"Where the fuck are you?" Max snapped instantly without a hello.

I rolled my eyes at how pissed off he sounded.

It had taken him a whole fucking week to call me, so I should have been the one who was angry.

Shitty parenting, right fucking there.

"Would you believe me if I said I was at the library studying?" I offered, a growl hitting my ears from him.

"No, I fucking wouldn't."

"Alright then. Well, I'm at Ty's, but we're about to head home," I replied, ignoring the smirk on Tyler's face as he toyed with the hem of my shirt.

"What the fuck are you doing there at this hour?" Max bit out, the volume causing me to wince.

"Oh, well it was Friday night. You know Josie mentioned the guys hang out regularly on Fridays for movie nights and shit."

"Who is *we?*"

"Me, Ty, Jense and Luke," I replied smoothly, not wanting to start an argument with the hangover from hell having a rave in my skull.

I heard him grumble before he snapped, "Just get home," then he hung up.

I glanced at Jensen and sighed, running a hand through my hair.

"Can you run me home?"

"Sure thing. You coming for a drive, Ty?" He asked, watching as Tyler bounced to his feet as if he'd had more than three hours sleep, swatting my butt on his way past to get changed.

We all got ready to leave, and once we were in the Camaro with the engine rumbling, I frowned.

"Where's Luke?"

Tyler gave me an amused grin from the back seat as he bounced around.

How the fuck did he manage to not make himself throw up?

"You thought he was going to stick around after you

humped him on the dance floor while you were high as fuck? He took off."

"Fair enough," I muttered, cranking the stereo up as Bad Mother Fucker by Machine Gun Kelly started, putting my window down and lighting a cigarette.

Jensen chuckled, glancing at me before pulling out of the driveway with a screech of tires, driving down the street and hitting the main road.

Tyler bopped along to the music in the back, rapping the entire song perfectly, which kept me amused for the whole drive, despite my headache still thumping.

Once Jensen had parked beside Josie's car, I climbed out and waited for them both to follow, laughing as Tyler tossed me over his shoulder and headed into the kitchen, where we found Josie and Max waiting for us.

I rolled my eyes as Tyler placed me back on the ground, cocking my head slightly at Max.

"Why do I get an intervention every time I walk through the front door?"

I stood between the guys and crossed my arms defensively, taking a step back when Josie reached for me.

She knew better than to touch me.

"Rory, we need a serious talk. Boys, can you come back later?" Josie asked carefully, but I snorted, stepping closer to Jensen who put an arm around my shoulders.

"Whatever you wanna talk about, I'll just tell them anyways. When can Caden come home?"

She seemed surprised, despite speaking in a calm voice.

"You want him to come home?"

"Why wouldn't I?"

"He hurt you," she frowned, her eyes taking in the small bruise that was around my neck that had nearly faded, her eyes darted to Jensen, a bitter laugh escaping me.

"You seriously believe my dad over your own son? Caden would never hit me. Ever."

Relief crossed her face, but she spoke firmly.

"You don't need to cover up his behaviour, sweetheart."

"I'm not! Why the hell would Caden hurt me like that? There's no fucking reason!" I exploded, watching her cringe.

"My son can be a handful but…"

"He'd never hurt me. He was checking on me after Dad fucking hit me. He caught me kissing Caden."

Her eyes went wide, but Max scoffed.

"Again with the lies, Aurora? When will you learn…"

"You let me think that Luke walked away from me, but in reality, you threatened him into staying out of it. I will kill you. Not today, not tomorrow, but I will fucking do it. In a few months I'll be eighteen and I'll be free from you. Until then, stay the fuck away from me."

"You listen to me…," Max started, but I cut him off, turning my attention back to Josie.

"I want Caden home by tonight."

She looked worried but nodded her agreement.

Max on the other hand, growled and stomped down the hallway, slamming the door like a child throwing a fucking tantrum.

Josie met my gaze, appearing unsure as she spoke.

"I'll talk to your father, sweetheart. You guys kick back in the pool or the movie room, okay?"

Fine by me.

We all headed out to the pool, staying there until we heard Caden's Challenger in the driveway at nightfall.

I instantly scrambled out of the pool and jogged through the house in my bikini, throwing my arms around him as we met in the kitchen.

He chuckled as I wrapped my legs around him tightly, his hands clamping onto my ass to hold me up.

"It's only been a day, baby. You miss me?"

"I did say I would," I murmured, burying my face in his neck and clinging to him until the others called to us from outside.

I thought he seemed tense, but I decided I'd imagined it as we headed outside and he kissed my cheek affectionately.

Jensen

After thinking about it all night and most of Sunday morning, I decided I really needed to tell the guys about Rory's past.

I'd been lying in bed for two hours, contemplating how to go about it.

I couldn't let them fuck her on Friday night, and I knew both of them were pissy at me for taking her away from them, but they didn't know what she'd already gone through.

She was fucked up on cocaine, as well as being drunk as fuck, so she'd probably pull the rape card on them.

Not that I'd really blame her, because Tyler got her fucked up on purpose, hoping to get her into bed that way.

I needed her to just fuck off to trailer park land or some shit where she belonged because this shit was going to get out of hand.

I was looking forward to school in the morning for the simple fact I'd get to see her again.

Pathetic, right?

It was as if I had a girl sidekick who just happened to be fuckable.

She was tough, I'd give her that, but that worried me too because that meant the guys would push harder to break her.

Don't even get me started on Skeeter's interest in her.

He played it cool, but I could almost hear his dick spring to life as he imagined all the fucked up shit he could do to her.

Lucky for us, she wasn't that type of girl.

He'd scare her away, if anything.

I heard the front door close quietly, perking me up slightly.

My dad had decided not to come home for the second month in a row, so Lukas usually showed up to hang out in the evenings.

His head poked around my bedroom door, a big smile on his face as he pushed his black hair out of his eyes.

"Thought you'd be up here. You wanna order pizza tonight? I'm fucking *starving*."

I shrugged, moving over on the bed to make room for him.

"Yeah, I guess. Can I ask you something?"

He sprawled out beside me, kicking his shoes off and letting them drop to the floor.

It had basically been his second home since we met a few years back, so he was pretty comfortable at mine.

"Yeah, sure."

"Should we try to talk Holloway out of this bullshit game with Rory? I mean, I don't think he hates her as much as he says he does, but if he knew the truth about her, maybe he'd cut her some slack?" I suggested, making him turn to watch me.

He was silent for a while before sighing, his face falling as he spoke.

"I think the whole thing's stupid and I don't want any part in it. I can't hurt her again, Jense. I finally got her back and now he wants me to fucking break her? I don't like it, and I think he needs to just admit that he likes her. So what if we let a girl into our group? She's tough, hot as fuck, and loyal. She's a nice chick."

"You still love her, don't you?" I asked quietly, his shoulders shrugging.

"Of course I do. It was just her and I for a long fucking time. She was basically the other half of me until Max went and fucked it all up."

I had to find a way to make Caden see sense.

We had to fucking tell him.

"Luke, we need to tell them, you know that, right?" I finally answered, making him groan.

"I don't want to get involved. She'll kill me if I tell her private shit to someone else."

"She told Caden that we could tell him and Ty, we'll just get her to give us permission on the day, so no one gets in trouble. We can sort it all out tomorrow at school, but for now I want that pizza you were talking about."

Lukas was my best friend, hands down.

I know I grew up with Caden and Tyler, but Lukas and I connected right from the start.

I remembered his mom dropping him off on his first day of high school, waving her money around and acting like the fucking Queen, which meant I instantly felt like I understood him.

He was fucking miserable, just like the rest of us rich assholes.

It had been a shitty week for all of us, actually.

Caden and his dad had gotten in a fistfight because his dad had threatened his mom, Tyler's parents decided to fire the housekeeper before taking off again, meaning he was alone completely, then there was me.

My mom took off when I was younger, and she'd gotten in touch with me that week and wanted to see me.

She never showed up, and all Dad said was he told me so.

It seemed stupid, but Lukas and I just ended up relying on each other for comfort from then on.

Like I said, he basically lived at mine most of the time, so we got really close.

The thought of not having him in my life was painful, so I didn't think about it.

I knew he wasn't going anywhere, mainly because he'd have to live with his mom all the time again, and that would be enough to push even the strongest person over the fucking edge.

She was in his face all the time, trying to feel youthful by having all of us around.

After two weeks of us tolerating it, we didn't hang out there again.

Lukas didn't blame us.

He loved her, but she was toxic for him.

I hated her for that.

Rory

"Slut," Claire scoffed as I walked into class Monday morning.

I turned to smirk at her, sarcasm lacing my voice.

"How's your face, Claire? Wow, took a bit of makeup to cover it up, huh?"

She seethed, stepping towards me with her fists clenched.

"You're nothing but a fucking trailer trash whore, you seem to forget that now you're living in Caden's mansion and driving around in Jensen's flashy cars and shit. Do you make their dicks feel good?"

Tyler waltzed in like king shit and plonked down at the desk I was about to sit at, yanking me onto his lap with a smirk.

"You bet Rory makes my dick feel good. Morning, baby," he added sweetly, kissing my cheek, which just seemed to piss Claire off.

"Seriously? You're actually fucking her too? You have no standards, Tyler Johnson."

He grinned, a nasty glint in his eye.

"I know. Fucked you, didn't I?"

She growled and stalked away from us, finally allowing me to turn around and raise an eyebrow at Tyler.

"This isn't your class?"

"Nah, I'm stealing you, but I know it makes you wet when I go caveman on you in front of other women," he winked, laughing as I whacked his arm with fake anger.

He stood, grabbing my books and putting an arm around my middle to lead me out of the room, but Claire's voice came from the back.

"Off for a quick fuck, are you?"

Tyler went to answer, but I gave her a small smile and cocked my head.

"Who said it was going to be quick? They like to take their time with me. You know, to make me feel *really* good. Climax comas are a real thing."

The class erupted in laughter and she scowled, sinking back into her seat as Tyler dragged me into the hallway with a big grin.

Fuck that bitch.

"Appears you're winning the school over slowly."

I shrugged, falling into step beside him as we walked past busy classrooms.

"I don't give a shit about being the queen of the school, I just don't want to cop shit when I'm here. Where are you taking me, anyways?"

"For a not so quick fuck," he joked, turning into an empty classroom where Caden, Lukas and Jensen were waiting for us.

I slowed, giving them a confused look, but Caden rolled his eyes with a grin.

"Come sit your ass on my dick for a minute?"

Always the charmer.

I snorted but walked over to him, lowering myself onto his lap to get comfortable.

"So, what's this about, guys? Secret power rangers meeting?"

Lukas gave me an unsure glance, instantly making me nervous.

"Caden said you gave us permission to tell him and Ty about the shit you haven't told them. I wanted to make sure we all knew it was okay with you."

My blood ran cold, despite Caden placing a kiss on my neck in an attempt to soothe me.

"You don't need to be here when we talk about it, but if everyone hears you say it's okay to talk about, then we all know we aren't talking behind your back."

I slowly nodded, Lukas sighing in relief.

"Thank you."

I was confused by his reaction but shrugged casually as if my whole body wasn't in complete panic.

"It's okay. I might head back to class then."

I had to get the fuck out of there.

Jensen stood with me. "Nah, come work out with me in the gym. I've got too much on my mind for class, and I already know what's going on with you. Lukas can tell them."

Caden frowned, but I smiled appreciatively.

"Okay, I'll see you at lunch?" I asked Caden, who simply gave me a kiss and swatted my ass on my way out the door, but I could see the look Jensen was giving him as we left, turning my panic up a notch.

I didn't want them fighting over me.

Once in the gym, we ran on the treadmills for ages, until Jensen suddenly slowed his down and glanced over at me, his voice laced with pain and regret.

"This place ruins good people, Rory. I'm sorry you were dragged into it."

I slowed my machine and frowned, not understanding what he was talking about.

"What do you mean? You've been acting weird all day, Jense. Talk to me."

"I didn't want to touch you. I swear I didn't want to hurt you, but I couldn't help but get closer than I was supposed to, and it's fucked a lot up and…"

"Jensen, what the fuck is going on?" I asked warily, watching as he climbed off his machine and sighed, giving me a soft kiss before patting my sweaty cheek, peering into my confused blue eyes with his broken ones.

"You've always been too good for us, baby. I'm just sorry," then he turned and took off before I could say anything.

My anxiety was officially through the fucking roof.

The fuck was that shit even about?

I gathered my things after another hour of running to try and ease my anxiety, but when I reached the parking lot, all the guys were gone, a frown tugging at my lips.

One of them always stuck around to take me home, so it seemed weird for them to have all left me.

I tried to call Caden, but his phone was off.

So was Jensen's.

Tyler's rang, but he didn't answer, so I trudged to the bus stop and headed home the old-fashioned way.

No one was home, and by the time I went to sleep that night, I was still the only person in the fucking house.

Jensen messaged me, the text tone making me sit up instantly to read it.

Jensen: I'm sorry.

I frowned as I typed my reply.

Rory: What for?

When he didn't answer, I tried to call him but his phone was off again, and he didn't turn it back on for the rest of the night.

Lukas

I felt fucking sick.

I glared at Caden as I flipped through the pages of Rory's diary, hating him for getting me to steal it in the first place, but hating myself even more for allowing him to push me around.

I should have told him to fuck off, but I didn't.

The diary was full of sadness and anger, but her recent pages were full of hope and happiness.

I wished it were all true, but it was all a big fucking lie.

We were going to destroy what was left of her, and I'd never get her back.

"Caden, this is stupid. I say we just leave her the fuck alone. She's been through enough shit," I said firmly, watching him roll his eyes, but I could see the hesitation on his face.

That was until he got his hands on the fucking diary and read all the cute shit she'd written about Jensen.

I didn't blame her, he was great, but it seemed to cement Caden's plan of revenge.

Jensen sat quietly as he listened to Caden read everything out to us, and every time I glanced at him, he looked even more miserable.

Jensen wasn't used to people not thinking of him as a fuck up, so hearing how important he was to her was ripping him apart.

He'd fallen for her, and Caden was being a fucking asshole to him, all because she was falling for him right back.

Caden didn't want to admit he wanted her, but no one else could have her either.

Tyler looked torn between keeping his best friend happy and shutting him up to keep the rest of us happy, but as usual, he took Caden's side.

It was how it always went, so I'd expected it.

It wasn't until I snatched the diary back and had another quick flip through, that I found a hidden pocket in the back.

I pulled a photo out and a shiver ran through me, chilling me to the bone.

She really kept a fucking picture of him?

Caden glanced over my shoulder, suddenly snatching it with a scowl.

"What the fuck does she have that for?"

I shrugged, the sick feeling getting worse inside me.

"Probably to fucking punish herself."

He paused, giving me a strange look.

"What does that fucking mean?"

"That's the piece of shit who raped her," I said flatly, but confusion took over when his eyes went wide.

He didn't say anything, so I sighed. "What? You know him?"

He turned the photo around towards Tyler and Jensen,

watching as Jensen somehow looked even more broken, but Tyler's jaw almost hit the ground as he met Caden's eye.

"Holy fucking shit, dude."

That didn't sound good.

Rory

I walked into school alone the next morning like a zombie, scrolling through Facebook and smirking at some of the pictures that the guys had tagged me in over the weekend.

I walked towards my locker and noticed a crowd of students lingering around it, instantly making me nervous.

What now?

As I approached, my heart sank as my eyes met Tyler's as he lazily leaned against my locker, Claire curled up to him with a nasty smirk on her face.

Something was wrong, and I held down the panic as Claire spoke with amusement in her voice.

"I told you it was all joke's on you, Aurora. You lose."

I kept my eyes on Tyler, who refused to look at me, making me snort in disbelief.

"Cowards way out? Nice touch, Johnson."

He winced.

It wasn't obvious to anyone else, but I knew him well enough to know I'd hit a nerve.

When he finally looked up, I could see the regret in his eyes, but I forced a smile and kept my voice strong.

"Joke's on you, because I'm used to losing people. You think I'll miss you and cry myself to sleep every fucking night? Don't count on it."

Fuck this shit.

I turned to walk off, but I almost ran into Caden who had a smirk on his face that I recognized all too well, managing to hide the hurt as it washed through me.

He was about to throw everything in my face and squash me like a fucking bug.

Claire was right, I'd been nothing more than a fucking game to them, and I'd let them play me.

My heart ached as he threw his arms out wide, cruel torment in his voice that matched his smirk.

"Bout time you got here, Aurora. Party just started!"

"Fuck off, Holloway," I bit out, but I was sure he heard the uncertainty in my voice.

"Now, now, don't be like that. Thought you loved me?" He tsked, giving me a look of confusion when I forced out a laugh, before he masked it again as I spoke.

"Was that your game plan? Make the poor girl fall in love with you, then break her heart? I don't even love my own fucking father, so why the fuck would I love you, Caden Holloway?"

He backed me into the lockers and grinned down at me, reaching for straws in his confused state.

He hadn't expected me to stand my ground, but he should have known I wasn't the type to lay down and take it.

I'd always bite back.

"You've mumbled it while I've been inside you before, but I get it, you were just talking to my dick, right? I'll take my comment back. Lukas stole your diary, you know? All those little secrets that you hold deep in your heart. Who you hate, who you want to hurt, who you think you fucking *love*."

He spat out the last one, making me flinch.

My eyes met Jensen's as he stood back in silence with a lost look in his gaze, but he kept his mouth shut and looked away from me, instantly dismissing me.

I looked back at Caden and sneered, sounding braver than what I was.

Then again, these boys had taught me to be stronger, so maybe I was actually being brave for once.

"Who gives a fucking shit? You don't know anything that could hurt me, Caden. Fuck off and stop wasting my time."

He laughed, but I could hear how fake it was as he tossed a picture to me, the image feeling like it burned my fucking hands as I saw who it was, causing me to drop it.

My eyes flashed up to his and my voice trembled without permission.

"Where did you get this?"

He got in my face, his kind hands becoming cruel as he yanked my hair back in his fist to keep my eyes on his.

"You believed we cared about you? You even wrote it in your little diary that we were your everything and you finally fit in somewhere. The page about how you could fall in love with Jensen because there isn't a mean bone in his body? Well, guess what? He *laughed* when we found this picture in the back hidden pocket of your diary, along with the old suicide note you wrote and obviously pussied out of doing. That man in the photo is Tristan Holloway. The man who ruined your fucking life is my father. *Checkmate.*"

What the fuck? No, no, no!

I scrambled backwards as my breath became heavy in my lungs, everyone breaking out into laughter.

They didn't even know what they were fucking laughing at, but they didn't care.

Caden Holloway ruled the school, so if he laughed, so did they.

Jensen looked frustrated as he went to reach for me, but I punched him right in the eye, my body shaking as the emotional train wreaked havoc on me.

"Don't fucking touch me, Jensen Gilbert. This is why you

were sorry yesterday? Why you wanted to spend just one last hour alone with me in the gym? Because you knew this was the plan? You fucking knew and went through with it, even after I confided in you? I don't give a fuck if you're sorry. I don't give a single fuck about *you*."

He watched me carefully, ignoring the burning in his eye socket from my hit as he spoke softly.

"I told you not to trust anyone. I told you why I couldn't touch you. I…"

"Oh, fuck you," I retorted, shoving past him and running out of the school yard before I could completely lose it in front of an audience.

I ignored my phone when Lukas called.

I ignored the hundreds of calls and texts from Jensen.

I headed straight to Caden's Challenger and stabbed two of his tires on my way past, jamming my pocketknife back into my pocket before making my way to the bus stop and jumping on the next bus that arrived, not climbing off until my old neighborhood came into view.

I had a cigarette on the front steps of my old home before deciding to make my way to the shed at the end of the road, nodding a thanks to the guy at the door who let me in after checking my I.D.

I hadn't had a cage fight in a long time, and I was well overdue to draw some blood.

I wished I'd never stopped fighting, but my anxiety became too bad to deal with, and Max was getting suspicious on my absence.

I couldn't have him snooping around there.

I knocked out my first opponent, tormented the second until they were tired, then I splattered their nose into a bloody mess.

I was on top of the fourth fighter for the night, hitting

them again and again even after they were knocked out cold, when I was yanked off them suddenly and pushed back.

I spun around and went to swing at my attacker, but my eyes met Skeeter's sharp light green ones a second before he pinned me firmly against the side of the cage with his tattooed arm, his voice low so only I could hear him.

I was surprised I could hear anything over the loud beating of my own fucking heart.

My adrenaline was pumping so hard that I wasn't even freaked out about being contained by a man I hardly knew.

"Enough," he demanded calmly, his voice stern.

He pressed his body against mine to keep me pinned there as he noticed my eyes narrow with every intention to fight him on it.

"Fuck off, Skeeter. You don't fucking…," I started to fight against him, but he held firm and glared at me.

"Calm the fuck down, or Slash will throw you the fuck out. We like a good bloody fight, but we don't like burying bodies if we don't have to. Got it?"

I was still fired up and fighting mad, but I nodded, his body instantly moving back to let go of his hold on me, jerking a thumb behind him towards the middle of the cage.

"All of what just happened? You're gonna talk to me about it right fucking now. Follow me."

For fuck's sake.

I went to argue but decided against it, following him through the crowd of cheering people until we reached an office out the back that I'd never been allowed in before.

I'd been well known at the shed a few years ago, but I'd never seen Skeeter before, which confused me since everyone seemed to know who he and his crew were.

It hadn't been that long ago since I'd drawn blood, had it?

"Sit," he demanded sharply, pointing to a chair in the

corner near a desk, grabbing a bottle of whisky and some glasses from the cupboard.

He sat down at the desk and poured me a glass, pushing it towards me before looking at me seriously.

"Now, what the fuck was that? I heard a few people talking, and apparently you were a regular teen fighter a few years back before the Psychos took it over. You sounded popular."

I downed the whisky, ignoring the sting it left on the cut on my lip from the fight.

I felt alive, and I thrived on the pain it gave me.

"I grew up just down the road. Mom took off when I was eight, Dad's always beaten me and treated me like shit, and I never really had many friends besides Lukas growing up. So, when Lukas and I stopped being friends and he went to a different high school than me, I started fighting as a way to deal with my pent-up rage."

He handed me the bottle and watched me pour another drink, dumping his cigarettes on the table with a lighter before pushing the ashtray towards me.

"Why the fuck are you here tonight, kicking the shit out of our best fighters, instead of cozied up in that big fucking mansion of yours? It's common knowledge around here that Aurora Donovan is on Caden Holloway's dick and living in his fancy fucking mansion. So, tell me your bullshit excuse why he'd let you come here alone. He'd never allow you to be here, and we all know it."

Allow me?

I angrily lit a cigarette and glared at him with either bravery or stupidity, I wasn't too sure which one.

"You gonna let me fight again if I talk about it? Because I'm gonna get fucking angry again."

"We'll see," he muttered, waiting for me to speak as he watched be intensely.

I took a drag and glared at the glass in front of me, not wanting to talk about my day, but also knowing he'd throw me out if I didn't.

"I went straight to my old place from school, then I came here, after Caden and his boys put on a nice little show about how they played me. I was a joke to them, Skeeter. They went through my diary, they fucked around with me to make me trust them. Jensen even knew that the man my dad lent me to as a fucking *rape* gift to pay off his debts, was none other than Tristan fucking Holloway, and I had no fucking clue. So, excuse me if I'm bleeding out your money makers, but I'm beyond fucking angry and this is the only place I knew I could go to burn some anger without going to fucking jail."

His eyes narrowed, something changing in him as he sat back with a thoughtful expression on his face as he tongued one of his lip rings.

"That's why Jensen told me not to touch you when I went to shake your hand, right? Because you literally don't like being touched?"

"Yep."

He watched me angrily finish my cigarette and down another glass of whisky before he stood, letting out a sigh.

"Not gonna lie to you, babe. Holloway's one of my boys, but even I know he's full of shit if he thinks you don't mean shit to them. Jensen's soft with you, when he's usually the hard ass out of all of them. Tyler doesn't share his coke with any girl either, and apparently he and Slash got you pretty fucked up over the weekend. Lukas wasn't there today, was he?"

When I shook my head, he snorted, "Because he was too pussy to tell you the truth about what was going down, but too much of a pussy to be part of it too. They're stupid, and they fucked up. I'll let you fight, but don't kill anyone, for fuck's sake. I mean, everyone knows nothing turns me on more than a chick with a criminal record, but I don't wanna add to mine. Okay?"

I nodded, standing and following him towards the door, but he stopped, glancing at me with a small smile.

"Slash's offer still stands. You need us, just holler, okay? I don't give a fuck about what game Holloway played. They wouldn't have bet on the fact that you'd still have someone on your side. Want me to threaten him with my gun? For shits and giggles?"

I smiled slightly, some of my heartache fading.

"Nah, I slashed two of the tires on the Challenger on my way out of the school, despite hating myself for damaging such a nice car. He wasn't that good in bed anyways, so who's really missing out, right?"

He burst out laughing, a real smile finally hitting his lips.

"I like you, Donovan. You want a good fuck, you come find me. Damn girl."

Once back in the cage, people started cheering, and I knew I was in for a long night of inflicting pain, even if it wasn't on the people who deserved it.

CHAPTER EIGHT

RORY

I changed my number two days later.

Jensen had messaged and called me hundreds of times in a panic as if I'd fucking killed myself, since I hadn't been seen since I'd taken off from school.

I had one text from Caden about his tires, telling me I was dead when he got his hands around my throat, and I had one missed call from Tyler.

I knew from the photos online that he'd been tagged in the previous night that he'd just been drunk.

Drunk apologies didn't mean shit, not that I'd fucking forgive him anyways.

Lukas hadn't even tried to contact me once, but he also knew it would have been pointless.

I climbed out of the spare bed at Skeeter's house early to use his treadmill for a few hours until my legs hurt, then I had a hot shower and did a line of cocaine, plonking down next to Skeeter on the couch.

He'd become a good friend over the past few days, and he didn't seem so intimidating anymore.

The cocaine helped, because I wasn't thinking straight.

He was a murdering machine, and I knew he'd kill me if I gave him a reason to.

He looked up from his laptop and raised an eyebrow at me with fake annoyance.

"Can I help you, hot stuff?"

I smirked as Or Nah by The Weeknd and Ty Dolla $ign blasted from the stereo in the corner, my body aching to dance and move along to it.

"Yeah, how long are you going to be doing manly gang stuff?"

He chuckled with amusement, leaning back on the couch to watch me.

"I've got a few things to do today. Also, not a gang, it's a crew. Why?"

I played with my snakebite piercings with my tongue for a second, biting my lower lip in a teasing way, his eyes zoning in on the movement.

I was going to hell.

"I was just wondering how well you ate pussy, actually."

He groaned, leaning forward to close his laptop before sitting back comfortably again as his eyes trailed over my body.

"About as good as I can fuck it. You asking? because baby girl, I'm fucking offering. I'll give you so many orgasms that you won't be able to move for a fucking week."

I was quiet for a moment in thought, not sure if I'd be able to handle him.

If he was as full-on as I'd heard, he was probably going to scare the fucking *shit* out of me.

I finally reached for the bottom of my shirt, decision made as I pulled it over my head slowly, watching as his eyes roamed across my skin with hunger.

They lingered on the bruises along my ribs from fighting

in the cage over the past couple of days, but when he met my eyes, he gave me his panty-dropping grin.

Everyone knew the bruised and bloodied look was his major turn on.

I didn't understand it, but I wasn't about to judge him for it either.

"Just so I'm clear, you're letting me touch you, right?"

The moment I nodded he pushed me onto my back, grabbing the top of my pants and yanking them down my legs aggressively.

Maybe it was a bad idea.

He unlatched my bra before kissing me hard, his tongue bar clicking against mine as his tongue assaulted my mouth.

I didn't get any warning before he pushed a finger inside me, my back arching as I let out a breathy moan.

He was rough, but I wanted rough.

No, I fucking *needed* it.

I wanted him to make me only think about what he was doing to me and nothing else.

I wanted it to hurt, despite any panic that would surface.

I needed to face my demons head-on, and Skeeter Maddox was basically the devil himself.

He kissed between my breasts, moving down my stomach and mound until his lips wrapped around my clit.

He added another finger and curled them inside me, an intense need to climax instantly racing through me.

Holy fucking shit.

My fingers ran through his shaggy reddish-brown hair, tightening my grip the closer to release I became until he had me cursing his name louder than I would have liked.

He sat back and grinned cockily as I recovered, yanking his shirt over his head and nearly causing me to drool.

He was just as fit under his shirt as I'd expected him to be, but he had a lot more ink than any of the other guys I'd ever checked out.

It was hot as fuck.

He had both nipples pierced too, but my surprised eyes flashed up to his amused ones as he stripped out of his pants and the piercing in the tip of his hard dick pointed right up at me.

I hadn't seen one of those before.

"Never seen a pierced dick?" He guessed correctly, moving closer as I reached out to touch it with fascination.

He gritted his teeth as I stroked his length, watching the ball move with surprise.

"No, I haven't. It doesn't hurt?"

"Guess I can figure out which of Holloway's boys you didn't jump on then. Nah, it doesn't hurt. You'll like it, trust me," he waggled his eyebrows suggestively.

I met his gaze again, ignoring his comment about the others and frowned.

"I'll be able to feel it?"

"It's great at finding your g-spot," he winked, moving over me and nibbling down my neck.

We were actually going to do it, and I was trying hard not to fucking panic.

I closed my eyes, letting out a surprised gasp as he pushed inside me suddenly, the metal ball instantly rubbing me in the right place, earning an amused chuckle from him as he thrust firmly in and out of me.

"Told you. Give me your leg."

He lifted one of my legs over his shoulder and thrust deeper, moving faster so that it was on the fine line between pain and pleasure.

He made sure to get me off twice before slipping out of me and sitting on his ass, patting his lap with a smirk.

"Hop on. I don't like my girls lazy, so show me what you've got."

Nerves kicked in but the cocaine was keeping me calm enough to give it a go, and once I sank over him, his hands grabbed my butt cheeks firmly and pulled me forward, a groan leaving him.

"Jesus, your pussy's so fucking good."

I finally figured out a good rhythm, and all we could hear in the house was flesh slapping together and heavy breathing, accompanied by Skeeter's mumbled curses the closer to relief that I got him.

He wrapped my hair around his fist and yanked me closer with a growl.

"Tell me right now if you're on the fucking pill?"

Most people asked that before sticking their dick in someone.

"Yeah, I am," I panted, startled when he lifted me off him with no effort and bent me over the side of the couch, kicking my legs apart before shoving himself into me deep enough to force a scream of discomfort from me.

It fucking hurt, but pleasure started overriding the pain as he kept going.

His chest pressed against my back as he thrust hard into me, my hair wrapped in his fist again as he fucked me harder and harder until I came loudly, his teeth suddenly sinking into my shoulder as he grunted and buried deep.

My shoulder burned as he seemed to keep sinking his teeth even deeper into my skin until he suddenly let go, an amused smirk on his face as he licked blood off his lip.

"Sorry about that, hot stuff," then he licked across my shoulder just as I felt a drop start to run down my skin.

I glanced at my shoulder as best as I could, my eyes going wide at the ripped skin and droplets of blood that slowly seeped from underneath.

I wasn't sure what I was supposed to be feeling, but surely it wasn't supposed to be arousal.

When I remained quiet, he ran his tongue across my bleeding skin again, earning a confused expression from me.

He grinned like the crazy fucker that he was.

"C'mon, baby girl. You fuck a Bloody Psycho, you're gonna fucking bleed. Trust me. If there's a next time, and there will be, I like knives. Just a heads up."

What the fuck?

"Knives?" I asked curiously as he moved off me, lifting me and carrying me towards the bathroom, despite my protesting.

My legs were weak, but I didn't need to be carried around.

I didn't want to rely on anyone for comfort ever again.

He turned the water on in the shower before answering with a smile.

"Yeah. I like inflicting pain when I'm fucking. I don't just go stabbing holes in people, but little cuts and marks here and there turn me on. C'mon, jump in."

I did as I was told, not surprised in the slightest when he shoved me against the wall roughly and wrapped his hand around my throat as he slid inside me again.

I wanted to panic.

I *should* have panicked.

But it scared me to admit to myself that everything he'd said had made me horny.

How fucked up was that?

Skeeter

Holloway's boys fucked up *big* time.

I'd never seen such a timid fucking bitch suddenly turn so bloodthirsty in the cage like she had, but Rory was a deadly weapon.

She let emotion control her, but she had potential.

I'd had to fuck so much pussy at the shed throughout the week to stop myself from jumping her in my fucking kitchen, because she literally walked around in those little booty shorts and a tank top all the fucking time.

I wasn't going to say no when she'd offered herself to me on a silver fucking platter.

I didn't give a fuck about the others finding out, and I honestly hoped they did.

I hoped they saw the bite mark on her shoulder and realized where she'd fucking been all this time.

Everyone knew I loved different pussy each day of the week, but I had every intention of diving into hers again the moment her broken blue eyes begged me to.

I knew it was an asshole move to just jam into her like I had, but she was either going to tell me to stop, or fucking love it.

Turns out, the timid bitch actually *loved* it.

Good girls love a little bit of danger in their lives, so I was only doing my community service by having my way with her and giving her that experience.

I mean sure, if she'd freaked out on me and wanted me to stop, I would have.

I'm a monster, but I wasn't *that* much of a monster.

Then again, I made a habit of fucking girls on the fine line between pleasure and abuse.

As long as both people got off, it was fine.

Right?

She'd passed out in my spare bed that she'd claimed for herself, and I shamelessly watched her like a creep.

I didn't date, ever, but Aurora Donovan was something else, and she was fucking mine.

It was like her demons were screaming out to join mine, wanting to drown together instead of alone.

I just hoped hers knew how to fucking swim.

Caden

"Stop fucking moping," I snapped, Jensen's eyes narrowing on me with anger.

He'd been a little bitch since Rory had taken off, and it grated on my fucking nerves.

"I never should have agreed to go through with that shit. Tell me it was a good idea, huh?" He snapped back, making me roll my eyes.

I expected the whinging bullshit from Lukas, but not Jensen.

He never gave a fucking shit about anyone.

"You knew what was going down from the start, and you were bouncing in your fucking seat when I first decided on it, so don't act all angelic with me now, asshole."

"At the start, she was just some annoying bitch that had moved into your house. She grew on me, and…"

"And it helps that she was falling in love with you, doesn't it?" I snorted as he flipped me off.

He was supposed to be the tormenting bastard out of all of us, but she'd fucked with his head somehow.

He was literally cut up because he made her fucking *cry*.

We hadn't seen her for nearly a week, and I hated that it bothered me.

I'll admit that I gave a shit, but no one else needed to fucking know that.

Mom and Max had been at me like a fucking dog with a bone and it was driving me insane.

They couldn't have been too worried, considering I'd told Max to fuck off and just call the cops, but he didn't seem to want them to find her.

I let her get too close, so I had to push her back out of my life, but was it what I really wanted?

I thought maybe she'd loved me, but she loved Jensen instead.

I'd bet she was a sobbing fucking mess somewhere, and that made me feel a little better.

I had to fucking hate her.

I had to, because if I stopped?

I knew I'd fall back in love with her, and I didn't love *anyone*.

That was why she'd had to go.

She was going to rip us all apart otherwise, but then again, it appeared she was managing to regardless of how far I pushed her away.

Jensen glanced over at Lukas, appearing bothered.

"Luke, I..."

"Don't fucking talk to me about it, Jensen. I promised her I wouldn't hurt her again, and I fucking did. You guys should have told me you were planning on being that cruel, because I would have stayed right fucking out of it," Lukas spat out, dodging Jensen's hand as he went to pat his knee for support.

Tyler groaned, running a hand over his face before plonking down on the couch beside me.

"I dunno, Holloway. I thought it was a fun idea at first, but what if she's gone and done something stupid because of us? No one's seen or heard from her. Do you know how fucking filthy I felt letting Claire climb all over me like that?"

I rolled my eyes at his dramatics, despite worrying that maybe he was right about Rory.

"You didn't feel filthy that time when you actually *fucked* Claire. C'mon, you stick your dick in heaps of shit, so Claire's a walk in the park. I don't get why you're all feeling so fucking bad, honestly. Everyone agreed on it being a good idea."

"Yeah, until we'd actually gotten to know her. Why'd you go and throw that shit about your dad in her face? That wasn't part of the fucking plan," Tyler muttered, my chest becoming tight at the memory of her face when I'd told her about my dad.

The moment Lukas had shown me the picture in the back of her diary, I'd wanted to throw up.

I knew Dad was a piece of shit, but he raped a thirteen-year-old girl?

As payment?

Jensen glared at me, shaking his head before standing.

"I should have just told her the truth, and I shouldn't have taken part in this shit. You wanted her gone because she was getting between us, but in reality, she was fixing us. That's what you didn't fucking like about it. She got under your skin, and we all know Caden Holloway's too fucking *tough* for all that shit. I see why you did it, but running from her like a little bitch isn't going to make it go away. You'd better hope nothing bad has happened to her."

"Or what?" I snorted, earning a dangerous look from him.

"Or, I'll fucking kick the shit out of you and leave you a bloodied mess on your perfectly polished floor."

It was fake, but I laughed and tried to keep my expression in check.

"You're seriously going to get in a fist fight with me over some bitch from the wrong side of town? Do you fucking love her? You honestly think someone like that would stick around for someone like you? We're only wanted because of our money and fancy shit, Jense. No girl's going to genuinely want us, just for being us. That's not how this shit works."

His face scrunched up for a moment before he shook his head at me, his voice surprisingly calm.

"If you really believe that she was only kicking it with us for our money, you're fucking delusional. She had no one, and she was more than happy to stay the fuck away from us. We pushed at her to make her like us, so you can't run off scared now that she does. Also, why *wouldn't* she want to be with me? Fuck you, Caden."

I wasn't surprised when Lukas sneered at me and left with him, but I was surprised when Tyler stood, heading towards the door, talking over his shoulder as he went.

"It still doesn't feel right, Holloway. I'll see you at school tomorrow."

"Wait, you're mad at me too? I did it for us, Ty. She was ripping us apart," I growled, but he smirked, not looking amused in the slightest.

"No, man. *You* ripped us apart, and you did it for yourself. I'll meet you in the parking lot before class," then he headed off without another word.

The house was suddenly silent, and I hated that my thoughts wandered back to the quiet nights I'd spent at home with Rory to keep me company.

Without the guys, I literally had nothing.

If I didn't hit the gym, I was going to lose my fucking shit.

I needed to get all the angry shit out of my system so I could fix all the bullshit with the guys.

I caught myself wondering what Rory was doing.

Ah fuck, she really was under my skin.

Rory

Going back to school sucked.

I had drinks tipped over me, my locker flooded, and then they became even pettier and decided to take my clothes from the showers after gym class.

I rolled my eyes, slipping on the bra and panties I'd stashed in case that had happened, then I snatched my bag from its hook and walked out of the bathroom.

Skeeter had hardened my heart a little, and I was proud by how strong I felt as I headed into the hallway, ignoring the crowd of students that hung around behind Claire to watch the amusement.

Claire and one of her posse members, Mandy, looked pissed that I wasn't completely naked, and I had a hard time holding back a grin of victory.

I knew when people started noticing the marks on my body, because the whispering started.

I'd been sleeping with Skeeter for a full week, so between getting bruised in bed and marked from his teeth and knives, I'd also been fighting and was covered in bruises.

Skeeter thought my black eye was hot, which had made me scoff at him.

I looked fucking terrible.

I went to keep walking, but I jerked to the side when a hand snaked towards me, my eyes darting up to meet Jensen's worried blue ones.

Caden, Tyler and Lukas were with him, and they looked just as horrified by the marks on me, but they covered it up better than Jensen.

Only I could tell they were bothered by it.

Caden's eyes raked up my entire body before his hard green eyes met mine.

I wasn't going to give him anything.

"The fuck happened to you, and where the fuck have you been? Mom's worried sick."

I snorted, not at all surprised that Dad fucking wasn't.

He'd just be angry that I was making him look bad in front of his new rich friends and girlfriend.

"Tell her I'm fine."

"Well, you're obviously not so..."

"Oh, you think I didn't like it? That's cute," I smirked, his eyes narrowing in thought, but I raised an eyebrow and cocked my head, speaking in a condescending tone. "Anyways, good to see you guys. Bet you've been fucking *fantastic*. Enjoy your afternoon," then I spun around and walked away without a backwards glance, knowing everyone was probably looking at the bite marks across my shoulders and back.

I hoped Caden noticed my bruised ass cheeks, because then he'd know *exactly* what I'd been up to.

I climbed into the white Chevrolet Corvette ZR1 that Skeeter had bought for me and I ignored everyone that had followed me outside.

It wasn't every day they saw a half-naked broke chick just climb into a 130k performance car.

It had over 5k of audio added in, which I was fucking in love with.

I revved the engine and lit a cigarette, giving the boys a little wave as I spotted them leaning against the fence with their arms crossed, confusion on their faces.

They knew I'd never be able to afford a performance car, so their minds would have been spinning with different scenarios.

They didn't know what to do with me, and it was fucking hilarious.

I headed off before they could follow, and once I got back to Skeeter's place and walked inside, I lit another cigarette and made my way through the house to find Skeeter, ignoring his crew member's gazes as they glanced over my nearly naked body.

Skeeter raised an eyebrow as I walked into the kitchen, where he was sitting at the table cleaning guns with Slash and a few others.

"Did you wear that to school, baby girl?"

I snorted, accepting his touch as he pulled me down onto his lap.

"No, I did have those nice black pants and red shirt on, but between Caden and Claire's little group, they were stolen from the showers. The guys actually looked concerned and wanted to know where I'd been. It was cute. Anyways, how was your day?"

He shrugged. "It was okay. Had a bit of a problem at the shed, but it's sorted now."

"Like a dead body problem?" I offered, ignoring the look that Slash gave him as he replied with a simple, "Yep."

"Well, fuck," I cringed, flicking the ash from my cigarette into the ashtray before noticing the irritated look in his eye. "Skeet? What's up?"

He scowled, giving me a stern look.

"*What's up?* Claire needs to back off before she's my next dead body problem, and I'm going to have a problem with Holloway's boys too if they don't back the fuck off from you."

I nipped his neck playfully, secretly loving how protective he was of me.

"How about we go upstairs so I can make you feel better? Then we can go to the shed so you can watch me demolish bitches for fun."

He smirked, biting my shoulder sharply.

"Fuck, you're the best. C'mon, let's fuck."

Slash rolled his eyes but gave me a wink on my way past as I led Skeeter up to his room, and after we'd finished, I watched him as he cleaned the slice he'd given me on my thigh.

He must have felt me staring because he smirked and glanced up.

"What?"

"Can girls fight guys in the cage?" I asked curiously, his eyes narrowing to slits.

"They're allowed, but not many guys will fight females. Honestly, I don't want you getting beat to shit by some guy, and when I mean some guy, I mean the big cunts. They're the only ones who'd get in the cage and swing at you. Most of the guys that fight wouldn't hit a girl, and they know how well you fight."

"I'm getting sick of fighting the girls, they fucking suck," I muttered, hearing him sigh as he watched me thoughtfully.

"I'll ask around, but it's only happening if I find a fair fighter, and if they win and you get seriously hurt, I'll shoot them."

"No, you won't."

"Bet on it!" He snapped, making me frown.

He sat up and yanked me closer by the throat, speaking in a firm voice.

"You promise to only fight a guy if I let you?"

I nodded, groaning as he kissed me hard before releasing my throat and stalking from the room to let me finish getting changed.

Moody bastard.

Most of the Psychos had cleared out by the time I got back downstairs, but Slash leaned against the wall with a frown fixed to his face.

"Guys would do some damage to you, babe."

"I know," I answered, halting as he put an arm out to stop me without touching me.

He peered at me cautiously.

"You're trying to block out the emotional hurt with physical, but the problem is that you're so fucking strong that you'll be dead before it soothes the emotions. You're a good fighter in the cage, Donovan, but I think it's best you listen to Skeet. He's watched you fight for nearly two weeks, so he knows what you can handle. He won't take it easy on you, but he won't let you get destroyed either. Trust me."

"I'm not trusting a single fucking person again. I know Skeeter knows what he's doing, so yes, I will listen to him. Can I go find him now?"

He chuckled and jerked a thumb at the front door.

"He said he'd meet you at the shed. I'll follow you."

Of course he would.

I snatched my keys and cigarettes before heading out to my car, waiting for Slash to climb behind the wheel of his Mustang, then we drove the short distance down the road to the shed.

I always felt powerful when I walked into the shed and people parted when they saw me, but this time I had to ignore the stabbing pain in my chest when I spotted Tyler talking to one of the fighters near the back of the room.

I saw him stiffen out of the corner of my eye when he noticed me stalking through as people cleared a path, and I grinned as one of the regular fighters bumped fists with me as I headed into the cage and moved over to Skeeter, who raised an eyebrow.

"I didn't know Ty was going to be here tonight. You okay to fight with him here? You know he's probably already sent word out to the others that you're here, right?"

"I'll fight *him* in the cage if he wants?" I offered, making him roll his eyes with a small amount of amusement that he couldn't hide from me.

"Just play nice and only fight the fighters, okay? You've got that blonde bitch up first."

I nodded, tying my hair up in a high messy ponytail before he nodded at the blonde girl to enter the ring.

People cheered as Skeeter left the cage and closed the gate, grabbing the microphone and smirking at the crowd.

"Alright you fuckers, you ready to see a good bloody fight? You're gonna fucking get one!"

I zoned him out as I glared at the girl in front of me who gave me a cocky smirk.

"Yo, Donovan. You ready to bleed, bitch?"

My lip lifted in a nasty smirk right back.

"Bring it, blondie. Show me what you've got."

The moment Skeeter called the start of the fight the bitch flew at me, but I was ready and swung around suddenly, knocking her back with a solid jab of my elbow, tripping her to the ground.

She growled as she scrambled to her feet and clenched her fists, but I kicked my foot out and clipped the side of her head, stunning her long enough to straddle her and pin her to the ground.

I laid punch after punch into her face until Skeeter ripped me off her so some of his crew could drag her out to clean her up.

My blood was pumping as I bounced on my feet, and Skeeter had to shove me against the cage hard to draw my attention.

"Hey, no dead body problems, remember? Once they're out, can you stop fucking hitting them?"

"Make me!" I snapped, giving him a feral grin as he gripped my throat hard and got in my face.

He was hot when he was angry.

"You wanna fight again tonight? Listen to me. I like how pumped up you get when you start seeing these bitches fucking bleed, but if you start actually killing them, then I have to do a lot of covering up, and you'll be doing it with me. You read me?" He growled loud enough for me to hear him over the crowds cheering.

I gave him a sharp nod and he released his grip on me instantly.

"Good. You've got the kicker up next," he muttered before letting another girl into the cage who I'd fought many times over the past week.

She was good, but she fought with her feet more than her fists.

I got the first punch in, but she got me in the eye twice pretty quickly.

I ignored Caden and the guys as they stood by the gate, Jensen getting in Skeeter's face, but I kept my attention on my opponent, kicking the girl in the kneecap and hearing the crunch as she screamed and hit the floor in agony.

I jumped on her and started punching her in the face until Skeeter pushed past the guys to rip me away, but I stopped on my own accord and stood back with a grin, just before he could grab me.

I clenched my bloody knuckles and raised an eyebrow at him as he scowled.

"Last warning tonight, babe, or I take your ass home."

"Give me a fucking challenging one then!" I shouted, one of his fingers jabbing into my chest with frustration.

"I've got a guy. Your height and close to your weight. He goes to the school I did, but the problem is he's known to fight dirty. He's been searched for weapons, but promise me if you're seriously hurt, you tap the fuck out and I'll split it up. You got it? I already told him if he does anything dodgy,

I'll put him in a fucking hole. Hopefully, it's enough to keep him in line."

"Bring it on," I gritted out, flexing my fingers again as he nodded at Slash who brought a young guy into the ring.

People went ballistic, but the guys were seething as Skeeter gave me an encouraging nod.

"Like I said, this goes south, tap out or I'll start shooting people."

"Fucking hell! Yes, Skeet!" I yelled, earning a dirty look from him before he nodded at the male fighter and left the ring.

The guy seemed irritated as I dodged a lot of his hits, but he got cocky when he landed one on my already blackening eye, and a solid one to my lip.

I tasted the blood and smirked, confusing him before I surprised him with two fist jabs and a crack with my elbow to the side of his head.

He jabbed me in the ribs and got a kick to my head, but after I headbutted his nose and managed to get him on the ground, I laid into him until he was out.

I scrambled off him and walked towards the gate as people whistled and cheered, Skeeter grinning at me with admiration.

"Nice, babe. Head into the office and get cleaned up. I'll be in soon."

To fuck me, I hoped.

I did as I was told, fist-bumping a few people on my way through as they parted for me again, and once I was shut in the office, I sat and lit a cigarette, thankful when one of Skeeter's guys delivered a bottle of whisky to me.

I'd had two glasses by the time Skeeter wandered in, instantly lifting me to plonk my ass on his desk so he could stand between my legs and lift my shirt.

He always checked my damage.

"How sore are you?"

"The usual. Can't really feel it," I mumbled as I had a drag of my cigarette, earning a grin from him as he leaned forward.

"Fucking liar. You've had broken ribs since your first fight here the other week, not to mention your face is bruised and bleeding. Your knuckles are ripped to shit too."

"I don't give a fuck, I need it," I glared, finishing my cigarette before he tugged me forward, shoving a hand down the front of my pants and jammed two fingers inside me firmly.

I heard the familiar click of his blade, and between being impatient and the adrenaline rush still flowing through me, I was nearly bouncing on the fucking desk.

He knew how to make me want him without a whole lot of effort.

He ran the blunt end of the blade down my chest before moving it up to the base of my throat, speaking sternly in my ear as he stilled the fingers in my pussy that was now soaking wet.

"If you *ever* argue with me in my fucking cage again, I will fucking slit your throat, Donovan. My guys can't think I'm weakened by the girl I'm fucking, or I start to lose my respect. I don't want to fucking hurt you, but don't think for a second that I won't think twice about it if I have to choose."

"Can I still tell you what to do to me in bed?" I smiled sweetly, watching him smirk as he pushed his fingers in and out of me again without moving the blade.

"You can tell me how to fuck you as much as you like, but I already know how to turn you to fucking jelly, so I wouldn't worry too much if I were you," then he pulled his fingers out and brought them up to my lips for me to suck my own juices.

He finally moved the blade from my throat once I'd

sucked his fingers clean, then he snatched a cigarette from the desk for himself and sat heavily in his chair.

He'd finish getting me off later, he always did.

I changed into a clean shirt before giving him a kiss goodbye and walking out of the room, nearly getting to my car before I heard Caden bark from behind me.

"Cage fighting? That's what you've been fucking doing? Ty told you not to fuck with them, Aurora. They fucking kill people for sport, and you have no idea how cage fighting even…"

"Why would I listen to Tyler fucking Johnson? I never listened to Jensen when he told me numerous fucking times not to trust anyone. Don't tell me that I don't know shit about cage fighting either, I used to come here and fight after I was fucking raped when I was thirteen years old. Don't you dare pretend to give a fuck about my safety, Holloway."

Tyler snorted from beside him as he joined the conversation, Jensen and Lukas standing off to the side.

"I've never seen you here before."

"So?" I asked curtly, watching him roll his eyes.

"I'm surprised Skeet even fucking lets you fight. He knew it would just piss us off."

A smirk stretched cross my face and I leaned back against the door of the Corvette, holding his dark gaze.

"You think Skeet gives a fuck if he pisses you off? Word of advice, guys. Don't fuck with the Psychos."

Lukas looked concerned as he finally spoke up.

"We didn't fuck with them?"

My gaze landed on him and I raised an eyebrow, my smirk widening.

"Well, Skeet's *pissed*."

Caden narrowed his eyes on the hickey on my neck, his voice sounding curious and pissed off all at once.

"Who are you fucking, and where the *fuck* did you get the Corvette from?"

"None of your fucking business, asshole," I retorted as I climbed into my car and put the windows down, cranking the stereo up as Oh My God by Hellyeah blasted, giving them a wink despite my insides feeling tight from the pain of them being there.

"Don't mess with the bull or you'll get the horns," then I tore out of the yard before they could say another word.

CHAPTER NINE

RORY

"Oh, fuck!" I gasped as Skeeter held my hip in one hand and thrust up, holding my tangled hair in his other fist tightly as I rode him hard.

He'd convinced me to pierce my nipples, and one of his buddies had given me a tattoo with the word *warrior* across my shoulder blade.

I was feeling more reckless, I guessed.

I ground myself down on him, my orgasm hitting me hard as his hand shot up and wrapped around my throat so tightly that my scream came out raspy.

The door opened, but we ignored it until Jensen's startled voice came from close by.

"What the fuck?"

Skeeter glanced up and let go of my throat, a taunting smirk on his face.

He totally knew they'd been standing there.

"Oh, hey guys."

I scowled before stopping and glancing over my shoulder, seeing all four of them in the loungeroom doorway, looking shocked at what they'd walked in on.

Caden looked pissed off, but Jensen seemed broken as his eyes met mine.

I could see all the regret that I'd noticed in his eyes since we'd first started hanging out, but now I knew he deserved to hurt.

I sneered at him, and Skeeter grabbed my chin hard, jerking my gaze back to him and speaking in a demanding voice.

"I'm not fucking *done*."

I was pretty fucking high, so I didn't care that we had an audience as I started circling my hips again, letting out a small groan as his piercing rubbed the right spot.

I had to place my hands on his chest to balance myself as my head spun slightly.

"Aurora, cut that shit out!" Caden snapped, but Skeeter gripped my throat hard again without taking his eyes off Caden, smirking when I kept fucking him.

I couldn't focus, but I just tried to ignore the fact that Caden was even there.

At least I could trust Skeeter to keep them in line.

"Don't fucking talk to her like that. Also, don't cock block me, or I'll be super fucking angry at you, Holloway, and I know you don't want that."

Tyler stared at me as I rode Skeeter, my ass smacking against his thighs as I picked the pace up, and Skeeter grinned. "Watch all you like, Johnson, she fucks like a porn star. Have a seat, guys. Get comfortable."

They all hesitated before sitting down on the couches, and Skeeter moved his hand from my throat to reach for his knife on the side table next to us.

Jensen's eyebrows shot up and he blurted, "You're the one who's been slicing her up?"

Skeeter paused before dragging the blunt end of the cool blade down my back, a shiver running through me.

"Yeah, why? You know I like to play with knives, Gilbert."

"I thought she was doing it to herself," he mumbled, Skeeter laughing hard as he turned the blade up the other way and moved it to my shoulder, sliding it across my skin with ease.

"You thought you guys drove her to self-harm? Don't be stupid. If anything, you made her fucking stronger."

Jensen frowned, but Caden growled and motioned to the blade with disgust.

"Can you not do that?"

Skeeter moved the blade back and licked across my skin as the blood trickled down my arm, warning in his tone as he spoke.

"You're in my house while we fuck, so if you don't like it, you can leave, Holloway."

"You're going to fucking hurt her."

"For starters, why do you give a shit what I do to her? And also, she can't feel it. You broke her hard enough for her to stop feeling. Nifty, huh?" He responded with a chuckle, moving to slice me again, but I spoke softly.

"You're wrong, Skeet."

"How so, baby girl?" He murmured, his light green eyes boring into me.

I lifted my eyes to his and ran a hand up his tattooed chest.

"I do it to feel, because I can't stand the numb, empty feeling."

"Either way, you like it, right?" He asked lightly, waiting for me to nod before looking back at Caden with a grin. "See? It's fine.

I kept riding him until he thrusted up with a groan, swatting my ass to dismiss me.

I was more than happy to get out of that room.

"Go jump in the shower and head to bed. I'll be up soon."

I gave him a quick kiss before climbing from his lap, ignoring the glances the others gave me as they looked my body over on my way past.

They had no right to fucking judge me.

After my shower, I annoyingly found Skeeter and Caden in the bedroom waiting for me.

I knew something was going on, and I knew I wasn't going to like it.

Skeeter sighed with a frustrated expression on his face.

"We've got a problem, hot stuff."

"Another dead body problem?" I offered, only half-joking, but Caden's eyes narrowed.

Skeeter smirked with amusement though.

"Not yet, but Holloway's pulled out the legal card. If your father thinks you're in danger, he'll bring cops into it. Since you know who I am and what I do, you understand that I can't have them show up here, right?"

I rolled my eyes and leaned against the wall, refusing to look at Caden.

"I can leave here to protect you, sure. Doesn't mean I'll go home."

Skeeter scowled. "Cops will think I fucking killed you or some shit if you don't. Everyone knows you've been on my dick for the past couple of weeks, so do us a favour and behave until your birthday, or I actually *will* have to kill you."

I finally glanced at Caden and shrugged.

"Fine, I'll go home, but if you think you're safe to sleep at night, Caden Holloway, you're in for a rude fucking surprise. If you think I'd even hesitate to gut you open in your fucking sleep..."

Skeeter groaned, pulling me against him and kissing my neck.

"You're making me horny all over again, stop it. Did you plan on fighting tomorrow?"

I said yes at the same time that Caden said no, and he actually looked slightly concerned for his safety when I pushed away from Skeeter and pulled the blade from his pocket, gently poking Caden in the side with it.

"What are you going to do if I do fight, Holloway? Call the cops to break up an illegal crew operated cage fight? Smart move, jackass. You'd end up in a fucking hole."

He held my gaze, but I saw the emotions behind the mask.

I knew him better than he did, and he was fucking cracking.

"Rory, I'm sorry. We fucked up."

You bet your ass you did.

I smiled with fake sweetness, turning the blade and dragging it down my own arm, feeding off the adrenaline my body threw out from the pain.

"Empty fucking words, rich boy. I don't give a *fuck*."

Skeeter snatched his blade back and tsked me.

"I'm meant to be the only one who marks you, and you know it. Grab your shit and bail, before I kill Holloway and the rest of his boys."

I shrugged, a taunting glint in my eyes.

"Might just take my fucking time then."

He chuckled as he left the room, leaving Caden to watch me as I started shoving things into my massive bag.

Skeeter had bought me a lot of stuff, and I'd won some decent money from fighting in the cage, so I'd treated myself with a pile of stuff too.

The rest of the money I'd stashed away for savings.

"We really are sorry," he insisted as he finally spoke again, earning an unimpressed glance from me.

"Like I said, I don't give a fuck. You're only sorry because it's hurting you, not because it hurt me. You want the guilty pain you have inside you to stop, but it won't. I hope it fucking eats you alive."

I shoved past him, dragging my bag behind me and snatching my keys from the table, making sure to give Skeeter a big kiss on the way past.

"I'll see you tomorrow night then?"

He shrugged. "Should do. Unless I get called out to do some shit for the crew, then I want you to stay away from the shed."

I snorted, narrowing my eyes on him.

"I've been going there since before it was even yours, Skeet."

His eyes blazed as they snapped to mine angrily.

"The fuck did I tell you today about arguing with me?"

"Not to do it in your cage. This is different, and you know it."

"Like fuck, Donovan. I'll still slit your fucking throat and watch you bleed out in the kitchen, just as easily as I would in the cage."

Jensen's eyes widened as I kissed Skeeter's cheek with a giggle.

"You'd miss my pussy too much."

He gave me a smirk, swatting my butt as I headed towards the door.

"I can still fuck you once you're dead, babe. Don't you forget it."

Caden cringed as I laughed and blew Skeeter a kiss on my way outside, climbing into my car without waiting for the others.

Caden walked past, pausing by my window as I put it down to light a cigarette.

"He really doesn't scare you? You know he's not bluffing, right?"

I glanced up at him, leaning my arm on the door.

"I know he's serious, but I'm not afraid of dying, Caden. I have nothing left to lose."

I started the engine and turned the stereo up, Lay Me Down by In This Moment hitting my ears before I revved the car and skidded from the yard without another word.

I beat the guys home, and once I parked the Corvette and switched the engine off, I swung my bag over my shoulder and stalked into the house, ready for a fight.

I'd only made it to the kitchen when Josie glanced up and gasped, running towards me with her arms out.

She was never going to fucking learn.

"Don't touch me! How many fucking times do you need to be told!" I screamed at her before she could make contact with me, causing her to flinch.

She ran her eyes over me with panic on her face.

"Oh my god, who…"

"Oh, this? Nah, it's fine. It was just a bit of fighting and good fucking," I shrugged as the front door banged open and Caden stormed in.

"Wait for us next time, for fuck's sake!"

"Why the fuck would I do anything for you, Holloway? Back off," I retorted angrily.

He stepped towards me, but I put my hand up to stop him.

"I wouldn't bother. I have a knife and I'm not afraid to use it."

"He's turned you fucking psycho!" Caden snapped, but his mother frowned with confusion.

"Who? Where have you been, Aurora?"

I narrowed my eyes. "My boyfriend's place. I'm fine, seriously."

"You don't look fine," she said gently, but Caden's eyebrows shot up in surprise.

"Boyfriend?"

"Well I *am* fine!" I snapped, ignoring Caden, but I tensed when Jensen moved closer to me, his voice soft.

"Rory…"

I'd never let them hurt me again.

I didn't trust them in the slightest, no matter how much they begged for forgiveness.

"No, you had the chance to stop it all. You had the fucking chance to tell me, but you kept dodging it. It's too late, Jensen. You guys fucked up, whether you wanted to or not. You chose to…"

"Lukas didn't do shit, so why are you pissed at him?" Caden demanded, but I rolled my eyes and pointed at Lukas.

"He stole my diary for starters, and he would have known who Tristan fucking was, and he never…"

"Tristan? What did he do? How do you even know him?" Josie managed to get out as Max walked in and froze, his eyes darting to Josie before I gave him a feral smirk, knowing I was about to fuck everything up for him.

"Oh, just old stuff. Dad owed Tristan a debt when I was thirteen, and I was the payment."

"What?" She tensed, her voice becoming tiny as Max started towards me with anger in his eyes, but I flipped my blade out and stopped him in his tracks.

"Like I said when we met, Josie, you're way too good for my dad. He throws people under the bus to save himself. He cost me my best friend, he sold my virginity to your fucking husband when I was thirteen, then he lied to my best friend when he said it would only be the once," I bit out sharply, watching as all four guys went rigid.

I never wanted them to know it had been a regular thing, but it was all coming out and no one could stop it.

I laughed as Josie stared at Max through new eyes.

She fucking hated him.

"He tried to originally get Lukas to do it, but Lukas loved me and never would have hurt me like that. Dad's beat me my whole life, and Mom left when I was eight because she couldn't handle him anymore. The debt, the lies, the cheating, and watching him hurt his own child. He's put me in the hospital more times than I can count, but I was always known for fighting, so people believed his stories about how I tried to take on older kids when I was younger. I was just something to trade to keep his head above water."

Josie turned to Caden, a disapproving tone in her voice.

"And you boys knew some of this?"

Caden nodded with shame, and she gritted her teeth, not at all impressed with him.

"When did you find out about your father?"

"The same week that Rory took off," he replied quietly, his mother scowling.

"And she took off because?"

He glanced at me, his shoulders slumping as I glared at him.

"Because, she was a game at the start, and we didn't realize we cared so much until we'd shown all of our cards. We drew her in just to crush her. Lukas hasn't met Dad, so he honestly had no idea until we went through her diary."

Was he fucking kidding me?

I let out a small chuckle. "Drew me in? You made me trust you first. Started warming me up to Jensen around the time I let you fuck me. Lukas got my trust back when he told me the truth about the night I thought he'd walked out on me, but then you wanted to start adding Ty into the little circle of trust too, and I fucking fell for it. Sure, I fell for Jensen, but the bits you didn't know that weren't in my diary, were that you guys weren't just everything to me, you were all I fucking had. I loved all of you, and I would have done anything for you. I let all of you touch me, whether it was just to hold my hand or sexually, but my biggest mistake of all was letting you fuck me, Caden. You were the first person to do that other than the times your fucking father raped me. That's what fucked me up the most. I trusted you enough to be my first chosen sexual partner after *years* of trauma, and you threw it all back in my face in front of the school. Leave me alone, or the offer still stands. I'll fucking gut you in your sleep," then I turned and headed up to my room, slamming the door behind me for added effect.

I'd never admit to them how hard it was to finally let it all out, but the moment I was alone, I sank to the floor and cried silently.

Fuck all of them.

It had been a long day without Skeeter.

I knew I'd been too reliant on him because it fucking sucked being away from him.

It was Friday night, and after a long day at school, dealing with Claire's posse and avoiding the guys, I pulled into the driveway to see the house already pumping.

Caden had warned me earlier in the day that it was his turn to throw a party, so I knew I was in for a long night.

I'd only just grabbed a bottle of whisky after doing a couple lines of cocaine in my room, courtesy of Skeeter, when I ran into Claire in the hallway.

She honestly seemed surprised to see me as she flicked her stupid long blonde hair over her shoulder.

"Aurora? What the hell are you doing here?"

"I live here?" I stated as if she was stupid, watching her frown and her waxed eyebrows furrow in confusion.

"But Caden..."

"My dad's still fucking his mom, you stupid bitch. You thought since Caden and I aren't fucking now, that I'd just vanish?" I asked, a grin stretching across her face as she stepped towards me, but Tyler's voice cut in from beside us suddenly.

"Claire, don't even bother."

"Don't tell me you actually pity her?" She exclaimed as she spun around to face him.

I smirked before grabbing her around the throat with my free hand, slamming her back into the wall and getting in her face.

"Oh, he doesn't pity me in any of this. He pities *you* right now, because I could break your fucking neck and no one would fucking know. I still live here, and I will throw you out if I want. If I were you, I'd stay out of my fucking way, you self-righteous prissy *slut*."

Her blue eyes darted around nervously, but Tyler didn't move until I'd let go of her.

He took a step towards me, making me snort.

"Don't even bother, asshole," then I headed down to the main party, swigging on my whisky bottle as I went.

I felt like a merry fucking pirate actually.

Feeling stabby with a bottle in my hand and all that kind of shit.

I'd only just lit a cigarette when the front door opened, and Slash walked in with some of the Psychos behind him.

Guys stayed back, while girls basically threw themselves at them.

I stayed right where I was though, they'd find me when they wanted to.

I was shoved from behind and Claire was suddenly in my face.

"What the fuck was that for, Aurora? You think you can just throw me around like that, you trailer trash whore?"

I took a long drag, flicking my ash on her shirt to her disgust.

"You're in my house, so yeah, I can. Besides, if you want a

real fight this time, I'll be sure to put you back on the ground where I left you last time."

"You want to fight me? You only got lucky last time, you crazy bitch," she seethed.

I was tempted to knock her the fuck out again.

I was done with people thinking they could walk all over me.

Skeeter chuckled as he walked over, and it wasn't a nice chuckle.

"Claire, she'd flatten you. She's my best fighter in the cage."

Her eyes flew to his and she frowned, irritated by his statement.

"Wait, you actually know her? C'mon, Skeet. She's trash."

He eyed her with anger and motioned for me to approach him, pulling me against his chest and smirked at Claire cruelly as I reached him.

"Know her? If I were you, I'd stay the fuck away from her. She's my girl, and if you fuck with her again, I'll let her put you in a hole. You feel me?"

Claire scampered away without another word like the little bitch that she was, a grin stretching across my face.

"She's such a pussy."

"Speaking of pussy," he said in a low voice before dipping down to claim my mouth, backing me against the wall with a thud.

I knew people were watching as Skeeter's hand went down the front of my pants, but I kind of liked it when he got possessive.

I liked it that he wanted people to see me with him, too.

"Hey, break it up and deal with this later. We've gotta bounce," Slash said as he popped up beside us, Skeeter growling like a feral animal.

"What the fuck for? We just got here."

He glanced at me, causing Skeeter to narrow his eyes.

"Do we have to deal with dead bodies, or are we raiding some cunt, or…"

"Dead bodies," Slash muttered under his breath and Skeeter instantly removed his hand from my panties with a sigh, putting his fingers in my face.

I kept my gaze on his as I sucked them into my mouth and swirled my tongue around them, receiving a satisfied smile from him.

"Good girl. Go and fuck someone, alright? I might be a few days, and I'd hate for you to be horny the whole time."

"What?" I asked as my entire body tensed up.

We were in a relationship, so why the fuck would I sleep with anyone else?

"Get laid, baby girl. I mean it," he replied casually before walking off with Slash who was laughing, reminding him that no one would touch me now they'd seen me with him.

I scowled, downing a mouthful of whisky and noticing Lukas standing across the room, eyeing me warily.

I was aware of the others watching me from close by, but I ignored them and headed towards Lukas, surprising the shit out of him.

"Uh, hey," he managed to get out, my lip twitching as I fought a smirk.

"Lukas. Having a good night?"

He seemed confused by the conversation but nodded.

"Sure. You?"

"Would be nice if I could get laid without someone barging in or dead bodies showing up, but yeah, it's alright."

"Skeet's a busy man, makes it difficult," he responded dryly, receiving a nod in agreement.

"Tell me about it."

I noticed a guy staring at me from across the room as I glanced around, my eyes lingering on him.

He was pretty hot, and I didn't know him, which was fucking *perfect*.

I smirked, Lukas frowning as he gave me the side eye.

"Rory, what are you doing?"

"Skeet told me to get laid, so I'd better get to it," I winked before moving across the room towards the hot guy.

He'd finally spotted me and was shamelessly giving me a panty-dropping smile.

The closer I got the more I realized he was hot as fuck.

Jackpot.

"Hey, sexy lady," he greeted with interest as I reached him, his eyes twinkling with mischief.

I looked him up and down appreciatively before answering him, my eyes lingering on the scar down his arm.

I was picking up Skeeter's kinks, apparently.

Scars were becoming a major turn on.

"Hey. You wanna get out of here?"

He seemed surprised by how forward I was being but nodded, putting an arm around my middle and drawing me closer to his side.

I ignored the alarms going off in my head as his hands touched me.

My anxiety could go and fuck itself.

I tried to enjoy it as he kissed me on the way out to his car.

But I wished I'd just stopped doing stupid shit when something hit the back of my head and it all went black.

Dumb bitch.

Lukas

I honestly didn't understand Rory.

She might have spent most of her life as my best friend, but I still didn't fucking understand her.

Dating Skeeter was the weirdest part because she was full of anxiety issues, and Skeeter was the reason anxiety was fucking *invented*.

He was reckless, unpredictable, and an actual fucking killing machine.

How he and Rory even got talking was beyond me.

Then she walked off to fuck a stranger?

That didn't make sense.

Jensen wandered over, leaning closer so no one else could hear him.

"Is she okay? What did she want?"

He'd been sucking up my ass ever since they'd pulled that stunt on her at school, and I didn't mind him grovelling in the slightest.

He was spending heaps of time at my place all of a sudden, basically begging me for forgiveness.

I'd always forgive him because he was my best friend, but I liked the effort he was putting in, so I let him sweat a bit.

I rolled my eyes, moving back slightly.

"Skeet gave her a hall pass for the night and she just left with some guy to get laid. I'd say she's fucking fantastic."

His eyes went wide and he shook his head, his hand going to my shoulder.

"Who was he? You just let her go with him?"

"Let her? Have you *tried* telling her what to do? Especially after fucking her over like we did. She'd be likely to stab me if I tried to keep her here. I've never seen him before, but Skeet told her to get laid, so that's on him," I snorted, hating that my insides churned at my words.

She was high as fuck, so fuck knows how with it she actually was.

Tyler walked over with a scowl on his face, motioning to the people around us.

"I'm already tired of us hosting this shit tonight. I say we shut it down and go run amuck."

Last time we agreed to run amuck, he set some assholes car on fire.

Not happening.

"Not tonight, Ty. I'm not in the mood to bail you out of jail," I muttered, making him frown.

"What's up your ass?"

Jensen cringed. "Ah, Skeet told Rory to find someone to fuck, so she left with some guy a little while ago."

His eyes narrowed on me, his voice low.

"You didn't think to mention that before? We could have stopped her."

I laughed, moving back from both of them.

"You could have tried, but she'd pull a fucking knife on you or some shit, and you know it. We fucked up with her, guys. She's never going to trust us again. We blew it," then I stalked off, needing my own space.

The party suddenly fucking sucked.

Tyler

Since Caden had started to come to realize that Rory was fucking important in our lives after all, he'd started to become a fucking mess.

It was usually me writing myself off, but he had his head in the toilet by midnight, babbling about being a fuck up.

I mean, we were all fuck ups, but that wasn't the point.

I was just glad that he was starting to see the truth.

He needed her, we all did.

I slid down the wall beside the toilet, bringing my knees up and watching him heave painfully into the toilet.

"You aren't looking too good, man."

"Thanks for your input, Captain Obvious," he mumbled, coughing before sitting back against the other side of the wall to meet my gaze. "Have you heard from her?"

"You're stupid if you think she'd get hold of any of us. If she wanted to make a scene about it, she would have just taken him upstairs to her room. She's doing this for her, Caden. Not to piss anyone off."

"Something's wrong, I can feel it," he insisted, and I couldn't hold back my chuckle.

"What, you two have some soul connecting shit going on? She's fine. You, on the other hand, are a fucking mess. Let's get you to bed, alright? I'll crash here to make sure you don't choke on your fucking vomit in your sleep."

"Kind of you," he mumbled before turning and throwing up in the toilet again.

I personally thought he was being selfish for having a pity party.

It was what he wanted, after all.

I could still see her face as her fucking heart shattered into pieces as she stared at me that day.

I thought I could go through with it easily, but I'd struggled to keep my shit to myself.

She saw the truth in my eyes, but she never fought me on it.

She was used to being let down, so I wasn't surprised when she put that big ass wall back up around her heart and stood her ground.

Caden broke her with the information about his father,

and he was lucky I didn't knock him the fuck out in front of everyone.

People didn't even know they were laughing about someone being raped as a kid, but they fucking laughed anyways.

Being kings of the castle sucked ass sometimes, and it was honestly getting old.

We always ran riot at school, doing as we fucking pleased to kill the time, but having Rory there made the days enjoyable, and it felt weird without her being with us now.

Nothing went back to normal like Caden thought it would, and he knew we all blamed him for the rift that was between us all.

Jensen and Lukas seemed alright, but I knew Lukas hated all of us for the first few days.

Hell, I fucking hated us for the first few days.

Hearing her tell us that Tristan Holloway raped her on the regular ripped my fucking heart out, and I knew it played on Caden's mind.

I helped my best friend into bed, watching him sleep for a good hour before deciding it would be safe to go to sleep on the couch in the corner.

Turned out, I was fucking wrong.

I should have gone looking for Rory after all.

Skeeter slammed the bedroom door open midmorning, a murderous glint in his eyes that actually made me think he was going to kill us this time.

He hauled me off the couch, getting in my face and yelling as if I were deaf.

"Where the fuck is she?! She's been missing all night and the burner phone I gave her was dumped down at the fucking docks! So tell me, Ty, who the *fuck* did my girlfriend leave with last night?!"

Shit.

Skeeter

I was ready to kill someone.

It had been three days since someone had kidnapped Rory.

Three fucking days.

I'd even reached out to the fucking Reapers of Chaos Crew down at the docks to see if they'd seen anything that night, but it was a busy night for business at their establishment, meaning there were dodgy people everywhere.

We didn't deal with other crews unless we had to, so whoever had my girl, had better pray that I didn't get my fucking hands on them.

Slash nudged me, pushing a beer towards me.

"Hey, we'll find her. Want me to reach out to the Devils?"

"You're fucking kidding, right?" I snapped, a loud snort coming from him.

"You wanna find her, or not?"

"They made their bed with us, so now they can lie in it. Don't fucking call them. Reapers don't know shit, and the phone was found in their territory. She must still be local, surely."

He watched me for a moment before scowling.

"See, women make us fucking weak, brother. You're here wounded, while someone could be planning a hit on us and take you out. Get your head in the fucking game. She probably just fucked off with her old man, anyways."

I lit a cigarette and ignored his comment.

We'd already fucking talked about that, and I knew for a

fact that she wouldn't just take off with that sad excuse for a fucking father.

I glared across the room at one of the new guys, not at all surprised that he didn't even flinch.

"Slash, seriously. I don't trust that guy."

"Liam? C'mon, brother. I checked his shit and he's cool. Why do you think he's bad news?" He asked, watching as I sipped on my beer with a shrug.

"Look, I just don't like him. He's too cocky for starters, but he's too eager to please. Look into him more, okay?"

He scowled about him being in charge, but he didn't bother to argue with me.

He knew fucking better than to push my buttons right now.

I had to find Rory.

I just had to.

CHAPTER TEN

RORY

For five fucking days, I'd been strapped inside a box on my back with my waist and legs sticking out a hole at the end, my legs braced apart.

I'd seen those sort of things in porn, but never in real life.

I was starting to wonder if Skeeter even noticed I was gone and was even going to rescue me.

I hated being the damsel in distress type, but I had no other choice but to wait.

After days of not knowing who'd been raping me, I was starting to think I never would.

The hands that had been touching me for what felt like hours were rough, so I knew it wasn't the guy who I'd left the house with.

This guy never said a word, and after that first night, I'd stopped shouting at whoever it was to not touch me.

It wasn't like I could stop them anyways.

I shivered as I was hit with the hose for my daily hose down, washing me off once he'd removed himself from me, and for the first time since being there, I heard his voice.

"Aurora Donovan, what the fuck did you do to make your father cut me another deal?"

I was going to be fucking sick.

I swallowed down the bile as he chuckled and jammed two fingers inside me.

"Looks like you're into some crazy shit, so maybe I need to make you like it a little more, eh? Do you like fire play? Or just the knives?"

"Don't fucking touch me, Tristan," I finally bit out, hearing him laugh just as something hot burned into my inner thigh.

I gritted my teeth, refusing to give him the satisfaction of hearing my pain, but he just tsked and jammed his fingers even deeper.

"No one likes a tough fucker, Aurora."

"Do you even know who my fucking boyfriend is, you piece of shit?" I snapped, causing him to hesitate before answering.

I hated using the Psychos name like that, but what choice did I have.

I was running on survival mode.

"Boyfriend, eh? But you left the party with someone I paid? So, who's this *boyfriend* you so willingly cheated on?"

"I didn't cheat on him, he *told* me to get laid. You'd know Skeeter Maddox, right? From the Bloody Psychos?"

I heard him curse before he left the room angrily, slamming the door behind him, his big bad attitude suddenly extinguished.

Even a stupid piece of shit like Tristan Holloway knew he wasn't going to be excused from the Psychos revenge if they got their hands on him.

I'd just started to relax when I heard him yelling upstairs, grinding my teeth with irritation.

Fucking obnoxious bastard.

I zoned him out, not realizing I'd drifted off to sleep until I heard the door creak open quietly.

I held my breath, waiting for the unwanted touch, but it never came.

I heard a small snort from somewhere in the room, and then they muttered, "Jesus, Dad. A fucking sex dungeon?"

My ears pricked up, too many emotions washing through me at the familiar voice as I manage to rasp out, "Caden?"

It was silent for a second before footsteps moved quickly towards me, the side of the box yanking open, causing me to blink against the sudden bright light.

Caden's eyes went wide when he saw me.

"Rory? What the fuck?"

Hot tears slid down my face as I reached for him, taking his hands and holding them for comfort.

"Get me the fuck out of here."

"Hang on, baby. I've got you," he said softly, unlatching the box properly before helping me sit up on the edge.

I winced, his eyes roaming over the damage his father had inflicted on me.

"Jesus, Rory. Dad did this?"

"Can we just go?" I sobbed, not even knowing when I'd started crying.

I was numb.

So. Fucking. Numb.

He yanked his hoodie over his head and helped me into it carefully, but when I went to stand, my legs wobbled from not using them in nearly a week.

He gently hooked his arm under them and one behind my back, cradling me against his chest without me even asking.

He knew I needed him, and for once I pushed my pride down and didn't argue.

We'd just reached the front door when Tristan's voice hit my ears, making me flinch on instinct.

"What the fuck are you doing, Caden?"

He met his father's eyes with a sneer.

"I'm taking her fucking home, you dirty piece of fucking *shit*. She's one of mine, so don't…"

"One of yours? She's a girl for starters but apparently she's with Skeeter Maddox. Don't try that bullshit with me, boy," he ordered, but Caden shook his head, obviously restraining himself from beating the shit out of him.

"I know she's a girl because I was fucking her for a while. For your information, Skeet's a really good friend of mine, and I might just tell him where to fucking find you. I never want to see you again," then he walked out the door, gently placing me in the passenger seat of the Challenger so we could leave.

I was shaking as I basically clung to him for most of the drive, terrified of him hurting me again, but also needing his familiar comfort that I knew he could give me.

I noticed we were at an unfamiliar house when he stopped the car, panic instantly rising inside me.

"Where the fuck are we, Caden? I…"

"It's okay, we're at one of Jensen's places, he has a couple. I'll call Skeet and get him to meet us here once I get you inside, okay?"

I let him carry me inside, despite the paralysing fear inside of me, and once he sat on the couch to cradle me, I realized how much my body hurt.

I fucking ached everywhere, and my head thumped like someone had stomped on it repetitively.

I wanted a bath more than anything.

A bleach bath.

Caden called Skeeter to let him know I was with him, then hung up and continued to just hold me in silence, waiting for me to be the first to speak.

"Max cut him a deal. He wanted me gone, so he got your

dad to take me," I finally forced out, his body tensing beneath me.

"Mom kicked Max out the day we had the party."

"So, he had me kidnapped and fucking raped for five fucking days as *payback*?" I snapped, calming as he rocked me, kissing the top of my head.

He knew I wasn't angry at him.

"I don't know. Slash thought maybe you'd bailed and gone with him, but we talked him into believing us that you'd never do that. Skeet's been looking for you with the guys since the morning after you fucked off. I only stopped in at Dad's today to raid through some of his paperwork and contacts. He knows a lot of dodgy people, so I wanted to hire someone to help find you. I had no idea you were even there," he stated, his voice breaking.

It was in that moment that I realized he really did care about me.

I didn't trust him in the slightest, but he cared.

We stayed like that for a while, until the door burst open and Skeeter stalked in, Jensen and the other two behind him.

The second he looked at my battered body, his light green eyes narrowed to slits.

"Where the fuck was she? What..."

"She's been locked up in my dad's fucking basement this whole time. Max cut him a deal to take her," Caden explained through clenched teeth, not looking at anyone as he kept me tightly in his arms.

Jensen's worried eyes landed on mine as he took a step forwards, slowly moving in my direction to ensure he didn't scare me.

I knew what he was going to ask before he even asked it.

"Babe, did he..."

I nodded once, letting him know that his thoughts were

correct, watching as he sank to the ground in front of me with his head in his hands.

He looked like he was in physical pain as he processed it, letting the truth sink in.

Skeeter's hands were in fists as he stared at Caden, looking like he was ready to murder someone.

Chances were high that he intended on it.

"Your fucking dad's had her all this time? Raping her? My fucking *girlfriend?*"

I lifted my head and reached for him, tucking myself against his chest as he lifted me from Caden's lap as if I were a child.

I was in Skeeter's arms again.

I was safe.

I kept my voice low as I spoke, not trusting myself to keep my emotions in check if I explained everything in detail.

"He had no idea I knew you. I told him about you today when I realized who he was, and he freaked out and left the room. Then Caden showed up."

"You didn't know who he was?" He asked, sounding confused.

"He had me in this box thing the whole time. He didn't speak until today," I whispered, his body vibrating with rage as I held on tighter.

"I'm going to kill him, Holloway. Your dad's a fucking dead man. Get in my way, and I'll fucking kill you too."

Caden snorted, his eyes not straying from me in the slightest.

"Have at him. He's no fucking father of mine."

"Should we take her to the hospital?" Tyler asked uneasily from across the room, but I shook my head in panic.

That couldn't happen.

Cops would get involved, and I was not okay with that.

"No! Take me to Skeet's guy! I don't want anything on record or..."

Skeeter nodded, running his hand down my back to comfort me.

"Sure thing, baby girl. I can get him to come here, if you want?"

I was too exhausted to go anywhere, so I nodded, letting him place me back on Caden's lap while he went and made the call, fighting tears as I met Jensen's gaze again.

Too many emotions swirled around inside me, and for a moment, I just wanted to go back to one of those days where me and Jensen just kicked back and joked around.

I missed him, despite him breaking my fucking heart.

Hot tears pooled at the memories and I reached both arms up at him like a child.

I needed him to tell me it would be okay, despite everything that had happened.

Relief washed through me as he moved onto the couch beside Caden and let me crawl into his lap, his arms wrapping around me tightly but not tight enough to hurt me, as I buried my face in his neck and clung to him.

We didn't speak, he just held me as we waited for Skeeter's doctor to arrive, placing me safely between himself and Caden when Skeeter led him in.

The guy frowned as he glanced at me but spoke to Skeeter.

"I'm unsure which damage I'm meant to be looking at, Skeet."

Skeeter scowled. "All of her. I mean, the cuts are all probably from me, but..."

"Yeah, alright man. Chill," he replied, his eyes softening as he looked into my traumatized ones.

I hated being so weak and helpless.

I'd fought too hard to claw my way out last time, so there

was no way in hell that Tristan was going to destroy me completely.

I'd never give him that.

"Okay, babe. I know you won't want to, but I need you to part your legs for me."

Fuck.

I hadn't thought that through.

My body stiffened, even though I knew I needed to show him, but Jensen kissed my shoulder to show he was there for support.

"It's okay. Do you want everyone to leave, or…"

"Why? Everyone except the doctor's basically seen my fucking pussy before," I snapped, but he ignored my tone.

Everyone could see I was shitting my fucking pants.

His voice was gentle as he spoke again, calming me the slightest amount.

"Alright. Give me and Caden your hands."

I hesitated before placing my shaking hands in theirs, and Jensen gave me a small smile.

"I'm going to hold your leg to the side, okay? Nice and slow."

His other hand went to my knee and gently moved it from the other, my eyes clamping shut as tears threatened to spill.

The familiar feeling of Caden's hand rested on my other leg, which somehow calmed me a little bit more.

The doctor was gentle and patient with me, giving me small breaks when I became close to a complete breakdown, and once he was done, he gave Skeeter a satisfied nod.

"Most damage appears to be emotional, but the burn mark on her thigh needs to be cleaned to stop infection. Maybe stop cutting her up, too. You're scarring her body," he scolded, but Skeeter smirked.

"I like them damaged. Thanks for coming around, I'll get Slash to pay you later."

He nodded, saying goodbye to us before leaving, and Skeeter instantly turned to Caden with a stern expression.

"I've got some shit to deal with. If anything happens to her, I'll fucking kill you."

I jolted up from my spot on the couch with wide eyes, panic in my voice at the thought of him going anywhere.

"You're leaving? You can't fucking leave me!"

"Babe, I've gotta deal with this amongst my guys," he replied with a sigh, but I knew he wasn't being impatient with me, he'd just known my reaction was going to happen.

I shook my head, my voice breaking as I kept begging him.

I didn't give a shit how pathetic I looked.

"You can't leave me with them, Skeet. Fuck no."

"Of course I can."

"But…"

He gave me a small smile, unfamiliar kindness in his eyes as he stroked my cheek affectionately.

"They aren't playing games, baby girl. I'd kill them if they even thought about it, but they love you, I promise you're safe," then he walked out, already on the phone to round up his crew.

I just wished he'd taken me with him.

Jensen

"I should have stopped her leaving that night. It's all my fucking fault," Lukas choked out as he paced in the kitchen later that night.

Rory had crashed pretty quickly once she'd had a long soak in the bath and Caden had tucked her into bed.

She surprisingly wanted to be left alone, so we let her be.

I grabbed Lukas's arm and tugged him in for a hug, his body tensing at my touch as I spoke.

"It's *not* your fault. You couldn't have stopped her from going, remember? She's home now, so…"

"Yeah, but she was fucking raped and abused for days, Jense. She's a fucking mess, and it's all because I let her leave the party with a random guy," he replied, trying to shake me off, but I grabbed his face in my hands and held his gaze, keeping my voice firm but gentle.

"Luke, it's not your fault."

He seemed ready to swing at me, but he finally nodded, allowing me to pull him in for a hug again.

He wrapped his arms around me, clinging to me as the guilt ate away at him.

I wasn't going to let him bury himself in hate over this.

I'd always have his back.

"Hey, head up to bed. I'll be up soon and crash on the couch, alright?"

"Thanks," he mumbled, giving me a small smile before heading off to bed, leaving me alone for a moment.

Caden and Tyler had already gone to bed, but I knew they wouldn't be asleep.

I doubted any of us would get much sleep to be honest.

Rory

"It's okay, babe. I've got you," Tyler soothed as I woke up covered in sweat at some ungodly hour in the morning.

I instantly grabbed his arm to anchor myself as he sat beside me, pulling my body against his to stroke my back in a calming motion.

I needed to get out of my own fucking head.

He rocked us gently until I peered up at him, desperation in my gaze.

"Do you have any cocaine stashed?"

He hesitated before nodding.

"Some. Come down to the den and we'll sit down there for a while. You want a shower?"

I noticed just how drenched I was and cringed, letting him lead me into the bathroom.

He turned to leave, causing panic to roll through me as I grabbed hold of his arm tightly.

"No, don't leave me!"

"Want me to sit on the sink then?" He offered cautiously, my grip on his arm tightening.

I took a breath before answering him.

"Come in with me?"

"Can I call Skeet first, so I don't get shot?" He asked with a small smile, but I knew he was serious.

I nodded and waited for him to be told it was okay, then he helped peel my damp clothes from my sweaty body, before stripping himself.

He led me over to the massive shower, turning the water on full blast and waiting for it to warm up enough for steam to fill the room.

I climbed under the hot spray and tensed as he stepped in behind me, worry taking over his handsome face.

"Rory, I can sit…"

"I need you in here with me," I shook my head as I moved closer, wrapping my arms around his bare middle and pressing my cheek against his chest.

He sighed, putting his arms around me gently, just holding me as we stood under the spray together.

"I'm sorry I hurt you. It was stupid," he murmured into my hair after a few minutes of silence, making me lean into him even more and close my eyes.

The memory of that day rushed back to me as I replied in a shaky voice, hating to admit the truth to him.

"You ruined me, Ty."

"I know, baby," he whispered into my hair just as there was a knock on the door and Lukas's muffled voice came through it.

"Yo, Ty. You in there?"

"Yeah."

"Have you seen Rory? Caden's freaking out because she's not in bed," he called out, my body going tense.

I didn't want them all barging in there.

Tyler's hand gently caressed my spine to soothe me.

"She's okay."

Lukas was quiet for a moment before speaking again, confusion lingering in his tone.

"She's in there with you?"

"Bad nightmare. She's okay, so let him know I've got her."

Once Lukas's footsteps walked away from the door, I peered up at Tyler with a frown.

"They're gonna think we're up to no good, you know?"

"Doubt it, but I don't give a shit. You need me right now, so I'm here," he said honestly, kissing the top of my head as if to prove his point.

I was too fragile to not believe his words, so I pushed the doubt down and nodded.

The water went cold after a while, so we climbed out

and he helped dry me off before handing me one of his shirts and some boxers, then we wandered down to the den.

They all seemed to have their own clothes at each other's houses, lucky for me.

Caden was sitting behind a desk, looking lost in thought when we entered, his gaze running over me before he spoke.

"Lukas said you had a nightmare. You okay?"

I gave him a nod, curling up on Tyler's lap as he sat down. "I'm okay."

"You can go back to bed if you'd like? Nothing else planned for today for you."

"Nah, I got out of bed for a line, and to be honest, a cigarette would be nice."

He shot Tyler an unimpressed glance but stood and placed his cigarettes in front of me before turning to leave, but I grabbed his hand to stop him.

"I loved you too, Caden. Just as much as I loved Jensen. I never had a favorite with any of you. I just wanted you to know that."

Why did I tell him that?

His expression softened and he sighed, sitting beside me and absently pulling me onto his lap while Tyler lined up for me.

"And now?" He asked almost timidly, meeting my gaze.

I'd never seen those green eyes look so vulnerable before, but big bad Caden Holloway looked ready to fucking crumble as my hand rested on his cheek.

"The only reason I haven't killed you myself is because I still love you, but I can't do any of that again. I'm with Skeet now, so you'll just have to deal with the fact that you let me go."

He looked ready to argue but nodded, letting me up to do a line before I curled up against him again.

Jensen and Lukas joined us after a few minutes, and for a little while, I was okay again.

Skeeter

They were all curled up on the couch talking when I wandered into Jensen's place.

Slash seemed pissed off that Rory was on Holloway's lap, her legs sprawled across Tyler, but I put a hand out to calm him.

I watched as Caden spoke softly to her, the tiniest smile forming on her beautiful face in response.

She seemed so fragile, but at the same time, she was so fucking strong.

It was at that moment that I knew without a doubt, I was fucking poison to her.

I'd protect her with my fucking life, but I knew it was time to keep my dick out of what I didn't deserve.

I couldn't give her the life that she needed, and the way she'd always looked at Caden was back on her face.

She was right where she fucking belonged.

"Hey," I spoke up, startling them all at the sudden voice.

When Rory realized it was me, she moved to climb off Caden with a timid smile on her face.

She didn't look at me with the same love as she'd always looked at Caden's guys, she looked to me for safety and protection.

I'd never admit to her how badly it hurt to let her fucking go.

"Stay with Holloway, baby girl. I've come over to say a temporary goodbye. I'm pulling a vanishing act for a while."

Panic flashed across her face, but I gave her a small smile, grateful that Slash didn't say anything about my bullshit lie.

"You don't love me like you think you do, Rory, even you can admit that to yourself. Stay with the guys, alright? I'll be around keeping an eye out for trouble but let them look after you so you can heal."

"But…," she whimpered, hating myself as I forced a wider smile, pretending that I wasn't stabbing myself in the heart as I spoke.

It had been nice while it had lasted.

"I'd say it's not you, it's me, but that's a lie. It is you. I won't let you drown with me, you're too good for this life," then I ran my gaze over her once more, turning and walking off with Slash behind me, leaving her staring after me.

I almost turned back.

Almost.

Rory

Tyler gently removed my legs from his lap and jogged after Skeeter and Slash the moment they walked out, but Caden stayed where he was, sensing the emotions washing through me as I stared at the door.

I finally glanced at Jensen, suddenly feeling the need for conversation.

I never got to ask him the important questions, and I needed a fucking distraction before I lost my shit all over again.

"Do you have your dick pierced, or does Lukas?"

He smirked, stretching out on the couch like the cocky sex god that he was.

"Why on *earth* would you think one of us has a piercing like that?"

"Skeet made some crack when I first started fucking him because I'd never seen one before. He said something about knowing which one of you guys I obviously hadn't fucked. So, is it you, or Lukas?"

"Both, but he'd be talking about me. Luke doesn't wave his dick around as publicly as I do," he chuckled, making me roll my eyes.

"So I've noticed."

"Any other weird questions?"

"Yeah, which is the ass man? Apparently one of you likes ass more than pussy, but I've never been able to figure out which one," I frowned.

Guess it was hard to pick a habit like that when I hadn't actually slept with them all.

"You're sitting on him," he winked, and I glanced up to see Caden smirking at me.

I winced, deciding to never let him try that shit with me.

Not that I'd actually forgiven him for all the bullshit he'd put me through.

"You fit your fucking dick in those tiny holes?"

He laughed with pure amusement at the horrified look I must have had on my face.

"Trust me, babe, it feels good when it's done right. Skeet never fucked you in the ass?"

"No," I scrunched my nose up, watching him shrug.

"Maybe one day you could ask him to. You might like it, you never know."

I gave him a dirty look, speaking flatly at his stupid idea.

"He just fucking dumped me, Holloway."

"Ask me any day then," he grinned, an unsure expression crossing my face as it suddenly became awkward.

It had taken a long time to build up to the idea of sex after last time I'd been assaulted, so I wasn't going to be climbing into bed with anyone in the near future.

Jensen instantly scowled, jumping to my defence like he always had, Lukas giving Caden a similar expression.

"Damnit, Caden. Don't fucking scare her. Why the fuck would she want butt sex right now?"

Caden's face fell, but I waved it off, pretending I was alright with it.

"It's fine, it's just not something I'm really into."

He didn't seem convinced as he assessed my face and sighed.

"Either way, I'm sorry. I didn't think. We have a few things to do this morning, so will you be okay if we leave you here with Jense?"

I nodded, letting Caden up to stretch before he and Lukas headed off to find Tyler.

Jensen led me up to his room and put a movie on, curling up with me so we could relax.

I appreciated it to be honest, but I had other things on my mind.

Like his piercing.

"Can I see your piercing?"

He looked amused, not seeming to believe my request.

"You want me to get my fucking dick out?"

"Yes."

He hesitated before unzipping his pants and popping the button on his silk boxers to pull himself free, my eyes going wide.

He was a similar size to Caden, but I didn't think he'd be hard.

He raised an eyebrow when I stayed quiet, his voice full of teasing.

"What?"

"Your dicks fucking huge!" I blurted out, my face heating with embarrassment.

I fucking sucked.

I was so awkward when I wanted to be.

"Thanks, babe," he chuckled, moving to put his dick away but I stopped him, speaking quietly.

"Can I touch it?"

He groaned, halting all movement without argument.

"You never ever have to ask me if you can touch my dick, Rory. Like, *ever*."

I rolled my eyes but reached out, grasping him and gently running my thumb over the tip, hearing him suck in a sharp breath through his teeth at the contact.

Pre-come beaded near the piercing, and I lowered my head to lick it, his hands fisting by his sides.

"Fucking hell, Rory."

I held his gaze as I licked along his length, sucking the tip into my mouth slowly.

I was gentle, but after swallowing him whole a few times I picked the pace up, his fingers running through my hair gently.

I knew he wanted to grab my head and control it, but he was too worried about scaring me.

He was always the gentler one out of the four guys when it came to me, so I gave myself an internal pep-talk before moving back and smiling.

"You don't have to hold back so much, Jense. I can feel you fighting with yourself."

"I'll scare you, and I can't do that to you. Fuck, I shouldn't be letting you do this either," he murmured, his fingers running through my hair absently as confliction crossed his face.

He hissed out a breath as I lowered my head again to swallow him, one of my hands moving between his legs to gently squeeze his balls.

I'd seen it in porn before, so I figured it was worth a shot.

I wanted him to get rougher with me.

I wanted to be okay.

Tristan wasn't going to fucking destroy me.

He rocked his hips up carefully, his fingers still in my hair as he groaned and pulled my head down further to where he wanted me.

The fear tingled inside me as his grip on my hair tightened, but I pushed through it and let him get rougher, knowing he wouldn't hurt me.

I needed the connection with him again so I knew I'd be okay.

He became rougher the longer it went on, and I knew he was getting close to finishing when I choked slightly and he kept going.

He jerked his hips up to meet my face until his grip on my hair tightened almost painfully as he slowed, the hot salty liquid hitting the back of my throat as I swallowed.

He pulled me nearly on top of him, holding me as his body calmed down, and I felt a small amount of victory build in me for taking control of my demons.

When he finally spoke, I could hear that the apology in his broken voice was genuine.

"Can you ever forgive me? I know I don't deserve it but fuck, Rory. I'm so fucking sorry for hurting you."

I laid there without moving for a while until I lifted my head and met his concerned gaze.

"You have no idea how much it hurt to look at you and see the dismissal in your eyes as you kept your mouth shut while Caden ripped into me like that. You could have told me about Tristan or even warned me about what I was walking into. You could have…"

"I tried to stay away from you, but I couldn't. Jesus Christ, I fucking fell in love with you and I was too chicken shit to tell you. Lukas bailed on us at school that day because he didn't want any part in it, and…"

"Then why the fuck didn't you bail too? Why the fuck did you just stand there and let Ty and Caden do that to me? It wrecked me to know I'd fallen in love with people who had used me for their own personal fucking amusement, and everything had been a fucking lie."

"Fuck all was a lie. Caden wanted to kill your dad from the start for what he'd done to you. Lukas has fought Ty and Caden about them both climbing all over you constantly, and we all became attached to you. We just didn't realize how attached we'd gotten until we'd lost you."

"Feel like a beer?" I asked as I climbed out of bed, suddenly not comfortable with the subject.

I wasn't ready to have my heart shattered again, just because they pitied me.

I left the room before realizing he hadn't responded.

CHAPTER ELEVEN

RORY

"The fuck are you doing here, Donovan?" Slash asked with irritation as I walked into the shed a few days later, giving him a look as if he were stupid.

"Fighting."

"Like *fuck*. Skeet would kill both of us if I let you up in that cage," he bit out, my fists clenching until my knuckles cracked.

"Let me get this straight. Skeet dumped me, so now I'm not welcome in the cage anymore?"

"Do your boys know you're here?" He asked, ignoring my question completely, a snort of annoyance leaving me.

Fucking bastard.

"No one tells me what to fucking do. I don't give a fuck if any of them have a problem with me being here, because if I don't fight in the cage, I'll pick a fight elsewhere. Probably outside in the yard *here*."

He ignored my protesting as he grabbed my bicep and dragged me into the office, slamming the door behind us and getting in my face, ignoring the crew members that were standing around the room.

"You fucking listen to me, okay? You're not fucking fighting in the cage *or* outside. Get it through your fucking head that you need to go home and stay out of trouble. I won't let you in that cage, and if you pick a fight in my yard, I'll personally fucking kill you. You think just because you were Skeet's girl that you're untouchable? I don't give a fuck about who you got on your fucking back for. I'll shoot you, and I'm not fucking around."

I shoved him hard, sounding tougher than I actually was.

"Fuck you. I was a good money maker for you guys, and I've been coming here since before you guys ran it, so back off. I don't give a fuck who I make bleed, so move before it's you."

The door banged open just as Slash furiously reached for his gun, Skeeter's voice cutting through our arguing like a knife.

"Touch her and I'll shoot you, Slash. Rory, what the fuck have I told you about throwing your weight around here?"

He was angry as fuck, but I didn't care.

I was ready for a fight and I didn't care who it was that I took on.

I pushed off the wall and went to jab him in the chest with my finger, but he grabbed my throat and slammed me back against the wall.

"And what the *fuck* are you doing here?"

"I wanna fucking bleed some bitch and Slash won't let me!" I snapped, earning a look of disapproval.

I knew I was going to get fucking lectured.

"I also told you not to come here without me," he said in a level voice, my body slumping as the anger started to vanish.

"I just need to fight, and I figured here would be the safest option."

He eyed me for a moment before stepping back and rubbing his temples as if I was giving him a headache.

I probably fucking was.

"Babe, I left you with the guys for a reason. This shit is toxic for you, *I'm* fucking toxic for you. Don't get me wrong, you can handle yourself just fine and I like you, but it's gotta stop before you either kill someone or end up dead yourself. If you killed someone in that fucking cage, it would ruin you. Not to mention you could end up thrown in jail, which you wouldn't deal with."

"Don't fucking tell me where I belong or what I can and can't handle. I'm not leaving until I fight, so give up and fucking let me. Then I'll go home."

Slash scoffed, plonking down in his chair and lighting a cigarette.

"You're gonna end up fucking dead, Donovan. By my fucking hands if my right-hand keeps threatening to fucking shoot me over you. You need to fuck off so he and I can have a fucking chat."

I turned to tell him that *he* could fuck off, but Skeeter grabbed my chin to keep my gaze on his, his thumb digging in more than necessary.

"Stop arguing with my guys, especially my fucking boss. One fight, and then you get in that fucking car of yours and get out of here. You read me, hot stuff?"

I narrowed my eyes, a smirk rising on his face as he sighed dramatically as if I'd asked him for a million fucking dollars. "Fine, two fights. Then I don't wanna see your ass back here."

Wait, what?

"Ever?"

"Ever," he confirmed, releasing me and glancing at his phone as it rang.

He grunted, looking back at me with irritation.

"And you need to fucking stay home, so these fuckers stop harassing me," then he answered the phone with a scowl.

"Yes, Holloway? Matter of fact I have seen her. She's right in fucking front of me."

I heard Caden yelling about something, but Skeeter growled, "I didn't fucking take her anywhere. She drove her own ass here and conned me into letting her fight, so make sure you're home when she gets back. I assume she'll need help cleaning herself up," then he hung up before Caden could reply, giving me a pissed off scowl.

"Now get out there and fight so you can go home. Not that it matters, I know they'll fucking show up anyways."

Chances were high.

I shrugged, standing on tippy toes to kiss his cheek, my voice sweet.

"Okay. Thanks, Skeet."

"No worries," he grumbled before shooing me out the door, muttering about me being a pain in his ass, just as Slash scruffed him and slammed the door behind me.

I probably got him into trouble, but it served him right for banning me in the first place.

He wandered out a few minutes later, pissed off and ready to strangle someone.

Probably me.

He motioned for me to get ready to fight, so I knew he just wanted me to hurry up and get my ass home.

Once I was in the cage, people went crazy, Skeeter's voice booming through the speakers over the top of them.

"Alright, fuckers. I retired this bitch, but she wanted one more go! You better enjoy it, because she won't be fucking back after this!"

People booed, a smirk stretching across his face.

"Yeah, I know, real shame. Let's turn this shit up!"

People cheered as Can't Go To Hell by Sin Shake Sin cranked up and he let a girl into the cage.

I'd fought her years ago, so I knew she was good at fighting dirty.

She smirked at me, yelling over the music.

"Retiring already? Skeet getting soft and doesn't want you to get hurt?"

I sneered at her, clenching my fists.

"I don't fucking answer to Skeet."

"Surprised to see you here to be honest. After he dumped you and everything I mean," she laughed, but I kept my face blank.

"How do you know he dumped me?"

She threw me a nasty smile that I really didn't fucking like, instantly putting me on edge.

"Well, I hope so, or he cheated on you. Man can eat a pussy *real* good."

Bitch was dead.

I saw red and went to swing at her, but hesitated when Caden angrily shouted at me from the gate.

"Aurora, get the fuck out here right now!"

She smirked. "Back with Holloway, eh? Hear he fucks alright too."

I wanted to do as Caden asked and go out to him, but the mouthy bitch pissed me off and I wasn't about to start doing whatever Caden Holloway demanded.

I suddenly turned and swung, surprising her enough to cause her to stumble.

I hardly felt any of her punches that connected with me, and I didn't realize I'd zoned out until arms went around me and yanked me back sharply.

I glared at Skeeter and he glared right back, startling me as he grabbed me and threw me down to the ground and held me there with pure rage in his eyes.

What the fuck!

"Skeeter, fuck off!"

"*Me*, fuck off? You've nearly killed her. Out of my fucking cage, you aren't focused. You're done," he snapped, my back arching as I tried to buck him off me.

"Like fuck!"

He moved off me and scruffed the front of my shirt, dragging me out of the cage and through the crowd until we were outside in the cool air.

He slammed my back against the wall, making me wince at the impact.

"Oh good, you felt that? Snap the fuck out of it," he growled in a low voice, slamming my back against the wall again when I struggled. "Now, Rory!"

I stopped fighting him and glared.

"Thought you liked your bitches fucking crazy?"

"I do, and you're making me fucking hard, so stop it. Seriously, calm your ass down. You nearly fucking killed her."

"Are you worried about me, or her?" I spat bitterly, a scowl taking over his face.

"The fuck does that mean?"

"You'd hate me to kill her before you're done with her, wouldn't you?" I snapped, an amused smile slowly spreading across his face.

"Baby girl, are you jealous?"

"Why the fuck would I be jealous?" I exclaimed, struggling against his hold, but his grip softened as he moved against me, his lips running along my sweaty neck before grinning against my skin.

"Just so you know, I fucked her once, and that was it. She isn't like you, babe. I actually like you when your clothes are on too."

The adrenaline slowly left my body, and my hands shook as I spoke softly.

"You aren't seeing her?"

He grinned. "C'mon, babe. I don't date, you were the

exception. I only care about you killing her because I don't wanna clean her skanky ass off my fighting cage. I don't give a fuck about her, but it's hot to see you try to kill her over me. I'm flattered, honestly."

I smacked him hard in the chest, making him chuckle as he pressed more firmly against my front and nipped my neck.

"Now, I'd like you to go home, okay? It's Friday, so go get ready for the party that you and your boys will be having."

"Do you have time to fuck before I go?" I asked hopefully in his ear, a pained groan coming from him in return.

"No more, okay? You need to stay away from me, I've created a fucking monster."

"I can just suck you off if you want?" I tempted, but Caden's voice came from close by with zero amusement in his tone.

"If you wanna suck someone off you can choke on my dick, as long as you get your ass in the car and get home first."

I scowled, but Skeeter grinned. "There you go, problem fucking solved. I'll leave your horny ass with Holloway to deal with. Look after yourself, hot stuff," he winked, giving me a sharp crack on the butt before he headed back inside, leaving me with Caden.

He stalked towards me with a glare firmly set on his face.

"Fighting, again? Aurora..."

"I'll fucking fight if I want to, Caden. Fuck off," I snapped, but there wasn't any anger in my tone.

I was tired, and I just wanted a hot fucking bath.

I knew I had a cut on my eyebrow too, because it had started to sting.

He hesitated, his expression softening as he moved directly in front of me, lifting his hand to cup my cheek.

Yeah, it hurt there too.

"Hey, let's go home and clean that cut up. You alright?"

I nodded silently, not arguing with him as he took one of my bloodied hands in his and led me towards his car.

I tensed up when he reached into my pocket and took the keys to the Corvette, but I relaxed when Lukas showed up out of nowhere and took them, walking towards my car to drive it home for me.

Caden opened his passenger door for me, closing it again once I was buckled up inside, then he quickly got into the driver's seat and started the engine to head towards home, changing the subject to my fucking relief.

"Party's at Ty's tonight. You up for it?"

I glanced at him with a small smile.

"Yeah, I guess. Can I have a bath when we get home? Do I have time?"

"Sure. We're allowed to be fashionably late anyways. How much damage did you end up with this time?" He asked gently, earning a shrug.

"Just bruising."

He reached his hand out to take mine as we drove along the main road, giving it a gentle squeeze.

"Make sure you clean your hands. They're cut to shit again, baby."

Yeah, I'd noticed.

The concern in his voice weakened me more, and I nodded, keeping my hand in his until we reached the house.

Once inside, Josie glanced up, looking torn as her eyes travelled over my damage, but I moved up to her hesitantly and gave her a hug.

I needed a hug that only a mother could give.

Caden was lucky to have her.

I knew I'd surprised her, but I honestly felt bad for being such a bitch to her since we'd met.

She was there for me without being obligated to, so it was time I acknowledged my appreciation to her.

"Everything okay, Rory? What happened to your eyebrow?" She asked, but I just held her tightly and sighed.

"I'm okay, I just wanted to give you a hug. I'm sorry about my dad being a piece of shit."

She cringed, her face becoming upset.

"I honestly thought you'd gone with him. Have you been okay? Have you heard from him?"

Caden snorted, heading towards us and taking my elbow.

I didn't argue as he led me over to the kitchen sink, gently washing my hands with warm water as he spoke to his mom.

"Max cut a deal with Dad to get rid of her. She was in Dad's basement office for five fucking days. Both he and Max are dead cunts."

Her eyes went wide. "Tristan had her? Did he hurt you, Rory?"

I kept my eyes glued to my hands as Caden continued cleaning them, but he looked up at her with anger in his voice.

"He raped her for days, Mom. We've had her healing at one of Jensen's places ever since I found her a few days ago."

"She needs a hospital, Caden!" She exclaimed with horror, but he shook his head.

"No, we've had her checked out, and nothing needed surgery or stitches and shit. She didn't want to make a report."

"Who checked her out? There needs to be a police report! What dodgy shit have you gotten her into?" She hissed, Caden's lips flattening into a line of irritation.

"Mom, it's fine."

"Like hell. You…"

"A guy from the Psychos checked her out. It's their emergency doc, so it's fine," he sighed, but I knew that was going to make it fucking worse.

"I thought you'd stopped all connection with that gang? They're bad people, and I don't want Rory near them!" She screamed at him.

She was panicking, but he just smirked, not at all fazed by her mini melt down.

"Cool it, they're fine. Besides, Skeet just banned her from the fights and stuff, so…"

"Let me get this straight. Rory's been illegally fighting at a gang event, and you let her?"

He shrugged. "I couldn't stop her, she was dating Skeet, so she kind of lived in the middle of the crew stuff when she took off. He looked out for her, and now that they aren't together he's making sure she's with us."

"Hang on, her boyfriend was *Skeeter Maddox*? Jesus Christ, Caden. He kills people for a living!" She snapped but I rolled my eyes, speaking up as Caden left the room to grab a clean towel.

"Skeet looks after me and doesn't let anything happen to me. I'm safer having him on my side, than not. I know Dad isn't here anymore, but since he's taken off and Skeet and I have broken up…"

"You stay here as long as you want, sweetheart. You're family still," Josie cut in with a big smile, making me sigh with relief.

She'd never replace my mom, but I'd always see her as someone I could turn to.

Caden walked back in and wrapped my hands to carefully dry them, giving me a cheeky smirk.

"You can't go anywhere, anyways. It sucks ass without you here. Come up to your room and sort some clothes out, I'll run that bath you wanted, as long as you keep your hands out of the water."

Josie watched us suspiciously but let us leave the room without another word, thank fuck.

I didn't feel like having one of those awkward sex talks that night.

She knew she couldn't stop us, regardless.

CHAPTER TWELVE

CADEN

Having Rory home was so fucking good.

I didn't know how she could even look at me after what I did to her, but she was somehow okay with me again.

I knew I wasn't completely forgiven, and I didn't blame her for that, but I was going to do everything I could to get her to trust me again.

The guys were right, we fucking needed her.

It had been a few weeks since Dad had assaulted her, and she was slowly coming out of her shell as more time passed.

I wanted to beat the shit out of Jensen for letting her blow him after what she went through, but Rory threatened to knock me the fuck out.

I knew that she needed to prove to herself that Dad wasn't going to ruin her, but she still needed to take it fucking easy.

I'd kept a close eye on her at our parties, but she seemed content just sitting with us and sipping on her beer.

I knew she'd be okay, but I also knew she was going to

become a fucking train wreck first, especially if she didn't lay off the fucking cocaine and whisky.

Tyler thought he was doing the right thing by letting her get high, but he was stopping her from processing all the bad shit properly.

She couldn't heal if she wasn't facing it, and he knew how we felt about her being doped up all the fucking time.

She wasn't addicted, but I was worried she'd rely on it too much.

It was Tyler's weekend to host our party, and he'd already fed her up on powder and whisky as if it was going out of fucking fashion.

She was more handsy tonight than she'd been recently, and I wasn't sure how far we could push her.

She'd gotten drunk and convinced Skeeter to fuck her the week before, but despite her saying she was fine with it, he told me another story.

She'd freaked out, cried a lot, then taken off on him for three fucking hours until he'd found her walking around in the dark.

He swore he'd taken it easy on her, but I highly fucking doubted it.

Skeeter didn't know what that even meant.

She'd tried conning Jensen into bed a few days ago, but he was too scared of freaking her out.

I was proud of him, until he said he went down on her and she blew him again as the negotiation.

Maybe it was best that we did as she'd asked?

After all, at least if she freaked out on us, we'd stop.

A stranger mightn't, and then we'd have to send Skeeter off to murder-land again.

He'd found the guy my dad had hired to kidnap her, and it wasn't fucking pretty from what one of the Psychos, Diesel, had told me.

I watched Rory from across the room as she did shots with Jensen, and I sighed in defeat as she kept climbing all over Tyler.

One of us were going to have to fuck her to help her prove to herself that she was in full control of her body.

She appeared to be having fun, but I could see her thought process from where I stood.

To get laid and prove my dad had no control over her demons.

Maybe I was a piece of shit for thinking it, but Tyler and I could fix that for her.

We'd reassure her and all that, but I just needed to get inside her and feel whole again.

Jensen would kill me, and Lukas would fucking help him, but I wasn't going to watch her walk off with a stranger again.

I was too fucking sober to deal with that shit, and I had no idea where my beer had gotten to.

It was going to be a long night.

Rory

I ground my ass against Caden's groin as I danced, my hands in his messy hazel-brown hair as we grinded to the beat of I Don't Dance by DMX and Machine Gun Kelly.

His hands held my hips firmly as he moved with me, and I laughed as Tyler moved in our direction from across the room, dancing like an idiot until he reached us.

I was pretty fucking high, a groan slipping from my lips

as he moved a leg between mine to sandwich me between both of them with a sly smirk.

"Nice shorts, they'd look better on my bedroom floor though."

I giggled as Caden nipped my shoulder, lowering my arms and threading them loosely around Tyler's neck to pull him closer.

Lukas frowned in disapproval as he walked past, but I hadn't seen Jensen all night.

I had no idea if he was even there.

The bass thumped in my head and I closed my eyes, letting the music move my body as I continued grinding between them.

When I noticed that Claire was in the corner scowling, I tensed slightly, Caden kissing down the side of my neck and along my bare shoulder to relax me.

I was wearing my favourite strapless crop top and denim shorts, feeling turned on as Tyler's hands moved up my bare sides, while Caden's stayed firmly on my hips as he kept his face buried in my neck.

Everything felt so fucking good after a few lines.

Tyler shot me his panty-dropping smile, not being able to help myself as I pulled him down with my arms and kissed him strongly without a second thought.

He kissed me back with desperation, and I became hyper aware of Caden's erection pressing against my ass all of a sudden.

I heard him curse as I swayed my hips harder, grinding against him more until his voice rumbled in my ear over the music.

"Calm down, the last thing you need right now is me and Ty going caveman on you together. I know we'd scare you."

Did he seriously ask me to stop?

I moved my mouth back from Tyler's, peering over my shoulder into Caden's smouldering gaze.

"You're saying no to me, when I'm turned on and wet for you?"

He growled, one of his hands threading through my hair and yanking my head back so that he could kiss me.

Yeah, that's what I'd fucking thought.

I moaned at how demanding he was being, and I was pretty sure I heard Tyler chuckle.

We stumbled backwards as Caden moved us through the mass of people and into the hallway, my hands fumbling with the button on my shorts, which seemed to amuse Tyler.

Once in Tyler's room, he helped me yank my shorts down my legs, instantly dropping to his knees in front of me.

He kissed down my stomach as Caden pulled my crop top over my head, his fingers getting tangled in my black hair as he kissed along my shoulder blade while unlatching my bra.

I wasn't sure if sober me would do it, but I wanted to so badly.

I just wanted to feel like myself again.

My attempt with Skeeter hadn't gone so well, and it was time I tried again.

Maybe both guys at once was a bad idea, but I knew they'd take their time if I asked them to.

My head fell back against Caden's shoulder as Tyler tugged my panties down, instantly burying his tongue inside me, his hands holding onto my thighs to pull my pussy closer as his nose rubbed against my clit.

Fuck, yes.

Caden slid a hand down my bare back and down to my ass, teasing it as he continued kissing and biting his way across my hot skin.

My senses were already fucking overloading, and my legs

became shaky, feeling more stable when Caden's free arm went around my middle to keep me steady.

I'd never hear the fucking end of it if I literally fell on my ass from pleasure.

I arched as Tyler pushed two fingers inside me, sucking on my clit firmly until my quiet gasps turned into a loud moan of surprise as I came hard, Caden's arm tightening as my legs gave out from the intensity of it.

I didn't care how desperate I looked as I rode Tyler's face until I couldn't handle it any longer.

If anything, it just turned them on more.

He moved back, his eyes full of need as he stood and pulled me against him for a kiss, tasting myself on his tongue.

It shouldn't have been hot, but it totally fucking was.

Warm skin pressed against my back, and I realized that Caden had stripped off while I'd been distracted, his hand going down his front to stroke himself.

Why did that make me moan?

He slowed and gave me a naughty smile as he noticed me watching him with interest over my shoulder through hazy eyes.

He suddenly turned serious, his voice stern.

"You say you've had enough, and we stop, okay? I don't give a fuck if I'm about to bust, you tell me to stop if you want me to, and I will."

I nodded but gave him an unsure glance, starting to worry that I'd look stupid or panic.

Or both.

"I've never..."

I shivered as Tyler's lips suctioned to my neck, Caden speaking before I could finish my sentence, not that I remembered what I was going to say, thanks to Tyler.

"I know. We'll take care of you, baby. If it gets too much though, you let us know. Or, if you wanna try something."

I nodded nervously, feeling cold liquid drip between my ass cheeks as Caden's finger smeared it over my ass until he eased it inside.

I kissed Tyler, letting Caden stretch me until he knew I'd be ready.

It was uncomfortable, but he knew what he was doing.

He placed a soft kiss on my neck, trying to keep me relaxed since he knew it wasn't how I usually rolled.

"Climb on the bed, you'll be more comfortable."

Tyler stripped off and moved me forward slowly, making sure he didn't startle me, laying back and pulling me over the top of him to continue kissing me.

He smirked slightly as Bouncin' On My Dick by Tyga blasted downstairs from the party, but I tensed up as Caden moved behind us, pressing the tip of his dick against my ass.

Fuck, we were really going to do it.

"It'll burn for a second, but it stops, okay? Try not to tense up, baby. Kiss Ty and let him take your mind off it. I'll take it slow, I promise," he murmured, waiting for me to do as he asked before pushing in further.

I managed to stay relaxed, but I knew it was the coke I'd snorted before we'd started dancing.

I groaned as he moved back before pushing in again as his hands firmly gripped my hips, pulling me back gently to meet his thrusts.

It wasn't bad, despite the uncomfortable burn at first.

Tyler's hand moved between my legs, and I let out a breathy moan as he pushed two fingers inside my wet pussy, driving my senses crazy.

"*Fuck*, you're so wet," he said roughly in my ear, a shiver rolling through me.

Yeah, I was officially impatient.

"Fuck me," I breathed out, a devilish grin stretching across his face.

"As you wish."

I gasped as his dick pressed between my legs, a different feeling of fullness than I was used to.

He took it easy for a while until I had adapted to the extra intrusion, then he picked up the pace along with Caden.

I knew they'd had some practice before, because they were in pretty good sync together when it should have been more fumbled and awkward.

I kissed Tyler hard as I fought the urge to take off, Caden's lips kissing down my back as he moved in and out of me at just the right pace to get me off quickly.

I hoped no one else heard me, because I was a little loud.

Well, I fucking screamed.

When I'd recovered slightly, Caden shifted behind me.

"I'm going to come in your ass, okay?" He growled in my ear, waiting for me to nod before he gripped my hips more firmly and thrust deeper and faster until it was almost painful.

Tyler stilled, waiting for him to finish, nibbling on my lower lip to draw my attention, a sly smirk on his lips.

"Once he's done, ride me?"

I winced as Caden suddenly jammed deep and came with a grunt, Tyler glaring at him with warning.

"Easy, Holloway. You fucking hurt her."

Caden was still for a moment before easing out of me, placing an affectionate kiss on my butt cheek, flopping onto his back with an apologetic expression as he sprawled out to cool down.

"Fuck. Sorry, baby."

I went to speak but Tyler sat up, giving me no choice but to sit back and straddle him.

He swatted my butt with a playful wink. "C'mon, babe.

I've seen you ride a dick, so ride me. It's all I think about when I jack off."

That shouldn't have made me feel all warm and fuzzy, but it fucking did.

His dick pressed against my g-spot as I rolled my hips, moaning the more I did it until my nails were digging into his bare back as the orgasm ripped through me.

I was suddenly on my back as he hammered into me, his fingers digging into my thighs as he buried deep and came, his sweaty body collapsing on top of mine without a word.

We all caught our breaths for a few moments, glancing at Caden who smiled as his hand took mine.

"You okay? Bet you need a beer now, huh?"

"I'm good, and a hot bath would be more like it," I replied, his eyes lighting up like a fucking Christmas tree.

"Lucky for you, Ty's hot tub is fucking massive. Want company? I'll even get some booze."

Having a soak in the hot tub in the middle of our own party?

Fuck yeah.

Being a queen sure had its perks.

I nodded, waiting for Tyler to roll off me, surprising me when he grabbed a towel and carefully moved my thighs apart to clean me up.

It suddenly felt more intimate than what we'd done moments before, and I quickly shoved my clothes on and ruffled my hair, moving towards the door, needing a minute to myself.

Caden frowned at my sudden escape.

"Where are you going?"

"Whisky. I saw Lukas had some," I grinned.

Whisky in the bath was such a good idea.

It also gave me five minutes away from them.

"Alright, I'll run the bath," he shrugged, letting me head down to the party to find Lukas without argument.

I stumbled into the kitchen, ignoring the judgemental glances from people as I passed them and headed over to Lukas, who raised an eyebrow at me.

"Where have you been?"

"With Caden and Ty," I grinned, leaning on the bench to balance myself.

Maybe I didn't need more whisky.

"You mean, between them?" He frowned, suddenly seeming annoyed as he toyed with my messy hair, but I shrugged.

"Yeah, whatever. I'm looking for whisky to drink in my bath."

He hesitated, taking my hand and leading me into the other room, and I was surprised to find Jensen talking to Slash.

Lukas grabbed a bottle of whisky from the cupboard without letting my hand go, and I noticed Slash take a step towards us just as he spoke.

"Yo, Donovan. Got a job for you tomorrow."

Huh?

Jensen scowled, looking ready to rip his fucking face off.

"I said no, Slash. Not fucking happening."

I eyed Slash as I grabbed the whisky, uncapping the lid.

"What job?"

"I need you to come to the shed tomorrow night," he replied casually, earning a dirty look from me.

"I'm not allowed to fight, remember?"

He smirked. "Oh, you won't be fighting. Do you trust me?"

As if I'd trust that asshole.

"Fuck no."

His smirk grew wider, and I wanted to punch the smug look off his stupid face.

"Good. See you at the shed then," and before I could demand answers, he turned and left.

Jensen was frowning at me as he reached out and ran his fingers through my tangled black hair.

"Have you been getting laid?"

"Yes. Where have you been? I was looking for you earlier," I asked, sipping on my drink casually, enjoying the burn it left in my throat.

His fingers paused in my hair for a moment before continuing to pull the small knots out, his voice sounding tight.

"You should have called me if you wanted a booty call. Did you find someone better?"

I scowled, but his lip twitched as he pulled me closer. "I'm kidding, babe. Who were you with though?"

Lukas snorted, jerking his head towards the door as Tyler and Caden stumbled in, Tyler appearing to be wiping powder off his nose, while Caden snatched a beer from the bench and downed it in one go.

Jensen rolled his eyes. "Both of them? Rory, you could have gotten hurt."

"I'm pretty buzzed, it's fine," I replied, squealing in surprise as Caden yanked me against his chest, nipping my lower lip sharply.

"*There* you are. I thought you were just coming down to steal Luke's whisky?"

"I got talking to Slash and Jensen," I replied, making him growl.

"I don't give a fuck, I want you naked in that bath ten minutes ago."

"So impatient, Holloway," I giggled, but Jensen crossed his arms firmly against his chest.

God, he had a nice chest.

"What the fuck, man? We talked about this."

He rolled his eyes at his friend's dramatics.

"She was up for it, trust me. Back off, Gilbert."

Lukas caught Jensen's attention, a sigh leaving him.

"Fine, but if she ends up an emotional mess, I'll kill you," then he stalked off with Lukas trailing behind him.

Tyler snatched my whisky with a *whoop* as Caden tossed me over his shoulder to drag me back upstairs like the romantic cavemen they were.

"Holloway, put me down!" I laughed, groaning as he swatted my butt with a swift smack.

I was really starting to like that.

"I'll put you down once we're in the tub, okay? I even put bubbles in it for you."

Tyler led us into the bathroom and locked the door behind us, and once we were all in the tub, we passed the whisky around and relaxed.

I sank into the hot water more and groaned, Caden's arms going around my middle from behind as he tugged me onto his lap.

Tyler shot me a lazy smirk as he lit up a joint.

"You'll be tender in the morning. We weren't too rough, were we?"

"Nah, it was fine, might have to do it again later," I teased, earning a groan from both of them in response.

It was going to be a long fucking night, and you bet your ass we fucked again before going to sleep.

Take that, Tristan Holloway.

Tyler

"Do you think we did the wrong thing?" I mumbled as I watched Caden run his fingers through Rory's hair as she slept between us later that night.

We'd scared her a little in the second round, but once we slowed it down, she seemed okay again.

I felt like fucking shit for freaking her out, but she'd insisted she was fine to keep going.

Caden glanced up at me, a mix of emotions on his face as he spoke quietly.

"It's what she wanted. Better us, than some fucker who doesn't give a shit about her."

I had to agree, but I hoped she wouldn't hate us in the morning for it.

She was pretty fucked up on powder and whisky, after all.

She looked peaceful as she slept, and I couldn't help but brush the hair from her face and smile.

"She's pretty fucking great, isn't she? Do you think she'll get over everything that's happened? The shit with us, and the shit with your dad and Max?"

He snorted, shuffling closer to her back and curling himself around her protectively.

"She'll never get over it, Ty. She'll eventually learn to live with it, but it won't just go away."

"I know, but do you think she'll be okay, for real?" I mumbled, a pained sigh leaving him.

"I honestly don't know. I'm just happy to have her back here where she belongs. Do you think Jense and Lukas are going to strangle us?"

"Oh, one hundred percent," I chuckled, watching a soft smile take over his face.

"Totally worth it."

It was weird seeing him like that.

He fell asleep long before I did, but watching my best friend wrapped around Rory soothed something inside of me.

She was putting us together again, piece by piece, and there was nowhere else I'd rather be.

CHAPTER THIRTEEN

RORY

"Pancakes, babe?" Jensen offered, as I stumbled into Tyler's kitchen the next morning.

Pyro by Shinedown was already cranking, and I rubbed my head with a wince.

"Seriously? It's not even fucking lunchtime yet. Why are you having a one-man party down here?"

"Not a one-man party," Lukas chuckled as he wandered into the room, already sipping on a fucking beer as he plonked down at the table.

I rolled my eyes as I walked across the room, surprising him as I sat on his lap.

As much as my night with Caden and Tyler had been amazing, I needed my best friend to anchor me again.

The cuddle was nice.

Jensen finished cooking, before bringing everything over to the table for us.

"So, where's your prince charming's at?"

"Sleeping, I wore them out," I joked, moving to climb off Lukas's lap so he could eat properly, but his arm went around my middle to keep me there.

I glanced over my shoulder at him with question, receiving an affectionate smile in return.

"You can stay there, Rory. I can still eat with you on my lap."

I gave him a nod, stuffing a pancake into my mouth, causing them both to snort.

I wasn't known to eat like a lady, not that they had a problem with it.

Too bad if they did, because I was fucking hungry.

Apparently, it was nice to have a girl around that wasn't high maintenance.

Jensen had told me so.

Once I'd eaten my share of breakfast, I leaned back against Lukas's chest, sighing contently.

"What are we up to today?"

Jensen mumbled around his food as he finished his plate.

"Probably just hang around here, then we'll take you to the shed tonight. Why?"

"I'm going to the shed by myself," I replied bluntly, earning a dirty look in response.

"Like hell, you are."

I raised an eyebrow, getting sick of the fucking conversation already.

"I can handle myself fine there."

"I know, but I don't like any of it."

"Do you know what he wanted me to do?" I asked curiously, watching him shrug.

"Could be anything with Slash. They do a lot more than run the shed. I don't like the idea of you meeting him there when Skeet's away, either."

"He's away?"

"Yeah, he is. Slash tolerated you hanging around the shed because you were Skeet's girl, and Skeet was always around to keep an eye on things. Now, you're not his girl and Skeet's not there, I don't know where Slash's loyalties will lie. Can you take one of us, at least?" He asked, a look of hope in his eye, making me feel bad as I let out a sigh.

I didn't want them involved, regardless of what it was that Slash fucking wanted.

"I'd prefer you guys to stay out of it in all honesty. Trust me, okay?"

Lukas snorted, his arm tightening slightly around me.

"We trust you just fine, it's Slash and the Bloody Psychos we don't trust."

"Well, I trust them."

"You don't trust *anyone*, and you know it. Don't lie to us," he muttered, kissing my shoulder softly.

Jensen stood, cleaning up from breakfast and letting me and Lukas argue for a while, but I finally sighed after a few minutes, wanting the argument to stop.

"Well, it's not until tonight anyways, so I'm going to head home and probably nap for a few hours. Tell the other two I'll see them later."

Jensen gave me a look that stated he knew I was full of shit, but I ignored it.

Lukas on the other hand nodded.

"Yeah, sure. You okay to drive? You were pretty fucked up last night."

I stood and stretched, kissing his cheek with a smile.

"Yeah, I'm fine. I sweat it all out of my system before bed."

He rolled his eyes, a small smirk tugging at his lips.

"Maybe use the gym next time? Drive safely."

Warmth spread though my chest at his concern for me, and I gave him a nod before kissing Jensen's cheek on my way out to my car.

God, I'd never get enough of my Corvette.

I mean, Skeeter bought it for a good price, which I took

to mean it was dodgy as fuck, but I wasn't going to question it.

I drove until I passed my old house and drove through the run-down neighbourhood, turning off at the end of the road and parking out the front of the Psycho's shed.

I walked up to the door and strolled inside like I always did, not wanting to stand outside knocking forever.

It was too early for people to be there for any cage fights, so it was pretty empty.

Slash's head popped out of the office, apparently spotting my arrival on his cameras, giving me a scowl.

"You're early. Like, all fucking *day* early."

I shrugged as I continued to walk towards him, starting to wonder why I'd even decided to show up.

All he did was piss me off, and I honestly didn't like him one bit.

"Jensen and Lukas were hounding me about it, so I told them I was heading home then came here instead. Figured you might not want them here for whatever the job is."

He smirked, opening the door wide to let me pass.

"They'll show up anyways, those boys aren't stupid. I have a proposition for you, Donovan." That didn't sound good, in my opinion.

I sat at the desk and helped myself to his whisky without bothering to ask.

Fuck him.

"Go on, I'm listening."

He sat opposite me and chuckled, eyeing the drink as I drank straight from the bottle.

"Thought you might be curious. While Skeet's gone, I need some help dealing with some shit."

"Like, cleaning the shed kind of help? Or dead body kind of help? Need to be a little more fucking specific, boss man," I snorted sarcastically, making him laugh as he leaned back and lit a cigarette.

"Dead body kind of help, but if you wanna clean the shed, I won't stop you, babe."

"I won't go to prison, Slash. Does Skeet know about this? You know he doesn't want blood on my hands. I'm not even meant to fucking be here."

He leaned forward, raising an eyebrow.

"Actually, he told me to stay the fuck away from you, but since when do we listen to him, hmm?"

"Sounds like trouble," I sighed, his shoulders shrugging lazily.

"He can fucking get over it. He seems to have forgotten that I'm in charge, not him. I let him have his way when it came to the cage fighting and his relationship with you, but he needs to learn to take a step back. You aren't his girl anymore, so I don't have to do shit that he asks. You're lucky I actually like you, or I'd use you to remind him in some cruel fucking ways of his place here, but since we're pals and shit, this will have to do. Besides, you like blood on your hands, so fuck him, right?"

I was uneasy but gave him a confident shrug.

I was actually starting to feel nervous as fuck.

"Just tell me the deal and I'll tell you if I think it's stupid."

"Fine. For starters, we've got a body here that we need to get rid of without Skeet finding out. Fighters got rowdy last night, and one ended up dead. You know what he's like about dead body problems here. Secondly, I need you to talk to one of our newbies. Skeet swears he's up to no good, so since it's crew business, I need to look into it. You're hot as fuck, so if anyone can get information out of him, it would be you."

"What information am I looking for, and what do I have to do to convince him?"

Not good.

I sucked at that kind of shit.

"Use your fucking imagination, Donovan. Fuck him if you have to. I need to know if he'll tell you about any of our business. If he talks, he's dead. Literally," he snorted, instantly making me feel uncomfortable.

I couldn't pull that off, even if I needed to.

Not after everything that had happened to me.

I was struggling to be okay with Caden, Tyler, and Skeeter sleeping with me, so a stranger would freak me out.

"You know what happened to me, right? I can't just fuck random people."

"I know it seems like a cruel job to throw at you, but I really need this. If he's a rat, he could bring us all down. To be honest, you'll get dragged into it too, since you're known to him. Skeet talks too much to you, and I know that, but the fact that you're like a fucking vault of secrets means I know you're fuck all of a threat. Lucky for you, or I'd have offed you by now," he suddenly grinned, but it just confused me.

Skeeter hardly ever spoke about crew business in front of me.

"He hardly tells me shit," I finally frowned, but he rolled his eyes and offered me his cigarettes.

Of course I took one, it was fucking free.

I lit it as he kept talking.

"You lived with him for a little while. He trusted you, and he doesn't trust anyone outside the crew, so I know he's told you shit. Besides, between the shit here at the shed, and the guns and drugs you've witnessed, you know enough to bring us all down. Trust me when I say your name's been at my table of concern by the others, and I'm the only thing standing between you and a shallow fucking grave."

I gave him an unamused glance as I sipped the whisky.

Fuck he was a prick.

I was secretly shitting my fucking pants though, I wouldn't lie.

"So basically, if I don't help you, I'll get to meet this shallow grave? Am I reading this right?"

He chuckled, but it wasn't very nice.

"Smart girl. Not like you're killing anyone for me, you're just…"

"I'm part of it, so I can't talk about it without burying myself in the process?" I offered, his dark grey eyes holding mine for a moment before he nodded.

"Bingo."

He glanced up as the door opened and one of his guys walked in without knocking.

He was young, and I'd seen him at Skeeter's house before.

We'd picked up drugs from his place a few times too.

He was one of the newbies, and by the way that Skeeter acted around him, I knew for a fact that he didn't like him.

"Ah, Liam. You know Donovan, yeah?" Slash grinned, motioning towards me.

I could read Slash's body language, instantly informing me that it was the problem newbie we'd been speaking about.

I sat up straighter and forced a smile that I hoped looked convincing.

"Good to see you again, Liam. Have you been working out more since I saw you last?"

Gag.

I hated girls who said shit like that.

Slash raised an eyebrow at me, but Liam smirked and turned his attention completely towards me.

Sucker.

"Yeah, I have. I heard you aren't fighting anymore. Why not?"

I faked a pout, my skin crawling at the sound of my own voice.

I could fucking kill Slash for this.

"Skeet won't let me now we've split up. He doesn't like me here, but I'm naughty and never do as I'm told. I like it here too much to stay away."

He was eating it up as he leaned against the wall and crossed his arms, annoyance on his face.

"I think he should just let you fucking fight. Everyone comes to see you."

"I don't think I'm the best fighter here," I giggled, but he shot me a sly grin.

"Oh, don't you worry, babe. You fight good, but you're hot as fucking sin, and that's why people come to watch you. Skeet's a fool for letting you go, if you ask me."

Slash snorted, despite his amusement.

Bastard.

"Ease up there, Liam. You'll bust in your fucking pants."

Before he could respond, I held back another gag and winked at Slash.

"Never you mind that, boss man, I'd help him clean up."

Liam's eyes tracked my tongue as it ran across my lower lip and toyed with my lip rings.

He was completely sucked in.

Hook, line and fucking sinker.

Slash was holding back a laugh as I stood, Liam's interested gaze remaining on me as I sighed.

"I'd better get going. I'd hate to get in the way of crew stuff. I know how busy you guys get."

Liam pushed off the wall before I'd even finished speaking.

"Let me walk you to your car."

I battered my lashes at him, giving Slash a smile.

"What a gentleman! You could learn something from him, Slash. I'll see you later?"

"You sure will," he chuckled, watching Liam lead me out of the room and through the shed.

He even opening the car door for me like the idiot he was.

I went to get in, but he backed me against the side of the car, a lazy smirk on his face that made me uncomfortable.

I swallowed down the fear that clawed at my insides, giving him a soft, fake giggle.

"Liam! People will see!"

"Like I give a fuck. It turns you on to know we might get caught this close, I can tell. What are you doing later, babe?"

I faked that I was deep in thought for a moment, biting my lip and placing a hand on his chest.

"I guess the thought of people thinking I'm fucking you *does* make me a bit excited. I mean, you're so hot. I'm not up to much in a few hours, why?"

He pressed against me, his breath hot on my neck, and I had to force myself to stand still.

I was starting to feel bad for pulling him along, actually.

Apart from being a cocky prick, he didn't seem to be a bad person.

"I'm hoping you'll be doing me later, to be honest," he answered, so I faked concern.

"You aren't worried about Skeet finding out? I'd hate for him to hurt you."

Skeeter would fucking murder him.

He smiled against my neck. "I can take Skeet on. He ain't shit, trust me. You should see him out on the job. He stands back while we do the dirty work."

I hadn't even gotten fucking naked and he was already blabbing what I wanted, so I giggled again for good measure.

Also, if he thought he'd have it over Skeeter, he was on some seriously good crack.

"Really? What a pussy. I bet you do *lots* of dirty work."

He hardened against my leg, so I arched into him slightly, making him groan.

"Oh, I get *super* fucking dirty. Give me a few hours to finish this drug run with the guys, and I'll meet up with you. Let's say, in three hours we meet at mine. You know where that is, yeah?"

"The brick place a few blocks from Skeet's? With the hedge around the property?" I asked, knowing exactly where he lived.

Skeeter scowled every time we drove past it, and like I said, we'd stopped in once or twice to grab drugs and shit.

"That's the one. Go and rest, you'll need it," he chuckled, giving my neck a sharp nip.

I had to cement this shit in, so I bravely scruffed him by the shirt and pulled him down for a kiss, his hands clamping onto my waist as he thrust against me with another groan.

He bit my lip harder than fucking necessary, moving back with a smirk.

"Three hours, okay? Let yourself in if I'm not there yet. Key's under the brick by the chair."

"Be careful," I faked more concern, letting him kiss me again, earning a wink before he turned and walked back towards the shed, talking over his shoulder.

"Trust me, babe. I'm untouchable."

I slipped into the Corvette and drove to my old house, not surprised in the slightest when Slash called me.

I never should have given him my number to sort cocaine deals out with him.

"I watched you on the cameras, Donovan. You've got him eating out of your fucking hands already. You're a natural," he exclaimed with a hoot.

Fucking pig.

"A natural whore?" I offered, hearing him bark out

laughter that Liam probably fucking heard from wherever he was in the shed.

"I prefer the word *seducer*, babe. Keep it up, I need him to trust you."

"I'm meeting up with him in a few hours at his place, and he's already talking more than he's meant to. Should be easy," I replied as I strolled into the kitchen, hauling my ass up onto the bench.

"That's my girl," he replied, and I could hear the grin in his voice.

"I'm not your shit," I bit out, his loud laugh almost deafening me.

"Cute. Call me later, babe. I'll meet you," then he hung up.

I glanced around the house and sighed.

I knew Max had put the house up for sale, and I hated him even more for it.

It was my safe place, and he was taking it away from me like I knew he would.

I hoped he just stayed gone, to be honest.

I wanted my mom.

Liam's house wasn't even fucking locked when I got there, making me roll my eyes as I wandered inside.

I looked around and helped myself to a beer from the fridge, just as I heard a car pull up out the front.

Liam strolled inside with a big smirk on his face when he noticed that I'd shown up.

"You came."

"Of course I did," I smiled, convincing myself to place my beer on the bench and move towards him.

His eyes blazed with desire as I ran my hands up under the front of his shirt, moving against him more.

"Wow, nice abs."

They hardly existed, but whatever.

He ripped his shirt over his head with a grin, flexing his arms like a fucking college football meathead.

"I've upped the weights lately. I think it's starting to pay off for me."

"Oh, it is. I love the tats as well," I breathed, trailing my finger along the tattoo on his chest and biting my lip in a way I'd noticed set any guy off.

It worked.

I gasped as he pulled me flush against him and kissed me hard, his hold on my body firm.

I forced myself to stand there and let him assault my tongue with his, faking a moan as I dug my nails into his back and wrapped my arms around him.

He automatically lifted me, placing my butt on the bench and standing between my legs.

I didn't think I'd be able to fake it so well, but he was all over me, his hands moving up to fondle my breasts.

I winced slightly as a sharp pain jolted me.

"Take it easy with those, I only recently got them pierced a month or so back."

"That's fucking hot," he muttered to himself, tugging at my shirt until I gave in and pulled it over my head.

He jerked me forward to get my pants off, and I wondered how far I'd be able to go with him, not that I really had a choice.

I knew Slash wasn't bluffing about killing me for starters, but I had to make sure Skeeter and the rest of the crew were safe.

He kissed down my neck and chest, his hand moving between my legs to slip into my panties, pushing two fingers inside me.

I was tender, like Tyler had warned me I'd be, but I bit back the discomfort and rocked against his hand.

"I love a bad boy. Make's me super wet."

I was going to panic and wreck this whole thing.

I just fucking knew it.

I was starting to think he wasn't even a threat and I was wasting my fucking time.

He looked way too happy about my comment as he moved back, removing his gun from the back of his pants and placing it on the table beside us.

"Lucky for you then, because I'm the baddest out there, babe."

"Really? How so? Because you're in the Psychos?" I asked with a breathy moan, trying not to shy away from him.

I didn't like his touch.

I'd fuck him to protect Skeeter, but I was going to melt down afterwards.

Slash could pay for the fucking counselling I'd need, too.

"You have no idea. We had to kill this guy the other week, right? Since I'm still proving myself, I offered to do it. Killing him was the best fucking feeling, and now I'm going to offer to do it all the time. I love taking someone's life and watching the panic all over their face as I do it. I don't like running the drugs too much though," he replied, moving his fingers faster.

He had no fucking idea what he was doing with a woman's body, so I knew I wasn't going to get off as a reward for putting up with this bullshit.

Fucking hell.

"You can get good cocaine, right? I could live on that stuff," I continued as he kissed down my neck, the stubble on his chin grazing my skin.

I felt dirty.

So. Fucking. Dirty.

PRETTY LIES | 239

"Whatever you want, I can get it for you," he promised, faking interest as I peered into his eyes.

"Can you get your hands on a Glock for me? I think it would look sexy tucked into my shorts."

"Anything you want, I can find it. I think it's a bit fucking pathetic that Skeet never helped you out, and you were his girl. Stick with me, babe. Trust me."

He laid me back and kissed down my body, but just before I thought he was going to go down on me and finally give me a fucking orgasm, he stood and yanked his pants down.

Shocker that he didn't give a fuck about getting me off first.

Selfish bastard.

"Oh, I don't think that will fit in me," I stated, putting a hand over my mouth for dramatics, pretending it worried me.

He was below fucking average, not that he knew that.

He grinned smugly. "We'll make it fit. Get ready for the best sex of your life, babe."

"Tell me all the bad stuff you've done while we fuck? I love how badass you are. I get so horny, I'd do basically anything," I forced out, knowing I'd regret that comment as I watched him lick his lips in thought.

"Yeah? What kind of bad stuff?"

"Anything. How you killed that person? Skeeter doesn't think it's that hot to talk about, but I'd fuck on a pile of dead bodies if I'd been allowed to. I think people who kill for a living are just *so* powerful."

"Skeeter's a fucking idiot. He won't last long anyways, I'm after his spot in the crew. Don't tell him or anything, though."

I bit his neck playfully and smiled. "I don't give a fuck

about him. He dumped me for some trash whore fighter. You'd be way better as Slash's right-hand man."

He looked at me for a moment, speaking gently.

"Can you keep a secret?"

"For you? Anything," I giggled, noting his hand had stopped moving.

Shit, he was going to tell me what I'd shown up to find out.

"My dad's a cop and I'm trying to impress him. He walked out on me and my brother when we were kids."

Oh, no.

Dread washed through me, but I gave him a big smirk, trying not to let my panic show.

"Oh wow, a cop? You really are bad, aren't you? Wouldn't it impress him if you just killed Slash?"

I was going to kill Slash myself when I got my fucking hands on him.

This was *bullshit*.

"That's my fucking plan," he mumbled against my neck as his hand tugged at my panties.

I didn't even think as I grabbed his gun from beside me, pressing it into his side and pulling the trigger before he could register what was happening.

It was silent, but I knew it hit as panic filled his eyes and he cursed.

He clutched the wound and looked at me with wide eyes.

Yeah, I'd officially lost my fucking mind and shot someone.

"What the fuck?! You shot me!"

I grabbed his throat tightly, tears stinging my eyes as I pulled him closer so that we were nose to nose.

"Don't fuck with the Psychos, because when you do, you don't get out alive."

Complete fear washed over his face, his eyes begging me for mercy.

He was just a little boy who'd do anything to get his father back.

I hesitated, until he started speaking, his voice shaking.

"Rory, please don't…"

"I'm sorry, Liam," I whispered, lifting the gun to his temple and pulling the trigger again.

This time, his body slumped over me as blood started to leak from the wounds and onto my skin, the life leaving his eyes almost instantly.

Fuck.

I shoved his body off mine and scrambled to my feet, glancing around the room in a panic as the shock raced through me.

It had to be done to protect the Psychos, but then I started to panic about everything I'd touched in the house.

I was going to get arrested and go to prison for fucking murder.

My eyes darted to the door as it opened, relief washing through me as Slash walked in.

He'd know what to do, he covered up murderous activities all the time.

His eyebrows shot up as he took in the scene around me, and he closed the door quickly as he watched the blood drip down my skin as I stood there in my bra and panties.

"Holy fuck, Donovan. What the fuck happened? I hadn't heard from you and got worried."

"He was planning on killing you to impress his cop father that abandoned him and his brother. You obviously didn't fucking look into his background properly before you recruited him. We've got to get the fuck out of here, can we talk after?" I snapped, but he looked back at Liam's body, surprise in his voice.

"You killed him to protect us?"

"Slash! Let's go!" I begged, but he put his hand out to silence me.

"Calm down. I'll get the guys to clean this mess up, and I'll get rid of the body and gun. You won't get dragged into this, I promise. He didn't hurt you, did he?" He suddenly asked, but I shook my head, my eyes landing on Liam's body as I sucked in a breath.

"I can't believe I fucking killed him."

He chuckled, irritating me slightly.

I didn't see what was so fucking funny about a dead body.

"Saves me doing it, but you weren't supposed to. Help me wrap his body up, yeah?"

I nodded, helping to wrap him in a massive blanket from the couch, before I grabbed my clothes and beer bottle.

I had to get rid of any sign that I'd been there.

Fuck, my ass cheeks were probably imprinted into his bench.

Slash brought a beat-up Chevy van around the back, praise the lord that the hedges covered the whole property, and I helped him put the body in the back in silence.

Why wasn't I a mess?

I'd wait for the shock to wear off, then it would happen.

I'd fucking killed someone.

Fuck.

I'd just started helping him clean up the blood in the kitchen when he glanced over at me, his voice gentle.

"Hey, the other shit I needed help with? Don't worry about it. Loyalty proven, okay? Just make sure you keep this to yourself. Thanks, by the way."

I shrugged.

I wasn't about to tell him I wasn't going to help him ever again, regardless.

"Hey, if seducing people and bathing in their blood once I've killed them is what keeps the crew happy and under the radar, then I'll do it. I don't want to, but I won't let you guys go down."

"Did you really do it for the Psychos? Or just for Skeet?" He asked, making me smile, despite wanting to strangle him for putting me in that position to begin with.

"Both. I owe Skeet more than anything, but the crew is his life, so both are important to me."

"He's gonna kill you if he finds out about this, you know that, right?" He snorted, and I rolled my eyes dramatically.

"No, he won't. Skeet's a big puppy with me. Besides, he won't find out about it."

"Wanna fucking bet, baby girl?" Skeeter's voice cut in sharply from the doorway, and Slash actually fucking grinned as I put my blood-covered hands on my bare hips, my voice sarcastic.

"Thank you for having your back is more fucking appropriate, don't you think?"

He gritted his teeth as he took in my blood splattered skin, his voice lethal.

"What the fuck did you do, is my first question, but since you and Slash are cleaning up this mess, I know it isn't fucking good. Get in the fucking car."

"I have to help Slash with...," I started, but he clenched his fists and glared at me, his voice making me jump as he raised it.

"Get in the fucking car, Aurora!"

I hesitated, grabbing Liam's large shirt and pulling it over my head to cover myself, Skeeter's jaw clenching as I walked past him and headed for the door.

I climbed straight into his white McLaren 600LT Spider, knowing he wouldn't let me drive myself home in the Corvette.

I was right as he walked out a few moments later, barking at one of the Psychos who'd just arrived, to get my car home, then he climbed into the driver's seat and slammed the door, putting his foot down and speeding in the direction of his house.

He didn't speak to me until we'd entered his bathroom, where he yanked the shirt off me with force, angrily shaking it in his fist as he glared at me.

"Since when do you and fucking Slash hang out, huh? And why the *fuck* were you at Liam's, nearly fucking naked and covered in blood? What the fuck did you do?!"

The half-dried blood was starting to crack on my skin, and I cringed.

"It's a long story."

"Then start fucking talking!" He exploded, causing me to take a small step back.

There was a small shake in my hand, and I knew the shock was starting to wear off.

It was about to become fucking breakdown central.

"Slash needed help with Liam, since you thought he was up to something. He figured you wouldn't let me, but since you were gone, he asked for my help anyways."

"Slash fucking brought you into this?" He growled, making me roll my eyes.

"It's not like he made me."

Liar.

"So, if you'd said no, he would have been all fine and fucking dandy about it?" He kept shouting, my reply coming out gentle, sounding more like a question than an answer.

"Um, Yes?"

He grabbed my throat and yanked me closer, violence in his eyes that honestly should have scared me.

"You know I hate it when you fucking lie to me."

"Fine, I didn't really have a say in the matter, but the plan was that I'd seduce Liam and see if he talked too much. When he told me his plan was to kill Slash and make his cop daddy fucking proud, I killed him. Slash only wanted me to get information then he'd deal with Liam himself, but I couldn't risk it."

"Risk fucking what?!"

"Risk him taking anyone down! He was coming after you too, Skeet! I couldn't let him do that!" I finally shouted back, his eyes closing as he rested his forehead against mine, speaking softly as if he were in pain.

"Did you fuck him?"

"No, but he had his fingers inside me," I responded, and he hesitated before continuing.

"*Would* you have fucked him?"

"Yes, if it meant protecting you and your crew. It was the original plan," I forced out, his eyes opening as his hand finally fell from my throat.

Now he just looked worried, not angry.

"What if he knew what you were up to, Rory? He could have hurt you or fucking killed you. I told you to stay out of crew business for a reason, and I told you to stay away from me for the same fucking reason. You aren't meant to kill people to keep me safe, babe. That's my job to do that for you."

"I'd do it again and again to keep you fucking safe, Skeet," I answered quietly, a rough edge to my voice that made him scowl, before my back suddenly hit the wall and he kissed me hard.

His fingers dug into my hips hard enough to bruise, but I didn't fucking care.

He yanked my panties and bra off, lifting one of my legs before shoving himself inside of me forcefully.

I gasped and dug my nails into his shoulders, his arms hooking under my legs to lift me higher, keeping one arm under my ass while the other tangled in my hair as he fucked me hard into the wall.

I'd never seen him so crazy, and the harder he went, the more I realized he wasn't fucking to make me feel good, he was fucking for himself.

My back slammed against the wall again and again, his teeth digging into my neck until the skin tore and blood dripped down my skin.

My nails dug deeper into his shoulders until I felt blood, and I bit back a scream of pain as he kept pounding into me, Liam's blood mingling with our sweat.

He buried deep inside me with a grunt, his body quivering as he finally slowed and caught his breath.

My voice was shaky as I said, "I'm sorry that you're mad, but I had to. I had to keep everyone fucking safe."

He finally lifted his head, meeting my gaze with a sudden calmness in them.

"I'm not angry, baby girl. I was fucking scared for you."

"Why? I'm fine."

"I can see that now, but when I first saw you in the middle of that bloody fucking kitchen, I wasn't sure if any of it was yours. I wasn't sure if someone had fucking hurt you. Jensen called me because no one had seen you since you left Ty's this morning, and he said you were meant to meet Slash at the Shed tonight. When they went to check on you, you weren't at home or at the shed. They think Slash offed you or some shit, and they're going fucking ballistic. Since Slash didn't tell me any of the plan and I wasn't back yet, I thought maybe they were right and Slash was getting rid of you. Fucking hell, Rory. I saw your car out the front of Liam's house, and instantly thought they'd taken you there to…"

His voice broke as he kept staring into my eyes, and I instantly felt bad for scaring everyone.

"I'm okay, Skeet. I'm sorry," I whispered, waiting for him to nod before he placed my feet on the ground.

fucking proud, I killed him. Slash only wanted me to get information then he'd deal with Liam himself, but I couldn't risk it."

"Risk fucking what?!"

"Risk him taking anyone down! He was coming after you too, Skeet! I couldn't let him do that!" I finally shouted back, his eyes closing as he rested his forehead against mine, speaking softly as if he were in pain.

"Did you fuck him?"

"No, but he had his fingers inside me," I responded, and he hesitated before continuing.

"*Would* you have fucked him?"

"Yes, if it meant protecting you and your crew. It was the original plan," I forced out, his eyes opening as his hand finally fell from my throat.

Now he just looked worried, not angry.

"What if he knew what you were up to, Rory? He could have hurt you or fucking killed you. I told you to stay out of crew business for a reason, and I told you to stay away from me for the same fucking reason. You aren't meant to kill people to keep me safe, babe. That's my job to do that for you."

"I'd do it again and again to keep you fucking safe, Skeet," I answered quietly, a rough edge to my voice that made him scowl, before my back suddenly hit the wall and he kissed me hard.

His fingers dug into my hips hard enough to bruise, but I didn't fucking care.

He yanked my panties and bra off, lifting one of my legs before shoving himself inside of me forcefully.

I gasped and dug my nails into his shoulders, his arms hooking under my legs to lift me higher, keeping one arm under my ass while the other tangled in my hair as he fucked me hard into the wall.

I'd never seen him so crazy, and the harder he went, the more I realized he wasn't fucking to make me feel good, he was fucking for himself.

My back slammed against the wall again and again, his teeth digging into my neck until the skin tore and blood dripped down my skin.

My nails dug deeper into his shoulders until I felt blood, and I bit back a scream of pain as he kept pounding into me, Liam's blood mingling with our sweat.

He buried deep inside me with a grunt, his body quivering as he finally slowed and caught his breath.

My voice was shaky as I said, "I'm sorry that you're mad, but I had to. I had to keep everyone fucking safe."

He finally lifted his head, meeting my gaze with a sudden calmness in them.

"I'm not angry, baby girl. I was fucking scared for you."

"Why? I'm fine."

"I can see that now, but when I first saw you in the middle of that bloody fucking kitchen, I wasn't sure if any of it was yours. I wasn't sure if someone had fucking hurt you. Jensen called me because no one had seen you since you left Ty's this morning, and he said you were meant to meet Slash at the Shed tonight. When they went to check on you, you weren't at home or at the shed. They think Slash offed you or some shit, and they're going fucking ballistic. Since Slash didn't tell me any of the plan and I wasn't back yet, I thought maybe they were right and Slash was getting rid of you. Fucking hell, Rory. I saw your car out the front of Liam's house, and instantly thought they'd taken you there to…"

His voice broke as he kept staring into my eyes, and I instantly felt bad for scaring everyone.

"I'm okay, Skeet. I'm sorry," I whispered, waiting for him to nod before he placed my feet on the ground.

He kissed my cheek and sighed, glancing down at the blood that was now smeared all over both of us.

"Let's get cleaned up before we get blood all through my house, then I'm taking you home. I don't know how to tell Holloway's boys about all of this, because we aren't supposed to talk to them about this kind of shit."

"I'll just tell them I've been at my old place all day, which isn't a complete lie. I was there for a few hours," I mumbled as his eyes assessed me before he turned the shower on and helped me under the hot spray, climbing in with me to wash the blood off his sweaty front.

Note to self, fucking while covered in blood was messy as fuck.

CHAPTER FOURTEEN

LUKAS

"I'm seriously worried about her. Shouldn't Skeet have called us by now?" Jensen asked as he bounced his leg anxiously on the couch beside me.

Yes, he fucking should have, but between Tyler nearly writing off his BMW when we went searching for Rory earlier, and Caden smashing half the kitchen to pieces when we arrived at his place to find she still wasn't home, I didn't need Jensen having a meltdown too.

I put my hand on his knee, halting the jerky movement instantly as his distraught blue eyes peered over at me.

"Luke, what if Slash..."

"Hey, Skeet will find her. She's probably drunk somewhere with a bottle of whisky, you know what she's like," I stated, earning a snort.

"Yeah I do, so she's probably off with Slash somewhere, trying to prove to the big boys that her balls are fucking bigger. He's wanted her gone since she started affecting Skeet's attention, so he's probably taken her out the back roads somewhere and fucking shot her."

Well, when he says it like that.

I tried to keep my face blank as I held his gaze.

"Jense, Skeet's going to find her."

Tyler scowled as he sat down on the other couch in front of us.

"I agree with Holloway and Jense. I think Slash has fucking hurt her or some shit."

"Do you really think he would? C'mon, Ty, he's a friend of yours," I mumbled, but his gaze flashed up to mine, his eyes darkening.

"I also know my friend is a murderous bastard who likes inflicting pain as a hobby."

Couldn't argue with that.

I went to speak, but Caden barrelled down the stairs and skidded to a halt in front of us, frustration all over his face.

"Skeet's just pulled in with Rory. Some other guy dropped the Corvette off."

"Holloway, calm down and let her explain herself," I groaned, his eyes narrowing.

"Why the fuck would I give her the chance to make up some bullshit? You're too fucking nice to her, Lukas."

He was going to fucking kill her for sure this time.

Caden

I was going to fucking kill Aurora when I got my hands on her.

Rory

"Caden," Lukas warned in a low voice as I walked in the front door at home, but Caden instantly stalked over to me and grabbed me by the throat, slamming me back against the door.

"Where the *fuck* have you been all day?!"

I winced at the impact, but I knew his reaction was similar to Skeeter's.

I'd scared him.

"I was at my old place for most of it," I replied, his eyes hovering on my neck before his lip lifted into a sneer.

"With who?"

"No one, why?"

He slammed me against the door again, his grip tightening.

"Whose teeth marks are in your fucking skin then?"

I was exhausted, and tears stung my eyes as I started to burn out after the hectic afternoon I'd endured.

I tried to push him away as I kept my voice level somehow.

"Skeet picked me up and I hung at his for a little before coming home. You would have heard him drop me off in the McLaren. What's the big deal? I just want to go to bed."

He looked even more pissed off as he got in my face.

"I know you weren't at your old house all day, because I fucking checked there this afternoon. Skeeter wasn't with you two hours ago, so where else were you? What aren't you fucking telling me?"

He stiffened when I let the tears finally fall, Jensen scowling and putting himself between us to shield me.

They knew I wasn't a fucking crier, so something must have been seriously wrong.

"Fucking hell, Holloway. Back off a minute."

Once I'd started crying though, I couldn't fucking stop.

Loud sobs wracked my body, my legs shaking slightly as Jensen pulled me against his chest, trying to hold me up.

The shock had worn off, and I wished it would come back to shelter me.

I'd killed someone.

A fucking person.

That had a fucking *cop* as a father.

"Fuck this, this isn't because of Caden. I'm calling Skeet," Tyler muttered, yanking his phone from his pocket as Jensen lifted me into his arms to carry me into the loungeroom, cradling me on the couch.

By the time Skeeter and Slash arrived, I was a complete fucking mess.

Caden shot Skeeter a look of rage instantly.

"What the fuck did you do to her? This isn't because I yelled at her, something fucking happened and she won't tell us shit, so start talking!"

Slash took a step towards him, but Skeeter moved in front of him to block his path, giving him a filthy look.

"This is why I didn't want her fucking involved in our shit. She's not made for this, and she's crashing from it."

Tyler crossed his arms with annoyance.

"What shit?"

"Nothing," Slash growled, but Caden pointed at me and got in Slash's face.

"Nothing? Does that look like fucking *nothing* to you? Look at her!"

I reached for Skeeter who didn't hesitate to lift me, letting me wrap myself around him and cling on as if I were a monkey.

I didn't care how pathetic I looked right then and there, I just needed him to ground me again.

Caden motioned to my neck with a growl.

"Oh, and if she's such a fucking mess, why the fuck did you think a good fuck would fix it? She said she hung at yours for a bit."

Slash rolled his eyes at Skeeter and asked, "Seriously? You took her home and fucked her to try and fix her?"

"Who said anything about trying to fix her? I fucked her to fix *me!*" Skeeter snapped, holding me even tighter.

Caden frowned. "Skeet, seriously. What the fuck happened today?"

Skeeter looked at Slash who gritted his teeth with frustration.

"Fine, but if you tell anyone and us three get locked up, I'll slit your fucking throat, Holloway."

That made all of them shut up and look at him, but Caden spoke sternly, and if I hadn't been such a mess, I would have swooned at him standing up for me.

"What the fuck did you get her into, Slash? Tell me, before I fucking swing at you."

"Fine, Jesus. Skeet told me to stay away from her, but obviously I'm in charge and I don't fucking answer to him. I cut her a deal that she'd prove her loyalty to us if she helped me deal with a new member."

"And by that you mean what, exactly?" He asked bluntly, Slash leaning against the wall with a bored expression on his face.

"Skeet told me he didn't trust Liam, so I convinced Donovan to seduce him and see if he'd talk. He was all over her in minutes and asked her to meet up after crew business was finished for the day."

Caden was staring at me, and I knew he was thinking the worst as Skeeter rocked me gently, but Skeeter's eyes were on Caden as Slash kept talking, as if we were talking about our plans for fucking brunch.

"She met him at his house, managing to get more information out of him than I thought she would. His dad's a cop, and he was going to kill me and take down Skeet to impress him. I showed up to make sure she was okay, since I hadn't heard from her, and she was standing in the kitchen in her bra and panties, covered in blood. She'd shot him twice to keep Skeet and the crew safe. It wasn't the plan, she was meant to just report back to me what he'd told her, but she didn't want to risk it. She helped me put the body in the van, and we were cleaning up when Skeet found us and took her back to his. End of fucking story."

Jensen's head was in his hands, Tyler and Caden looked murderous all over again, but Lukas shook his head sadly.

"You should have fucking known she'd look out for Skeet and your guys like that. You shouldn't have fucking put her in that position to begin with. Damnit Slash, she won't be able to deal with that shit, she's not like you!"

I lifted my head, meeting his gaze.

No one had noticed how quiet I'd become until I spoke.

"Deal with it? I'm not fucking *done* yet."

Skeeter tensed, but Lukas frowned.

"What do you mean?"

"If I can kill a guy our age for someone else, I can fucking kill the two men who wrecked my fucking life. Then I'll be able to live with it," I responded firmly, Skeeter kissing my cheek affectionately.

"Hey, I'm dealing with them, okay?"

"No. They're fucking mine, Skeet. I mean it," I growled, wriggling until he put me down, but he took my wrist gently, pulling me around to face him.

"Can we talk about this tomorrow? You need a good night sleep. You've had too much shock today, and your body and mind are crashing on you. I've got other shit to deal with tonight, so get some sleep and…"

"No! I have to start looking for them and sort a plan

out!" I snapped, yanking back from him, but he just followed me and wrapped my hair around his fist to keep me still.

"I know where they *both* are. We can sort out a plan tomorrow, but you need a clear head before going into this. I promise, I won't go behind your back if you promise to get some sleep."

My expression softened as I gave him a nod, leaving the room the moment he let my hair go.

I'd only just made it to my bedroom door when I heard footsteps, and I was surprised to see Lukas behind me, not one of the others.

"What are you doing?"

He raised his pierced eyebrow as he stopped in front of me, a sad look deep in his almond eyes that I didn't think he was supposed to let me see.

He forgets how easily I've always been able to read him.

After all, he was my best friend and my first love, despite the fact that we never acted on it.

"The guys were fighting over who should keep an eye on you tonight, so I figured since we're just at a friendship level unlike you and them, that it's best I just sleep in here with you."

I opened my bedroom door, giving him a confused glance.

"You think I just see you as a friend?"

"Well, yeah?" He mumbled, closing the door and watched warily as I stripped out of my clothes, leaving only my panties on.

I moved towards him, his back hitting the door as he held my gaze. "Aurora..."

I pressed my naked chest against him, my hands resting on his lean waist as I got on tip toe, brushing my lips lightly over his as I spoke.

"You know I've always loved you, Luke. You don't think I still do?"

He swallowed, his eyes still on mine.

"I've stayed out of it because you and Caden…"

"I wasn't kidding when I said I loved you all, Caden and Ty have just been more forward about climbing on me. Jensen's always unsure how far to push me, and you choose not to at all. Doesn't mean I don't love you."

"I came in here to make sure you got a decent sleep, Rory. I won't fuck you," he forced out, a small smile tugging at my lips.

"It's one reason I fell in love with you all those years ago. You always put me first," then I gave him a quick kiss and turned around, padding over to my bed and waited for him to join me so we could get comfortable.

Once curled up in his arms, I kissed his chest, a shiver running through him as I said, "Thank you."

He hesitated, kissing the top of my head affectionately.

"What for?"

"For everything," I mumbled, the exhaustion taking over as I dozed off.

"Morning, baby," Caden said gently as I padded into the kitchen to make coffee the next morning.

I smiled softly at him, instantly warming at his voice.

He always seemed to soothe my demons, even if it was only a little bit.

"Morning."

"Sit, I'll get your coffee," he insisted, grabbing a mug from the cupboard, while I got comfortable at the table.

I watched him walk around shirtless, wondering how someone like that could want someone like me.

I honestly didn't fucking understand.

I wanted to trace his tattoos with my tongue and let him bend me over the bench, too.

Lukas walked in, silently lifting me so I could curl up on his lap, which I was grateful for.

I'd woken from nightmares multiple times through the night, but I'd managed to get back to sleep with Lukas mumbling calming words to me.

Caden glanced at us as Lukas whispered in my ear before kissing my neck softly, causing Caden to raise an eyebrow.

"You two fucking now?"

My eyes moved across the room to his, my face remaining blank.

"No, but if we were?"

"I'm just surprised, that's all. You can do what you want, Aurora," he replied with a shrug, but I could hear something unfamiliar in his voice, making me frown.

Lukas smiled against my neck as I watched Caden fumble around the kitchen to finish making my coffee, and he whispered, "Go give him some affection. He's feeling replaced."

I hesitated before doing as I was told, moving over to Caden and wrapping my arms around him from behind, his body going tense.

"Rory..."

I kissed his bare back and buried my face between his shoulder blades, breathing him in.

"I'm sorry for scaring you yesterday."

He relaxed as he turned in my arms, sighing and pulling me against his chest.

"I seriously thought we'd find your body somewhere. I'm sorry for how I acted when you got home. I was going fucking crazy not knowing if you were okay. Did I hurt you?"

I wasn't going to tell him that he had, but Lukas spoke bluntly from his seat.

"Yeah, you did. You've bruised her back up, asshole."

Fucking hell.

Lukas hadn't been happy when he'd brought up the bruises while we'd been lying in bed, so I knew he'd be straight on to Caden about it.

I also told him most of them would have been from Skeeter fucking me against the bathroom wall.

Caden would just feel fucking bad and fuss over me.

"Can I look?" He asked with concern in his voice, meeting my eyes as I nodded and turned around, pulling my shirt over my head.

His hands lightly skimmed over my back, my eyes fluttering closed as his lips kissed over the tender parts.

"I'm so sorry, baby," he murmured, and I knew he meant it.

Despite the fact that they had lured me in before, I knew they were all genuinely sorry for everything that had gone on since we'd met.

"Most of that is Skeet's fault, but I forgive you, Caden," I whispered, letting him turn me to meet his gaze that was full of questions.

"For last night?"

"For all of it, but if you hurt me like that again, I'm done," I said firmly, his eyebrows going up in surprise.

"You really forgive us? For all that shit?"

Nodding, I snuggled up to his bare chest as his arms tightened around me.

It was so fucking nice.

It was still weird to have people care about me, but I was grateful.

"What's going on in here?" Tyler asked as he walked in with Jensen, and I glanced up, giving him a lop-sided smile.

"*Not* a gang-bang."

"Fuck, you sure? Nothing can change your mind?" He waggled his eyebrows, but Jensen's eyes hovered on my exposed back, glancing at Caden as unspoken words passed between them.

I really didn't want them fucking fighting about it.

I moved back, letting Caden help me back into my shirt so I could take my coffee back over to Lukas.

Once back on his lap, we all sat at the table chatting until Josie walked through the front door, seeming surprised to see us.

"You guys still here? It's nearly lunchtime."

Caden shrugged. "Yeah, figured we'd all have a sleep in."

She nodded, but her eyes went to me.

"Can I talk to you, sweetheart?"

Lukas swatted my butt as I stood, but Caden's hand shot out, pulling me back until my ass hit his lap, making me laugh.

"Can I help you, Holloway?"

He smirked. "Always. Come get me if you need me okay, baby?"

"I will," I promised, giving him a quick kiss as he lifted me back out of his lap, ignoring the look from his mother.

Once in the other room, Josie cleared her throat.

"I don't appreciate those friends of yours coming up to me in the street, telling me they're taking you away for a while. I don't want you going anywhere with them."

Huh?

I frowned. "Who?"

"Some guy from that gang."

"The Psychos? Catch a name?" I asked with confusion, knowing Skeeter wouldn't approach Caden's mom like that.

He might be an asshole, but he had respect amongst his friends.

"I know he's good friends with Tyler."

Oh, for fuck's sake, Slash was still causing shit.

"That would be Slash. I'll tell him he was out of line," I sighed, earning a flat look in response.

"But you're going with them, right?" she asked dryly, making me shrug.

"I wasn't aware I was going anywhere, but yeah, if they want me to tag along, I will."

"Caden won't mind?" She asked lightly, an amused snort leaving me.

"Why the fuck would Caden care?"

She seemed unsure as she blushed.

Like, an actual fucking blush.

"Aren't you dating him?"

"No."

"Oh," she frowned as Caden strolled around the corner and leaned against the wall, mischief swimming in his green eyes.

"We just fuck, Mom. Besides, she's still fucking Skeeter."

"Caden!" Josie hissed, but he shrugged casually.

"What? Sometimes me and Ty get bored and wanna get laid, so…"

I rolled my eyes at him, playfully swatting his arm.

"Don't wind your mother up, asshole."

"Oh, he's joking?" She laughed with confusion, but I just snorted again, letting Caden drape an arm around my shoulders.

"Well, no. You just don't need to know what we get up to. That's weird."

Caden smirked, leading me back into the other room without being dismissed, and dumping me straight into Jensen's lap.

"Hey!" I laughed, Jensen instantly ruffling my hair with a shit-eating grin.

"Everyone but me seems to be getting your attention, so I complained until Caden got sick of hearing about it. He delivered you to me. Neat huh, baby?"

"I spend heaps of time with you!" I grinned back, watching as he shrugged lazily, pretending not to be too bothered.

"Not lately. If you aren't running off with Caden and Ty, you're off with Skeet. You used to spend nearly all your time with me, so I miss you."

Oh.

My expression softened as I ran my fingers through his chocolate hair affectionately.

"I miss you too. Can I stay at yours tonight?"

Caden and Tyler exclaimed their objections loudly, but Jensen smiled and ignored them.

"Course you can, babe."

Lukas raised an eyebrow at Caden, who was throwing the tantrum of the fucking year.

"Holloway, you and Ty spend the most time with her, get over it."

He scowled, leaning back in his chair and crossing his arms.

"Yeah, well, she's meant to be here with me all the time. She *lives* here."

"Surprised you still wanna fuck her to be honest. I mean, she isn't your sister anymore," Tyler teased, earning a thump to the leg from him, but Lukas laughed and gave me a cheeky smile.

"Hey, you wanna move in with me, Rory? I'll keep these animals away from you."

I rolled my eyes, nuzzling into Jensen's neck to get comfortable.

He basically lived with Jensen, anyways.

"I kind of like them fighting over me. Makes me feel

special and all that shit."

"Well, it's about to get worse. Skeet just showed up," Tyler stated over the racket just as Skeeter strolled through the door, instantly frowning at Jensen.

"Play fair, Gilbert. Give her here."

I rolled my eyes for what felt like the hundredth time, but climbed off Jensen's lap, walking over to Skeeter and hugging him tightly.

I knew we had a lot to talk about, but I also knew he'd refuse to fix our relationship.

I'd just have to try and convince him with sex and my charming skills.

We moved over to one of the loungeroom chairs, and he instantly pulled me into his lap, earning a smirk from Caden.

"Aw, Skeet, you got room on your lap for me too? Sharing's caring."

Skeeter chuckled with amusement, his tattooed fingers running through my hair absently.

"She bends over for me, you don't. No special treatment for you, Holloway."

Caden flipped him off as we all laughed, but Skeeter leaned back in the chair more, not moving his eyes from Caden as he raised an eyebrow and spoke.

"Afternoon, Josie."

We all glanced up to find Josie peering around the doorway at us, embarrassment on her face.

Caden groaned. "Mom, how long have you been spying on us?"

She stepped into the room with red cheeks, glancing at me with confusion.

"Are you guys all in one relationship?"

I thought we'd stated that we just fucked when we're bored?

Then again, Caden only mentioned Skeeter and Tyler.

Skeeter barked out a laugh, "Like, the six of us date? Don't think so, Josie. I love your son, but not like that."

She blushed even harder. "No, I mean are you all dating Rory?"

I looked thoughtfully at Caden.

We hadn't really talked about labelling that shit.

"Well, I guess? Dating's a strong word though."

He snorted, "I had you first, so you're mine. Nice try, baby."

"Doesn't mean shit," Jensen muttered, causing Skeeter to grin slyly, not being able to help himself as he tried to provoke an argument.

"True, my man. She loved you first, right?"

Argh, seriously?

I stood, moving into my own chair and giving him an unamused glance.

"No one likes a troublemaker, Skeet."

"I happen to know you like troublemakers quite a lot, Donovan," he replied in a low voice, his grin turning naughty.

Asshole.

I flipped him the bird before glancing up at Josie again, needing to shut the conversation down, pronto.

"I'm not technically dating anyone. Ever *again*, if this keeps up."

Tyler's foot tapped mine under the table, but I ignored him as Skeeter and Caden argued, no one realizing Josie had snuck off until I stood and dumped my empty coffee cup in the sink and headed up to my room without a word.

Boys, I'm telling you.

I got dressed, shoving my hair into a ponytail and lacing up my black boots, before jogging down the stairs and colliding with a solid chest as I turned into the loungeroom.

Jensen backed me into the wall, a sly smirk on his face.

"Going somewhere, cupcake?"

Fuck.

I scowled. "Don't call me that."

"Well, where are you going? Thought we were heading to mine for the night?" He pouted, as if that would change my mind.

"It's lunchtime, so I have hours till tonight," I argued, a small smile hitting my face as he lifted me and pressed my back against the wall.

I could lick his biceps, honestly.

Goddamn, he used the gym perfectly in my opinion.

Bruised back?

What bruised back?

Drool.

"Well, I wanted to have the afternoon with you too, so give me a good reason why I should let you go?" He murmured as I snaked my arms around his neck to lean closer and kiss him.

"What did you wanna do then?"

"I want to know where you were going in such a hurry," he chuckled, placing my feet back on the ground.

"The shed," I replied honestly, his eyes narrowing on me.

"Why?"

"I need to see Slash about something," I shrugged and went to walk off, but his hand pulled me back before I got two steps from him.

"Nuh-uh."

"Damnit, Jense, don't do this shit. Come with me if you fucking have to, but I have to talk to Slash."

"Talk to Slash about what, hot stuff?" Skeeter asked, sweet as honey, from close by.

I rolled my eyes, knowing he was going to over analyse it.

He was always fucking eavesdropping, too.

"That you guys are apparently taking me with you somewhere?"

He frowned, suddenly not looking amused anymore.

"Where the fuck did you hear that?"

"Apparently, Slash just strolled up to Josie today and told her you guys were taking me somewhere. She's a bit shitty about being approached, so I'm going to talk to Slash, since she thinks he was the person that spoke to her."

"Don't even bother," he growled, earning a filthy look from me as I went to fight him on it, but he pinned me against the wall carefully, his voice soft. "I don't know shit about it, so let me find out what the fuck's going on. I won't put you in danger. This is either a lack of communication, or Slash is up to something. Stay with the guys until I find you. Please."

Well, he did actually say please, this time.

I sighed in defeat, tucking myself under Jensen's arm as Skeeter turned to him.

"Keep her in your sights, no matter what. She needs to shit, you sit in there too. Got it?"

I rolled my eyes, but Skeeter's concerned gaze hit mine.

I knew he was seriously worried.

"Rory, this isn't a game. For once in your life, do as you're fucking told. I'll call you when I know what's going on, okay? Maybe go to Lukas's house or some shit. Somewhere you don't usually go."

Jensen tightened his arm around me protectively, and I couldn't lie, I swooned a little.

"We were heading to mine. She hasn't been there many times."

"Your main house, or the one she stayed at after the shit with Holloway's dad?" Skeeter asked with his jaw set hard, but Jensen replied calmly.

"Main house. She's only been there once or twice."

"Good. Keep your eye out. If Slash shows up and you haven't heard from me, call me," he ordered before pressing a kiss to my forehead and taking off.

Jensen sighed, already apparently over the drama that I'd bestowed on them.

"See why we talk about things before doing them? Let's get going."

I wanted to argue, but words never came.

I just nodded, letting him have his way this once.

CHAPTER FIFTEEN

RORY

Jensen: Where the fuck are you, Aurora? Answer the fucking phone!

Guilt ate at me as I read Jensen's text.

I'd waited until he'd gone to sleep before prying his arms from around myself and sneaking out, heading straight to the shed on foot.

I walked for an hour before reaching the turn-off, just as Jensen's text came through, so I knew I didn't have a lot of time before people turned up looking for me.

I jogged up to the door and let myself in, making my way towards the office and coming face to face with Slash, who chuckled with pure amusement.

"I fucking *told* Skeet you wouldn't stay put."

I sat my ass on his desk and stole a cigarette, raising an eyebrow.

I could kill the piece of shit.

"So, you did corner Josie in the street? Careful, Slash, that's not your fucking business."

"No offense, but you are my business. I needed to keep all

your fucking guys busy at watching you. Got you a gift, Killer."

I scowled at the nickname, taking a drag of my cigarette as I lit it.

"For me? You shouldn't have, seriously. Where's Skeet at?"

"Busy, but he'll be here once Gilbert tells him you've gone M.I.A."

The fuck?

That put me on alert instantly as I demanded, "How do you know Jense knows I've vanished?"

"If you think we'd let you run around all this time as Skeet's girl and not had a tracking device on your phone to track texts and calls, you're really stupid. Anyways, I'll take you to your gift, and I promise I'm not kidnapping you. Go slide your delinquent ass into my 'stang."

"How do I know you aren't kidnapping me?" I scoffed, but he shrugged.

"Well, you don't know that I'm not, but I've got bigger fish to fry, babe."

I warily followed him out to his car, holding back the urge to just tackle him and run.

He was totally kidnapping me, wasn't he?

I frowned when we'd driven a few blocks away and he pulled into a parking lot beside an abandoned building, parking close to the door.

Again, why did I keep doing stupid shit?

"This *screams* kidnapped to me, Slash. Just saying," I snorted, not at all amused, earning a genuine laugh as he climbed out.

"Can't kidnap someone who's willing, babe. You'll like this gift, trust me."

"I'm not trusting any shit that comes out of your mouth, boss man."

"Just follow me," he sighed impatiently and rolled his eyes, waiting for me to follow him inside and along the dark hallway, before stopping in front of a door at the end.

He unlocked it, startling me as he grabbed the back of my pants, his cool fingers brushing against my skin.

He chuckled at my panic. "Relax. It's just part of the gift."

I went to yell, praying that someone would hear me, but I hesitated when I felt cold metal slide down the back of my pants.

"Slash, is that a fucking *gun*?"

"Yep, fully loaded. You're welcome," then he opened the door and gave me a small shove, locking me inside.

The room was bright, causing me to squint as the panic rolled through me.

He'd actually fucking kidnapped me and locked me in an abandoned building, and I'd been stupid enough to just get in the car with him.

Skeeter was going to fucking kill me.

A noise sounded from across the room, and I looked up to meet eyes with a panicked Tristan Holloway.

I instantly froze up.

How the fuck could Slash do that to me?

How much did he pay Tristan to do this?

Or did Tristan pay Slash?

Fuck, I'd been set up.

"What the *fuck*?"

Tristan's eyes went wide in fear, and I realized he wasn't there on his own accord.

Slash had fucking taken him.

"Aurora, you have to help me. Your boyfriend's crew..."

"Don't think for a second that I'd *ever* fucking help you," I gritted out, taking a step back as he moved closer.

He'd been beaten, which made me smile a little.

Hang on, Slash had given me a gun.

"Why not? We can help each other escape, yeah? You can convince him to let us go, right?" he blabbered like an idiot.

I smirked, manic laughter bubbling out of me as I realized what was actually going on.

Slash was serious about giving me a gift.

He'd literally brought me there so I could kill my fucking rapist.

Holy shit, he did that for me?

Tristan frowned at my psychopathic melt down, but I waved a hand at him to dismiss it through my laughter.

"Oh, you think I've been kidnapped? My bad."

"But…"

"I wasn't kidnapped, I was brought in here to see you."

"For closure?" He asked with curiosity in his voice, making me grin.

"Yep."

"They'll just kill me, Aurora. Please help me…"

His mouth snapped shut mid-sentence as I pulled the gun out, pointing it at him with a sinister smile.

"I'd be pretty mad if they killed you, considering I'd called dibs. Final words, Tristan?"

I was shitting my pants, but at least I sounded fucking badass.

I needed theme music.

"Caden would never forgive you! If you love my son, you won't hurt him like this!" He begged, literally grovelling on his knees in front of me like the pathetic piece of shit that he was.

I cocked an eyebrow. "Caden wants you dead, but if you really loved him, it wouldn't have come to this. You didn't do any of that shit for my father, you wanted me beyond damaged to keep me away from Caden once you'd found out how close we were. News flash, all you did was bring us closer together. We're stronger than ever, and he can't stand the fucking thought of you. You touched what he sees as his, you know?"

"You'll never be able to live with yourself if you kill me! Having that kind of blood on your hands would destroy you!" He insisted, clasping his hands together, getting desperate.

"I'll just add it to my body count. You'll be two, Max will be three. Lucky you guys, huh?" I grinned, starting to feel more in control as I watched him fucking fall apart at my feet.

"You'll kill your own fucking father? You're a psychopath!"

Power surged through me as I pointed the gun at his forehead, pressing it firmly against the skin and watching the panic cross his face as I smiled.

"Caden did say Skeet had turned me psycho once, but you have no fucking idea," then I pulled the trigger without hesitation.

The sound echoed through the room as the blood splattered, spraying my shirt and neck from the close range.

I heard the door unlatch, so I headed out of the room and gave Slash a nod of appreciation.

I didn't like the asshole, but I had respect for him now.

He let me face my own demons, and I'd fucking won.

Skeeter barrelled into the building, his eyes landing on the blood on my shirt, his expression changing from pure rage to something else in an instant.

It almost looked like pity.

I turned to Slash, letting him take the gun from my hand to dispose of, just as Caden and the guys showed up, but Skeeter put an arm out to block them.

Caden's eyes took in my appearance, not hesitating to shove past Skeeter to reach me, but I met his eyes and he instantly froze at the emotions he saw in them.

I didn't hide a thing from him as I spoke, my voice somehow sounding steady.

"I wouldn't go in there if I were you, Caden. I don't fucking want that for you," then I walked out, gently pushing the others out of my way as I left.

No one followed me, but one of Slash's guys pulled up beside me after fifteen minutes of walking, and I climbed in for a lift home.

I was getting sick of burning my blood-stained clothes.

This shirt? One of my favourites.

The house was silent by the time I got there and burned the evidence before having a hot shower and managing to fall asleep quickly once I'd climbed into bed.

The silky sheets on my bare skin always helped, I guessed.

An arm went around my middle a few hours later, jolting me awake, and I was surprised to find Caden curled up behind me.

I rubbed my sleepy eyes with a frown.

"Caden?"

"Yeah. Just me, baby," he mumbled softly, my frown deepening.

I'd just killed his fucking dad, how could he want to be anywhere near me?

"Why are you in here? When did you get home?"

He was quiet for a moment, before kissing my bare shoulder.

"I just got here. I need you, as much as I think you need me."

There was too much raw emotion in his voice, and I rolled over, placing a kiss on his chest, a bit confused by what he meant.

"I'll always need you."

"I *need* you. Now," he murmured, his body almost sagging in relief as I tilted my head up to kiss him tenderly.

He always knew what I needed, and I was more than happy to de-stress with him in a way that would help heal the both of us.

I was only in my panties, so I kicked them off and tugged his boxers down before swinging a leg over to straddle him.

He groaned, his fingers running through my hair as he pulled me down to kiss him as I sank over him completely, rotating my hips as his kiss became desperate.

I sat back and put my hands on his chest to balance myself as I rode him, shyness taking over as I realized he was staring at my face.

I blushed at the intensity of it, slowing my movements as his thumbs stroked my hips gently.

"What?"

"You're just so fucking beautiful, Aurora," he replied without hesitation, my heart thumping harder.

I wasn't sure why, but his words seared into me, wrapping around my heart and lighting the spark inside.

"Really?"

He sat up, resting his back against the headboard and wrapped his arms around me.

His lips brushed softly over mine as he spoke, making me shiver.

"I love you."

"Even after…"

"I love you *more*, because of everything. You have no idea, baby," he murmured, trailing his lips down my throat as I whispered, "I love you too."

Caden

Skeeter had been the one to go into that room and tell us what had gone down.

Slash had watched me as Skeeter told us that Rory had shot my father in the head, and he'd seemed surprised when I'd told them she should have dragged it out painfully.

No one wanted their parents to die, but Tristan Holloway wasn't a father in any sense of the word.

He only helped make me, but that was where it ended.

We'd never been close, and I'd spent most of my childhood being beat on by him or watching him beat on Mom.

We were always going to be better off without him, and I was glad he was fucking gone.

I'd spent a few hours alone, needing to clear my head before deciding I'd needed to go home to my girl.

I'd watched her sleep for a while before climbing into bed with her, pulling her close as she woke from her sleep.

I felt bad, but we needed each other, and I needed her to know that I was there for her, no matter what.

I was shit scared of telling her I loved her, but watching her ride me like that?

I'd been in fucking awe of how fucking perfect she was.

She was the most beautiful, strong woman I had ever laid eyes on, and I couldn't keep that shit from her.

She deserved to know just how much she meant to me.

I'd never really slowed shit down in bed, but it felt right with her.

It was like our souls fucking collided amongst the chaos, and everything suddenly became calm and clear.

You know all that bullshit about soulmates?

It was totally fucking true.

She was mine, and I was hers.

I believed she had other soulmates out there, and I strangely didn't mind in the slightest.

She'd become part of mine, and that was all I gave a fuck about.

<u>Rory</u>

Skeeter didn't speak as I walked into the shed first thing the next morning.

He watched me cautiously, as if calculating what to actually say to me, but Slash shot me a wide grin like the proud piece of shit that he was, tossing me the cigarettes from his pocket.

"Get much sleep last night, Killer? I sure as fuck didn't, because I was awake all night with a fucking *boner* because of you. Fucking hell babe, you're one cold-hearted bitch."

I grunted, plonking down in his chair and put my feet up on his desk.

Pretty sure I was still in a sex induced coma from all the fucking orgasms Caden had given me through the night.

"I spent most of the night fucking Caden between naps, so I guess I got a little bit of sleep."

He cracked up laughing like a fucking maniac.

Trust him to get off on it.

"You offed his dad and he got *horny*? You guys are some sick fucks. Where is he, anyways?"

I glanced at Skeeter, who was still watching me, as I replied.

"He bailed to deal with some shit."

"What shit?" Slash asked with amusement, making me shrug.

"I didn't ask. I know you guys have my dad on your radar, so tell me where he is."

Skeeter's face stayed blank from emotion, but Slash chuckled.

"You really turned cold enough to off your own daddy? Shame you don't have a dick, I need men as tough as you in my crew."

"Sign me up," I joked, but Skeeter finally spoke up, a touch of sternness in his voice.

"You're not even funny, Donovan."

I ignored him, like the mature adult that I was, turning my attention back to Slash completely, finally lighting a cigarette and leaning back in the chair.

"So, where the fuck is he? Might be wise to tell me before I start firing shots at you, boss man."

He raised an eyebrow, obviously not amused by my demand.

"Are you threatening me, Donovan?"

"No, I'm warning you, big difference. Where the fuck is he?" I bit out, and he gave Skeeter a glance.

Skeeter gave him a flat look in return, but I stood up and headed towards the door, sick of wasting time.

"Fine, I'll find him myself. Don't get upset if I start sticking my fucking nose where you don't think it belongs."

Fuck them, I'd just deal with it by my fucking self.

I only made it halfway across the main room before Skeeter's hand wrapped around my throat and I was pushed back into the side of the cage.

I expected him to start yelling, but his voice was calm, his eyes holding mine with a mix of emotions.

"You calm your thirst for fucking blood and we will go. Okay?"

"Don't like me now I'm like you?" I gritted out bitterly,

sorrow flashing across his face as his grip on me loosened slightly.

"Baby girl, I don't like *me* like this, so of course I don't want you like this."

"Let me go or I'll cut you. I'm not fucking around anymore," I seethed, praying he'd let me go.

He didn't move, even as I yanked my knife from my pocket and pressed it against his throat.

"I mean it, Skeet. Let me go."

He moved forwards, the blade pushing against his throat until I saw a tiny drop of blood, his voice low as he spoke.

"Cut me then, because I won't let you go anywhere, guns fucking blazing, with your head in the clouds. Word's out in our world that we offed the big bad Tristan Holloway, so Max will be on edge and ready for it. You'll have to fucking kill me if you want to get past me, Aurora. Don't say shit without intending on going through with it. Don't *ever* make fucking empty threats."

His gaze was hard, and I finally pulled my blade back and put it back in my pocket, his lip twitching into a small smile.

"Well, at least I know you aren't *completely* cold inside."

"Where the fuck's my dad, Skeet?" I asked quietly, waiting for him to let me go before I reached out and ran my thumb over the small cut on his throat, lifting it to my mouth and licking the droplet of blood off the tip.

He growled loudly, "Jesus fucking Christ, unless you wanna go back to mine instead, I'd stop that shit if I were you."

I smirked, knowing he wasn't serious.

Well actually, he'd fuck me right there in front of everyone.

I really shouldn't taunt him.

"I'll play fair when you do."

"Get in the van, I'll be out in a minute," he muttered, rolling my eyes as he stalked back to Slash.

I headed outside and found the old beat-up black Chevy van and climbed in.

The vehicle screamed dodgy to me.

It had tinted windows and everything.

Skeeter emerged from the shed a few minutes later, hoisting himself up behind the steering wheel and slamming the door harder than necessary.

Once on the road, he glanced at me with a scowl.

"Three bodies in a week for a newbie is a little crazy, babe. When you off your old man, you're going to crash and burn. You thought your break down over Liam was bad? You wait till it's your own dad in a shallow grave. You sure you wanna do this?"

"Yes, I'm fucking sure. He showed no mercy with me, so I'll be fucking damned if I grant him any as his final wish," I snapped, relaxing as his hand rested on my thigh, his voice becoming gentle.

"Hey, it's fine. I'm there if you need me to finish it or anything. Either way, we aren't leaving till he's dead," he promised, revving me up more.

My mind was full of nerves, hate, and rage, as memories of Max flashed through me the whole drive.

I honestly didn't have a single good memory of him, and that was all I needed to keep me going.

Skeeter parked at the end of a street, making me frown as we climbed out of the van.

"Where are we?"

"Walking the rest of the way. Can't have him hearing us arrive in case he's ready," he answered as he started walking, and I had to jog to catch up to him.

Once we'd reached an empty-looking house right at the end, surrounded by overgrown weeds and open fields,

Skeeter signalled for me to stay silent as we moved along the side of the house and around to the back.

I followed him until we reached a door and he silently opened it, creeping in with me right behind him.

He hesitated just as Max's voice hit my ears from close by.

He couldn't see me, but if he had a gun, he could hurt or even kill Skeeter.

"What the fuck did I ever do to your crew, huh? Whatever Tristan did to get himself killed has nothing to do with me," Max hissed out, fear and anger rolling out of him in waves.

I heard a gun load, and I instantly pushed down all my doubts and fears, before moving into the room and standing right in front of Skeeter as a shield.

Max's eyebrows shot up in surprise.

"Aurora? What the fuck are you doing here? If they need information about shit and are using you as bait, it's pointless. I don't give a *fuck* about you," he bit out, a confident smirk stretching across my face

I knew Skeeter would have my back, so I spoke with more bravery than I normally would with Max.

"I'm not here as leverage, Max. They don't use the people they care about, unlike some. They didn't kill Tristan Holloway, I fucking did."

He glanced between us nervously as the ball seemed to drop, his voice becoming quieter as denial moved through him.

"No, you wouldn't…"

"Why wouldn't I? I already killed one of their fucking members for being a problem, so Tristan was an easy one, because it was fucking personal."

"Caden will never forgive you when he finds out. You just fucked up the only chance at love you ever fucking had. Then again, I think he's just using you again. Who'd fucking want you?" He sneered, but I could still hear the fear in his voice.

"Caden showed up after seeing me covered in his father's blood, and he still climbed into bed with me and fucked me while telling me how much he loves me. Maybe he and I do have more in common than we thought?"

"How so?" He swallowed, and I shrugged as I flicked my blade around in my hand, letting out a small chuckle.

"Well, neither of us give a shit that our dads were murdered, because we felt no fucking love towards them in the first place."

"I'm not dead, Aurora."

"Not yet, I'm getting to that part," I replied bluntly, halting the blade's movement.

He actually smiled slightly. "Seriously? You're going to kill your own father? You don't have the guts to for starters, but you wouldn't handle prison, honey. Just go home, trust me, I won't bother you again."

"She won't be going to prison, I'm here to deal with the aftermath," Skeeter stated, Max laughing at him with amusement.

"You and what army?"

"The usual," Caden's voice suddenly said from behind us as he and the guys walked in, standing behind me to give me the strength I fucking needed.

We heard cars outside, and a sadistic grin spreading across Skeeter's face as lethal torment laced his tone.

"Looks like the clean-up crews arrived early. Damnit, hey?"

Max took a step back, howling as I snatched Skeeter's gun and shot him in the leg, making him drop to his knees in pain.

I moved closer until I was squatting in front of him, giving him a smile.

"Yeah, damnit is about right."

"Wait! You'll never know about what happened to your

mother if you kill me!" He exclaimed desperately, but Skeeter scoffed and I tensed instantly.

He was too amused to not know anything, and I hid it well as he spoke, despite my insides being crushed by every single fucking word.

"Marla Donovan, age forty-three, worked at the local diner until she ran away when Rory was eight. She worked cash jobs here and there for a year, but then vanished without a trace for a month. Her body was found with distinct markings that I just happen to know is done by an acquaintance of mine. Turns out, you paid him to get rid of her, and you managed to keep it all on the down-low so your daughter wouldn't fucking know. She's spent the last ten years looking for a woman who's been dead for *nine*."

I stepped forward, my entire body going numb.

I couldn't fucking look at him.

"Why, Max?"

"Why? She didn't fucking run away, I made her leave, and she was working her way back to you! She wasn't going to fucking take you from me! If I was going to sink, you were fucking going down with me!" He snapped, and I finally looked him in the eye, my body warming slightly as realization hit me.

"She wanted me?"

"Of course she did, but if I told you that, you would have gone fucking looking for her. She had a nice little house, not many friends, a fucking *baby* on the way," he bit out, a shiver running down my spine.

I was meant to be a big sister?

"What?"

"Your mother managed to get herself knocked up by some prick that took her in for a while. He was paying someone to take you from me. The plan was, she'd steal you, and he was paying someone to keep you under the radar once she'd gotten you back. If they took you, I had no fucking hope," he spat bitterly, a frown taking over my face.

"At what?"

"Getting out of all of the problems I ended up in! You were my bargaining chip, and I was just lucky you were too scared to venture off because you knew I'd bring you back every time. You can't escape me, Aurora. When will you fucking learn that?"

I was still reeling about that fact that Mom wanted me.

"But she could have just taken me because I'm her kid! Why…"

His chuckle made my stomach twist, and I felt Skeeter's chest against my back, letting me know he was there if I needed him.

He could sense me weakening.

Everything was starting to spiral and burn as the man who was meant to be my father, completely wrecked me.

"Your birth mother died in the hospital the day you were born. You were a daily reminder of what I lost, so when Marla found out she was pregnant, I knew I didn't want more children. I hated you, and Marla loved you like her own, so I got rid of that baby while I could. Rich family adopted her. Marla thought her baby girl died, but she didn't. The kid was born premature and is the same age as you. Well, I technically knocked Marla up before your real mother died, while I'm being honest with you. It was easy to believe she was your birth mother because she had the same fucking blue eyes that your real mother did," he grinned like the fucking monster he was.

"Where's my sister?" I whispered, my throat going tight and the gun in my hand feeling heavy as he kept grinning.

"After seeing how well she grew up, I kind of like Claire more than I ever fucking liked you. She goes to your school, right?"

I heard one of the guys behind me suck in a breath, but my body shifted into an emotionless shell as I lifted the gun and gave my father a big smile, his eyes going wide.

"That's funny, I like that cunt more than I ever liked you too, and I fucking *despise* her. Fuck you, Max," I said, my voice steady and blank from emotion.

The single gunshot echoed in my head as I watched his body lie motionless on the floor in front of me, glancing up as Skeeter's guys made their way inside.

I tossed the gun to one as I turned, my voice completely cold as I spoke.

"Burn him," then I walked outside without another fucking word.

To be continued…

Watch Me Burn series.
1. Pretty Lies
2. Twisted Fate
3. Beautiful Deceit

Coming soon (2021)
4. Ignite Me
5. Perfectly Jaded
6. Don't fear the Reaper
7. Wrath of Rage

PRE-ORDER

Did you know I teamed up with C.A. Rene for the Romance After Dark Spring 2021 Anthology? It's dark, it's bloody, and it's steamy! Pre-order now!
https://www.amazon.com/Violent-Tendencies-Romance-Spring-Anthology-ebook/dp/B08CVPR8H1/ref=sr_1_1?crid=2G4EN8455Y98K&dchild=1&keywords=violent+tendencies&qid=1610942568&sprefix=violant+tend%2Caps%2C384&sr=8-1

ACKNOWLEDGMENTS

First off, a massive thanks to my Instagram soul sister, Megan! We might not have met, but you're my most cherished friend. You were the first person to ever read my book, and I'm only published today because you convinced me that people would love it.

Honestly guys, without her, this wouldn't have happened! Follow her book review account on Instagram! It's how I found her! Wideeyedbookreviews

Massive shout out to Samantha at TalkNerdy2me for my stunning cover! I am blown away, and I can't wait to see what else she creates for my book babies in the future! So grateful to have such an amazingly talented woman on my team! Follow Talknerdy2me on Instagram and Facebook for wicked book releases and all things books!

To my editor at Dark Raven Edits, and my second editor and proof-reader at Diamond Editing and Proof Reading, I can't thank you enough! I had so many questions since it was my first book and you guys just powered through all the answers and dove straight into this book!

To my first beta reader, Jocelyn, you are a fucking gem! I am so happy to have come across you in my mission to get this book published. Us Tassie girls gotta stick together, and I appreciate the hell out of you!

To my second beta reader, Steph, your comments throughout cracked me up, and you made editing fun. I'm so glad to have you as part of my team!

To my little psychopath beta, Kenia, thank you so much for all your help and keeping me sane with your insane ways. I appreciate all the help!

Massive thanks to my Street team and ARC team who supported me as I learned what the fuck I was supposed to do. I still have no idea, but I got here, so thank you for your patience, kind words, and never ending support!

Shout out to the authors who found time in their busy schedules to answer all my questions, and there were a lot! Special thanks to these four who were so patient with the long line of questions I threw at them, please check them out on Facebook and join their readers groups!

KT Strange: KT's Beauties

Loxley Savage: The Inferno – A Loxley Savage readers group

Harper Ray: Harper's Naughty Royals

Hellie Heat: Hellie's Garden

Special mention to my girl Roxy. You have been amazeballs at helping me with decisions and questions, and you'll never know how much of a help you really are to me. Follow fallen_angel.edits on Instagram for amazing book image edits by my girl!

Most importantly, thank you! To anyone reading this, you are awesome! I hope you love Rory and the guys as much as I do, and I hope you grab the second book in the series, Twisted Fate, on release day!

You think five guys is enough? Guess again!

Love you all! Xx

STALK ME!

Stalk the crap out of me you little freaks, I love it!

Facebook:

https://www.facebook.com/indieauthorrebond/

Facebook Readers Group:

https://www.facebook.com/groups/259020108635485/

Instagram:

https://www.instagram.com/author.re.bond/

Goodreads:

https://www.goodreads.com/rebond

SPOTIFY PLAYLIST LINK

Listen to the writing playlist for Pretty Lies
https://open.spotify.com/playlist/
16nokgWJ2qTyHQkjDNf90o?si=eDoLC-
XvQ4CAffYEKau8PA.

ABOUT THE AUTHOR

R.E. Bond is a dark romance author from Tasmania, Australia. She is obsessed with reverse harem books, especially if they have m/m! She collects paperbacks as a hobby, has read or written every day since she started high school, and constantly needs music in her daily life. She loves camping and rodeos in the summer, and not getting out of bed in the winter. Coffee and books are life, and curse words are just sentence enhancers.

CPSIA information can be obtained
at www.ICGtesting.com
Printed in the USA
LVHW030837200422
716605LV00006B/184